Nazareth

A Visual Biography

Martin Popoff
with Roni Ramos Amorim on Images

Nazareth
A Visual Biography

Martin Popoff
with Roni Ramos Amorim on Images

WP
WYMER
PUBLISHING
Bedford, England

First published in Great Britain in 2021
by Wymer Publishing
This edition 2023
www.wymerpublishing.co.uk
Tel: 01234 326691
Wymer Publishing is a trading name of Wymer (UK) Ltd

Copyright © Martin Popoff /Wymer Publishing.

ISBN: 978-1-915246-37-0

The Author hereby asserts his rights to be identified
as the author of this work in accordance with sections
77 to 78 of the Copyright, Designs & Patents Act 1988.

All rights reserved. No part of this publication may be
reproduced or transmitted in any form or by any means,
electronic or mechanical, including photocopying, or any
information storage and retrieval system, without written
permission from the publisher.

This publication is sold subject to the condition that it shall not,
by way of trade or otherwise, be lent, re-sold, hired out or
otherwise circulated without the publisher's prior consent in any
form of binding or cover other than that in which it is published
and without a similar condition including this condition
being imposed on the subsequent purchaser.

Every effort has been made to trace the copyright holders of the
photographs in this book but some were unreachable. We would
be grateful if the photographers concerned would contact us.

Design by Andy Bishop / Tusseheia Creative.
Printed in England by Halstan.

A catalogue record for this book is available from the British Library.

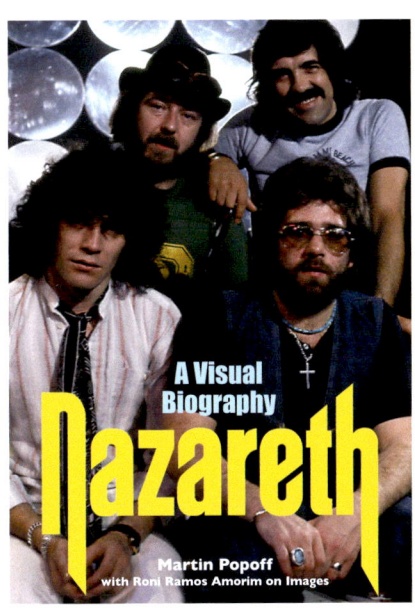

ROLL OF HONOUR

Wymer Publishing duly acknowledges the following people who all put their faith in this publication by pre-ordering it:

Gordon Aitken
Bjørnar Andreassen
Bruce Ashcroft
David Mackay Ballard
Jason Barber
John Bell
Sandy Brands
Jules Brazeau
Ralph Palma
José Ailton Claudino de Bastos
Arne Dahl
Bjørn Dalvang
Russ Evers
Schneider Fabrice
John Fell
Douglas Ferguson
Grant Finlay
Keith Fitzgerald
George Galloway
David Gauger
Vitaly Gorbash
Ulrike Graber
Mike Grieshaber
James Griffis
Derek Hall
Steve Haynie
James Hoffmaster
Ian Hunter
Roy Hutchinson
Aleksey A. Kononow
Ron Lewis
Julian Lewry

Danny Lucas
Pål H. Lund
Edenil Osmar Marques
Larry McGuffin Jr
Altair Antonio Muraro
Alan Murray
Bill Nelson
Andrew Newberry
Raymond Niemelainen
Mark Porrovecchio
Robert Pratt
Alex Pritsker
Susanne Rashed
Paul Robertson
Aaron Rautamäki
Jan Harald Roset
Richard Schultheiss
Vadim Grigorievich Shatskiy
Nigel Sheppard
Mark Skaar
Darla Soich
Karl Stanka
Jan Atle Steinsland
Chryssi Stout-Yonkins
Eric Sweetwood
Werner Temmel
Lee Thomas
Martin Thompson
Wes Waschuk
Brian Wilson
Karel Zdenovec

CONTENTS

Introduction	9
Origins Through 1974	13
1975 – 1979	49
The 1980s	101
The 1990s	155
The 2000s	189
The 2010s to 2022	211
Acknowledgements	239
About the Author	239
Martin Popoff – A Complete Bibliography	240

INTRODUCTION

Welcome one and all to this celebration of Scotland's finest, a band that surprisingly hasn't seen much elaborate pictorial presentation in the past. It took long enough, but here we are, 52 years since the self-titled debut album, extolling the virtues of Nazareth, a band near and dear to my heart because it was the favourite band of my deceased brother, Brad. But the reason my brother and I grew up listening to Nazareth is because, in addition, I'm pretty darn sure that *Razamanaz* was the first properly heavy rock record I ever owned, even if something tells me that either Led Zeppelin *II, III* or the untitled fourth was the first properly heavy rock record I ever heard.

And what would that make howler monkey Dan McCafferty? Well, he would be the first extreme rock vocalist I ever heard, although now it gets complicated: I did indeed own Steppenwolf Gold and a couple of Creedence Clearwater Revival records *(Cosmo's Factory* and *Pendulum)* before metal became my unceasing biggest hobby, and one could argue that John Kay and John Fogerty are somewhat extreme atop each's not very extreme musical backing, i.e. dated, pre-Nazareth-type music from the late 1960s and in CCR's case, the late 1860s!

But man, dropping the needle on *Razamanaz* and specifically "Razamanaz" back then in the summer of 1973, at ten years old, my world changed, and not just because of the unholy screech emanating from the spaces between Manny Charlton's stacked wall-of-sound power chords, but also because of Darrell Sweet's double bass drum madness. It's possible that right there something wormed into my subconscious that made me take up the drums, which I did immediately.

Not long after, me an' my buddies were lowering the needle on "The Ballad of Hollis Brown," and our brains were wrecked, forever destined to be metalheads, as Nazareth became the second band after Black Sabbath to wallow in what would become known as doom metal, not that these guys were ever deliberate about their heaviness, much less any obscure subgenres of heavy metal. That's one of the cool things about Nazareth: anything goes. And as the years piled up, anything went, much to the detriment of their career. It might be argued that all that '80s stuff made the '70s stuff sound even more special, but that one is up for debate. In fact, I really only thought of that now.

Another cool thing about doing this book is that besides the personal connection that my brother and I had with this band, there's an extra level of personal attachment, and that's because I'm from Western Canada, now living in Toronto, and Nazareth were a big deal in Canada, playing back and forth across the country regularly, and in later years, really staking an uncommon claim in BC and Alberta and Saskatchewan. Quite remarkable, really, to the point where my dad and my brother, long after I'd moved to Toronto, actually went and saw the band in a small bar in Nelson, BC.

But yes, the Great White North was a territory where most of those '70s records went gold and platinum. Now, something I just recently figured out. If you aren't particularly impressed with Canada's certification levels of 50,000 sold for gold and 100,000 sold for platinum, the wider point is that Nazareth could headline hockey arenas for years across Canada, meaning

that the upside impression that Canada had on the band's success was actually quite large. The band expresses as much, with the fond memories that they hold for this territory made clear in interviews across the ages, enhanced also by the fact that they made three records at Le Studio in Quebec, famed for its association with local heroes Rush.

Of course the other cool thing is that Nazareth are one of these world-travelling bands, particularly big in Germany and Brazil and Russia, besides the well wishes they receive across Canada. Good stuff, and it's made for an interesting life, even if that pirate lifestyle has sadly come to a close for Dan. After McCafferty had reluctantly bowed out of the band, bassist Pete Agnew soldiered on, hiring on first Linton Osborne and then Carl Sentance, with whom the band has actually made one studio album already. But the story doesn't end there: Pete's son Lee and guitarist Jimmy Murrison have been part of the band for what amounts to decades now, and so we shouldn't be so quick to declare Nazareth over when Dan has had to, quite literally, take a seat.

Crack open the pages of this book and these story points are all explained, in a format with which I'm familiar, and which readers of my books should, by now, also be familiar. What I've done is create a detailed timeline, just as Wymer Publishing and myself have done across four other books similar to this in recent times, as well as many other books I have done outside the Wymer umbrella. What makes this a little more special over and above my recent similar books on Blue Öyster Cult, Thin Lizzy, Van Halen and Uriah Heep, is that I've liberally marbled in quotes from the band, making this better than a timeline book, better than an oral history, because it's... both a timeline book *and* an oral history.

In other words, there should be more than enough literary substance to satisfy as you graze these pages filled with the band's fantastic album cover art, 45 sleeves and demonstrations of live camaraderie and friendship between each and all the various lineups of this band, even if—and they would agree with a chuckle—the mugs on the front of the Nazareth guys aren't exactly the most photogenic in the world. As well, this wasn't a band surrounded by stage props and pyro—they just kind of went up there and played, and so there's not a lot of drama in the live shots you're about to see, even if there is a more than ample display of the rainbow of human emotion and experience that comes from a bunch of Scottish lads plying their trade since the mid-1960s.

But like I say, the live photography is supported ably by the band's artistic flourishes in the graphics department, as well as the special fact that among the books in this series, with this one you really get to hear the guys explain their 50-year career in their own humble and bemused words. Finally, I've got to say that one of the crowning joys of doing this book besides the reasons cited so far is the fact that I find myself very surprised that the final three albums with Dan—in my heart of hearts, swear to God—are probably three of my favourite six albums the band has ever crafted, along with *Razamanaz, Loud 'n' Proud* and *Hair of the Dog*. I love that! And I love this band. And I love the fact that we're about to share our love for Nazareth together. So let's do that.

Martin Popoff
martinp@inforamp.net; martinpopoff.com

"It had never, ever even crossed my mind to play bass and the only times I strapped on a bass guitar was when our bass player would turn up late for gigs and I had to play 'til he arrived. When I listened to records it was always the singers and the songs that I concentrated on and never any particular instrument and certainly not the bass. I ended up playing bass because there was nobody else in our hometown that we wanted. Up until then, Dan and I used to do twin vocals and before that I was on rhythm guitar and vocals. But when we eventually fired the bass player the guys said to me, 'Why don't you play it? You play the guitar so why not the bass?' I thought, 'Well, I don't know.... and then again, it's only got four strings so why not?'"

"So I really got the gig by default, and since they never found anybody else I just kinda got stuck with it for the last 50 years.(laughs). Like I said, I always concentrated on singing rather than bass playing and have never consciously studied other bass players, although I have had and still have many excellent players as good friends. Guys like Roger Glover, Glenn Hughes, the late great Trevor Bolder—Uriah Heep and Spiders from Mars—and of course my own son Chris. But we never really talked about bass playing. We're not like drummers who are always talking about nuts and bolts when they get together. Bass players... they're usually talking about the quality of the beer."

Pete Agnew

ORIGINS THROUGH 1974

Just like their good buddies in Uriah Heep, Nazareth set themselves up for life across the span of two or three action-packed, sleep-deprived years in the early '70s. But it almost went pear-shaped before it got going. There was a debut that didn't make much of a dent, even if its considerable heaviness raised a few eyebrows. Then there was the career stumble that was Exercises, a bit like Deep Purple's classical album debacle, Zeppelin with III, Rush with *Caress of Steel* and even more similar to what Uriah Heep did with *Salisbury.* As Mick Box is wont to say, Heep found their sound with *Look at Yourself,* while across London town, Nazareth just as forthrightly found their sound with *Razamanaz.*

And again, like Heep and many other '70s greats, Nazareth found themselves putting out two records in one year, following up their heavy metal barnstormer of a third album with a fourth called *Loud 'n' Proud* before 1973 was out. Unlike Heep and Deep Purple (but more like Black Sabbath), there wouldn't be a live album, with Nazareth getting right back to work in 1974, issuing *Rampant*, which took a wee bit of wind out of the band's sails, although, fortunately, the decline was not to last.

An interesting question is to what extent Nazareth paid their dues, so to speak. One might say that they emerged relatively quickly onto the scene and became a working band, i.e., off to America with their very first album. But the fact is, through their origins as The Shadettes, the guys really did spend years learning their collective craft, even if these woodshedding years were relatively tranquil, having been spent close to home.

But yes, as soon as we got to the '70s, and especially 1973, the band got very busy, playing at home, to be sure, but also on the mainland and also in Canada and the United States, helped along by support slots with Deep Purple, sort of like Elf, although the residuals of that situation would take a much different turn than that of Nazareth's. Within the context of this story, what would happen is that Deep Purple bassist Roger Glover would produce the band, seizing upon their "live for today" material, teaching them the reality of reality, and framing the likes of *Exercises* as just that, exercises, or, conversely, the type of material one might save for a Roger Glover solo album.

The resultant explosive records, along with the cock-sure live shows, honed from years of experience playing covers and seeing what works and what doesn't in front of a demanding penny- and battery-chucking Scottish pub audience, resulted in a not insignificant amount of media buzz about this band, in the local UK music weeklies, but also rock and pop magazines on the continent. The fact of the matter is, in the early '70s, Nazareth were executing, bringing both quality and quantity, again, building a sturdy foundation upon which decades of rock was about to be piled.

February 13, 1692. The Massacre of Glencoe takes place, in the Scottish highlands, pitting government forces against the Clan MacDonald. Nazareth would write a song about it called "1692 (Glencoe Massacre)," which would appear as the last track on their second album, *Exercises*.

1935. H. Kingsley Long sees publication of his novel *No Mean City*, which would inspire a 1979 Nazareth album of the same name.

July 25, 1941. Manuel "Manny" Charlton is born in La Linea, Andalusia, Spain.

1943. The Charltons immigrate to the UK, settling in Dunfermline, Scotland, where Manny would make his way through Commercial Primary School and Queen Anne High School.

September 14, 1946. Pete Agnew is born in Dunfermline, Scotland.

October 14, 1946. William McCafferty is born in Dunfermline, Scotland.

May 16, 1947. Darrell Antony Sweet is born in Bournemouth, England.

May 4, 1949. Alistair MacDonald "Zal" Cleminson is born in Glasgow, Scotland.

1957. Pete Agnew's first show is a skiffle contest at the ABC Cinema in Kirkcaldy, which he won.

Manny Charlton:
"Originally Pete was a guitar player, and then he didn't play guitar and he just sang for a few years. And then when we lost our bass player—he left—Pete said, 'I'll play the bass.' So that was it. He became the bass player. Yes, Pete the happy bass player. Yeah, Pete always has a big smile on his face, bobbing around the stage; he's probably happiest when he's on stage. He's the original… It was kind of his band, because he started it way back, in the early '60s, and they were called The Shadettes. It wasn't until I joined that they changed the name to Nazareth. And that was Pete, Dan and Darrell and another bass player at the time, and the keyboard player was the original Shadettes. And they asked me to join when they lost their guitar player. They were all from the same town."

1957. Darrell Sweet's first public show is with The Fife Pipe Band, Burntisland.

1959. Manny Charlton plays his first gig, the Cowdenbeath Palais, with his band The Hellcats.

1961. Pre-Nazareth band The Shadettes open for business, with Pete playing guitar. Manny Charlton, who would join right at the end, had already been in bands, most notably Mark 5 and the Red Hawks. Dan says their first gig was at the Kirkcaldy YMCA.

Pete Agnew:
"In Scotland in the '60s, all the bands were heavily into soul music, as were the people who came to dance. The vocalists on the Stax and Tamla labels were—and still are to a great extent—the best in the world. To this day Dan and I would name Otis Redding as the best singer the world has heard. Also the great riffs that peppered soul music were an inspiration in later years to the

creators of heavy or 'hard' rock: many a' soul riff has been changed around a wee bit and used as the basis of some of our best known rock songs. The songs themselves were fantastic, and there seemed to be about five classics released every week. I still get a buzz when I hear Otis sing 'Mr. Pitiful,' when I hear Sam & Dave sing 'Hold On I'm Coming,' or Bob & Earl do 'Harlem Shuffle.' We used to do all those songs back then, and I suppose it must have rubbed off a bit when it came to writing and performing our own songs. At least, I hope it did." (w/ Dmitry Epstein, dmme.net)

1962. Bill McCafferty becomes Dan, at least to his buddies.

Pete Agnew:
"Everybody thinks it's William Daniel McCafferty. But Dan was Bill, Bill McCafferty, and Dan doesn't come from a middle name because he never had a middle name. We grew up with Bill—Bill and the boys. When he went to start work, when he was 16, he got this nickname Dan, from the guys. God knows how he got it, but we all started to call him that and it just stuck and he became Dan McCafferty. So it was just an old nickname. He was Bill McCafferty everywhere he went. I mean, his whole family, his wife calls him Bill (laughs). And I know his sisters and brothers, and everybody, the whole family, they all call him Bill. My wife still calls him Bill (laughs)."

1962. Bonnie Dobson includes her song "Morning Dew" on her live album *At Folk City*. Nazareth will cover the well-travelled classic on their first album.

Early 1964. Darrell Sweet is now part of The Shadettes, replacing Alan Fraser, and Des Haldane joins on guitar.

Pete Agnew:
"When The Shadettes started in '61, it was my band, and I was the singer and a rhythm guitar player and there were the four of us. And then when it got to 1964, the end of '63, the beginning of '64 the drummer, Darrell and Des Haldane joined. Des played guitar and he could sing. Up 'til then, I was only guy that could sing in the band; the other three guys couldn't sing at all. When Des came in it was great because it was another guy who could sing so we could do all these harmony things and I got to really like that. And when he left, it was really strange not having another singer."

November 8, 1964. Future Nazareth guitarist Jimmy Murrison is born.

1965. Keyboard player Ronnie Leahy is in a band called The Pathfinders, at which time he makes the acquaintance of Dan, Pete and Darrell. Later, Leahy would play with Stone the Crows and White Trash before becoming a member of Nazareth in the '90s, appearing on the *Boogaloo* album from 1998.

Early 1965. Dan joins The Shadettes.

> **Pete Agnew:**
> "When we lost Des, I always said it would be nice to have another singer again, and at the time, Dan used to travel around in the van with us, just as a pal. He was my mate from school; he used to come to all the gigs. And somebody just said, 'Well, Dan sounds good, he can sing.' So we thought why not? Let's give him a shot. And so we said, 'Dan, fancy a go?' 'Certainly, let's have a go.' So it was great to have another singer in so we could do the two-vocal things again."
> "Now Des used to play guitar but when Dan came in, he was just a singer standing on his own—he doesn't play guitar. So what happened was, for the first six or nine months of Dan in the band, he only did something like six, seven songs—because I was still the lead singer in the band. And of course he had to go off the stage, because he didn't sort of play guitar and wasn't singing and playing guitar like Des did. But we wanted more and more and more to get Dan to become the lead singer. I was still playing guitar and what happened is, later on—actually later that year—we added a keyboard player. At that time, '65, you've got to realize that around here the big thing was the Tamla soul stuff. That was going everywhere in the dance halls and was what the bands were all playing in Scotland. So we got a keyboard player in and what happened is that I stopped playing guitar. Because you had Sam & Dave, Bob & Earl, all these soul things, Four Tops, so we figured we'd just have the two singers then and I stopped playing the guitar altogether. So we had the keyboard replace my rhythm guitar, if you like—I never played guitar and it was just Dan and I as the two lead singers."

November 2, 1967. Cream issue their second album, *Disraeli Gears,* which helped set a new hard rock standard that would inspired bands like Nazareth to turn up the volume.

February 1968. Tomorrow issue their one and only album, a self-titled, on Parlophone. Opening track is "My White Bicycle," which Nazareth would cover and take to moderate hit status.

> **Pete Agnew:**
> "The secret of a good cover is not to think of the song as a cover. A great song is a great song and can be performed in a number of different ways. When we do someone else's song, we probably loved the original but would never think of doing a version of that version. If you can't change it enough to make it yours, don't do it." (w/ Dmitry Epstein, dmme.net)

July 1, 1968. The Band issue their debut album, *Music from Big Pink.* It includes a song called "The Weight" which would soon become part of the story of the band discussed in this book.

Pete Agnew:
"We loved The Band—as did almost every other musician on the planet—but I wouldn't say they particularly influenced our music, although everything you listen to must subconsciously influence. Being a rhythm 'n' blues-based 'hard rock' band, Nazareth have always listened to every other kind of music except hard rock, so our influences are wide-ranging. What we call Scottish rock—and that goes for most of the Scottish rock bands of the '60s and '70s—is heavily influenced by American music rather than the English rock bands who tended to influence one another. The Scottish settlers who went to America tended to move to the south and were largely responsible for what we know today as country music, which with black blues influence became rock 'n' roll. So in a roundabout way, you could say our ancestors had a great deal to do with creating Scottish rock. Little did they know what they were starting!"

"There have been a lot of good bands come out of Scotland, and indeed are still coming—Simple Minds, Texas, Travis, to name but a few—but although they play excellent contemporary music, I don't think you would describe them as rock bands. So yeah, I suppose you could say we are the only ones flying the Scottish rock colours—and certainly the oldest." *(w/ Dmitry Epstein, dmme.net)*

November 1968. The four members of the classic Nazareth lineup play together for the first time, although the band at this point is still called The Shadettes and there are six members in the group.

Dan McCafferty:
I went to school with Pete and I've known Manny and Darrell since I was 16. We all come from similar backgrounds. We have the same basic values, so it's much easier for us to get along together. Plus we're all coming from an identified prime musical influence, which was the original Jeff Beck Group, the lineup which had Ron Wood and Rod Stewart in it. Now *that* was an incredible rock 'n' roll band!" *(w/ Ritchie Yorke, Star-Phoenix, January 13, 1978)*

Pete Agnew:
"When Manny joined the band at the end of '68, the lineup was still Dan and me as the two lead singers, and we used to do one song apiece and that kind of thing. And then what happened was our bass player at the time, he just really wasn't interested. He'd come up when he felt like coming up. He'd never come to rehearsal for ages, and when we went to start a gig—we played in Dunfermline's Kinema Ballroom as a resident group—he was never there in the beginning of the thing. I would just put the bass on and I'd play the first two or three songs until he turned up. And eventually we got fed up with that and said, 'Look, you may as well not bother coming anymore. We're fed up with this.' And then we thought, well, who's gonna play the bass? And then Manny said, 'Well, there isn't anybody else in town so you could just play the bass, Peter.' I never really intended being a bass player; I was thinking of getting somebody else. Anyway I thought, well, it's only got four strings, I could play a guitar with six strings, so let's give it a go. So that's how I became the bass player—the job just became mine."

"As the year went on, the keyboard player went the same route as the bass player. He was one of these guys, when we were playing the Kinema, we'd go on break and he'd disappear to the bar. We'd come off the break and go back on and he was never there. We'd do two or three songs without him and so we said, 'That's it. You, off you go' (laughs)."

"By the way, the Kinema was one of the main stop-off points for big touring bands when they came to Scotland. For example, we played here with Cream,

The Who, Deep Purple, David Bowie, Jeff Beck, Rod Stewart... the list goes on forever. Before The Who went to tour America with *Tommy*, they did some warm-up dates 'up in the sticks' (laughs) to try it out. When they played the Kinema, we, as the resident group, had the dubious honour of playing before and then after their set! This was after Mr. Townshend spectacularly smashed his guitar to smithereens, as was his wont on any given evening. Yep, as resident group we had to open and then follow every guest band that came. Good training for our future career and it probably contributed heavily to the 'cavalier' approach we have to playing festivals—bring 'em on!"

"But yes, at this time, now we were definitely just a four-piece, and Dan was definitely the lead singer. Because we weren't doing Sam and Dave stuff anymore. Through '69, that all started to go, where we started to have Dan as our proper lead singer. Thank God we did, by the way, because he started to develop his own style as well then. He wasn't imitating people or copying people so much. He was starting to be the Dan McCafferty that the world got to know."

1970

Early 1970. The Shadettes change their name to Nazareth.

Pete Agnew:
"At the beginning of 1970, that's when the keyboard player, got the chop. So then it was very much, well, we had the same lineup as The Who and bands like that then, didn't we? It was a three-piece with a singer. And that's when we thought, well, we definitely have got to get a name change here. The Shadettes just doesn't cut it. Especially these days with other bands like Cream and Blodwyn Pig and all the strange names that people had. It was all what we called modern names, if you like (laughs). The Shadettes was so old-fashioned, like The Ronettes, that type of thing. So we thought it's definitely got to be changed."

"By this time, we had started playing at a place across the road from our old regular gig called the Belleville Hotel, and we started talking about changing the name, putting out all these different suggestions. And we were having a pint and 'The Weight' by The Band came on the radio, with 'I pulled into Nazareth.' And I said, 'What about Nazareth?' It just sounded good—'What about Nazareth?' And nobody said no, you know? But they didn't say, 'Oh yeah, that's great.' So we said, 'Let's write it down and see what it looks like.' So we wrote it down and it was pretty punchy, that. We went, 'Ah, that's good, that's it, that's it—Nazareth.'"

"But, you know what was funny? I've been watching that film that they did with The Band, *Once Were Brothers*, with Robbie Robertson, and I never realized that until then, he was telling the story of 'The Weight,' and he said that he was just diddling away trying to write a song and he's just thinking and he looked inside the Martin guitar, and of course it said 'Made in Nazareth, Pennsylvania' and he saw the word Nazareth and he just thought it sounded good. And I thought that's funny, that's exactly what happened to me (laughs). I got it from him, but he got it from the same kind of vibe as I did—the name sort of punched him the same way it punched me."

June 3, 1970. Deep Purple issue *In Rock*, while Uriah Heep and Black Sabbath also issue very heavy albums in 1970, two in fact from Sabbath. Hard rock is on its way, with Nazareth soon to participate in the movement boldly.

Dan McCafferty on *In Rock*:
"I just thought it was amazing. The Deep Purple before, they were a good band, too, but when Ian and Roger joined up, it was like oh, hello, this was something else altogether. The excitement. There was such a good vibe about it and energy that was like, whoa. The electric guitar, and the way Ian drummed, it was just new. And then Black Sabbath with that sort of anger, it was like whoa, these guys are not kidding. It was pure, raw energy that nobody had before. Ten years after Deep Purple came out, every band I heard was trying to sound like Ian Gillan—heavy metal was about singing like Ian."

1971

1971. Nazareth relocates to London.

Dan McCafferty:
In Britain, in that time in the music business and the early days, if you weren't from London and you didn't go to London, you couldn't get arrested. You would have to play the Marquee and all these places. But the Beatles came along and changed all that because they were from Liverpool. So everybody's like, 'Wait a minute, there's bands north of the Thames.' That's when it started to open up for everybody."

January 13, 1971. Lee Agnew is born in Dunfermline, Scotland. Lee is the son of Pete Agnew and became Nazareth's drummer when Darrell Sweet died in 1999, after first serving as drum tech. Pete has two other musician sons as well, Stevie and Chris.

May 3, 1971. Leon Russell issues his second album, *Leon Russell and the Shelter People*, which includes a song he wrote called "Alcatraz," soon to be covered by Nazareth.

June 1971. Joni Mitchell issues her *Blue* album; it contains "This Flight Tonight," which Nazareth will cover.

November 4, 1971. Nazareth issue their debut, a self-titled, on Pegasus Records, a Vertigo-like offshoot of B&C Records. The album, recorded at Trident, is produced by David Hitchcock with Roy Thomas Baker engineering. Also engineering on the record is John Punter, who will produce 1982's *The Fool Circle*. Pete takes a lead vocal on a song called "I Had a Dream."

Pete Agnew:
"We recorded this first album at Trident Studios in London. Neither ourselves nor our management had any experience of recording studios up until that time so we just went for somewhere famous and expensive. I remember we were told Elton John used Trident so we reckoned if it was good enough for him… you get the idea. I didn't like the place because of the layout and cramped control room but on the plus side the resident sound engineer was Roy Baker—soon to be Queen's producer with an added 'Thomas' in his name—who not only introduced us to the intricacies of recording but also became a good friend and producer of our next album. First albums are like the first time for anything, that is you mainly learn what *not* to do. It was recorded over 11 days and mixed in three days."

Dan McCafferty on the heavier songs on the debut:
"That's just what we wanted to play. We were young and full of piss and vinegar, and rock music had to be aggressive because that's how you felt. You know, you went to join the national 'blank' party or something. It was the energy and anger that went on with a lot of things that was going on politically in your home place. It was a difficult youth, really, and that's where that came from. I have no regrets about it, by the way. I have no regrets about it at all. But we were starting up at the same time as a lot of the other bands and heavier music was popular at the time. In the clubs and stuff, not too much on the air waves, but in pubs and clubs. But then people like Sabbath and Zeppelin came out and it was like whoa, what's this, then?"

1972

January 1972. Mountain/Pegasus issue a first UK Nazareth single pairing "Dear John" with "Friends."

Dan McCafferty:
"The decision to go professional was a hard one, because we are all married and have kids, and we had to have some kind of guarantee that when we were away, the wife didn't get evicted. We were writing our own songs and our manager brought the tapes to London and started taking them around the record companies. It was really nice. Because you read about bands that have been flogging their tapes around for ten years before they got anywhere, but we got right in, the first kick at the ball."
(w/ Rosalind Russell, Disc, June 9, 1973)

Pete Agnew on the Nazareth logo, in place already on the band's debut:
"For years we had no idea who did that logo. But then what happened was this: Dave Field, an artist who designed both our *Razamanaz* and *Loud 'n' Proud* album sleeves, contacted me last year a few months into this plague lockdown to let me know he was putting out a new book of his work. It's a big pictorial book something like this one you're doing but displaying all the album sleeves he's designed. I had a look at Dave's website to check out all the sleeves he'd done. It turns out that not only did he do loads of beautiful sleeves, he also did loads of great logos and, yep, you guessed, there was our logo right at the beginning of the bunch. I've known Dave for years and it never clicked that he was the guy our original record company had hired to design a logo for the first album because I never met him until he did the *Razamanaz* artwork. So there you go: now I know, and better late than never."

February 1972. The band play the Rainbow supporting The Faces. Dan and Pete consider this the band's first important public appearance.

April 5 – 8, 1972. The band play multiple shows at the Whisky a Go Go in West Hollywood, California.

May 1972. Little Feat issue their second album, *Sailin' Shoes*, which includes "Teenage Nervous Breakdown" soon to be covered boisterously by Nazareth.

June 1972. Nazareth's cover of "Morning Dew" is issued as a single, backed with "Spinning Top."

July 1972. Nazareth's first single in the US, issued by Warner Bros., pairs "Morning Dew" with "Dear John."

July 1, 1972. Nazareth issue their second album, *Exercises*. The record marks only the third project for producer Roy Thomas Baker, soon to be famous for his work with Queen. It is recorded and mixed at Trident Studios.

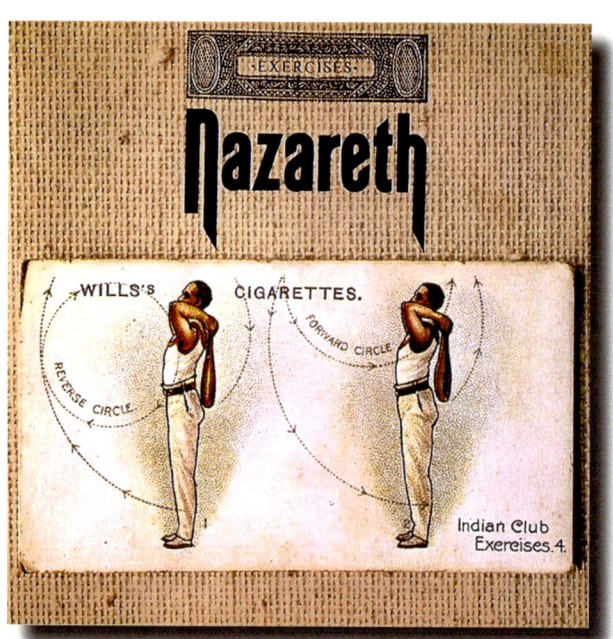

Dan McCafferty, on why *Exercises* was so mellow:
"I know, I think it was just because that was the stuff we were writing at the time. And because we were Scottish, and really the first band ever to succeed internationally from Scotland, I think we got a bit ethnic for a bit there (laughs). We were trying to create Scottish rock. I don't think it was a conscious decision, but looking back and analyzing it, that's what we did. At the time I liked it. Looking back that's the way it

worked. Do you like the songs? Yes. Do you think we should record them? Yes. Do you think people will like them? Yes. Well then let's do them!"

Pete Agnew:
"We'd done *Nazareth*, the first one, which was just a mix of songs that we did. Some were rock, some were… When we did *Exercises*, at that point we were listening to Poco, The Grateful Dead, all these kinds of bands, and we thought, 'What do we want to be?' What were we going to be as a recording band? We weren't a cover band anymore. So we saw ourselves at that point as playing acoustic stuff, electric, different things. And we did that album and it was a fucking disaster. But it was a learning curve. Roy Baker produced that album, the great Roy Thomas Baker. He was just an engineer then. So we did that album and the record company—and our management company—said, 'Well, boys, you got one more chance.' Because that record did nothing."
"Interestingly, we never named this album, never even had a say in the matter. It went like this: the album was recorded over 13 days. We finished recording on the Thursday night at 11:00PM, went back to the band's apartment and had a quick sleep, got up and packed our bags for an American tour, took our bags (and bodies) back to Trident at 8:00AM and began mixing the album. After a straight 21 hours of mixing, the album was proclaimed finished at 5:00AM (and so were our ears) so we picked up our bags and headed out to Heathrow airport, had breakfast and hopped on a plane to New York. If any of you think the mix on the album sounds 'not wonderful,' this might go some way to explain maybe why. During the fifth week of our American tour we got a phone call from our management to tell us that the album was to be named Exercises and that they had designed the record cover. We said, 'Eh?'"

September 1972. Mountain/Pegasus issue a non-LP single from Nazareth pairing "If You See My Baby" with "Hard Living."

Dan McCafferty, comparing *Exercises* with the debut:

"I still think *Exercises* is good music. But there were things we just couldn't get over. For our first album, we had only been professionals for two weeks, so we were lost then. It was our first time in the studio and it was a lot of fun because they put the drummer in a box. Darrell was like a big tomato in this box and we couldn't feel the drummer. And Manny and Pete were behind the screens, and I had to sing with cans and I hated that. I was really disappointed. That's why we changed the whole policy with *Razamanaz*."

"But there is one thing that Nazareth's first album has that I still like: excitement, which is another thing that we are about. We are excited when we play and try to shove it in plastic. Whereas with *Exercises* we were relaxed, because we were terrified of falling into the Black Sabbath riffy-type of thing. There was a lot going on at the time, and we didn't think it was for us. We were in a bit of a mess actually. I didn't think *Exercises* hurt us, because if we hadn't done that, we would still like to follow that direction. Now we can look back at this and think, 'This is where we go wrong, and we will have to avoid that in the future.'"
(w/ Tony Stewart, New Musical Express, August 18, 1973)

December 1972 – March 1973. Nazareth work with Deep Purple's Roger Glover at The Ganghut, Jamestown, Scotland utilizing the Pye Mobile on tracks to comprise their proposed third album.

Pete Agnew:

"After *Exercises*, we were writing these songs and they were all rock songs. We were heavily influenced by the rock bands and we were playing them live. You had Deep Purple, Zeppelin and all that thing. And funnily enough, we did a British tour with Deep Purple and we were playing songs from *Razamanaz* on the tour, and Roger Glover heard us every night, and we were looking for a producer to do the album. He said, 'I'm your man; I want to do this.' And of course we worked with Roger for the next three albums and it was a great, a match made in heaven."

"We were looking at Jimmy Page and Pete Townshend, but the thing is, Roger really, really wanted to do it. He actually said to us, 'I really, really want to do it.' And that makes a difference, rather than we were just hiring someone to do it and I think you can see that the few albums he did with us, he was a great producer for us. Hats off to the guy. He definitely helped to make those albums, and those were the albums that got us into the big time."

Manny Charlton on The Ganghut:

"We had turned professional and we needed some place at home as our rehearsal facility. And that's basically what it was. It was two rooms that we used to rent in this warehouse. They were maybe ten, twelve feet square, and we had one room for all the equipment. It was concrete walls and high ceilings though, and we had Marshall stacks in there and the drum kit and it was deafening. We used to come out of there after working all day and my ears would be ringing for hours. And the other room we had set up for mixing. We had a little Revox and we did our demos in there."

"When Roger came to produce the band, he said, 'Where are you guys happy playing?' 'Well, we're happy in our little rehearsal place in Scotland.' And he said, 'Well, then that's what we'll do. We'll record there and we'll bring a little mobile studio. We'll record in the place that you're happy.' And we thought that was so neat, to think of something like that, rather than put us in a commercial facility. He just brought the studio to us."

1973

April 1973. Nazareth, through their new label Mooncrest, issue "Broken Down Angel" paired with debut album track "Witchdoctor Woman." The single reaches #9 on the UK charts. In 1974, Dan calls this the band's first big break—as well as biggest disappointment, when the track didn't reach #1.

Pete Agnew:

"It's very funny with 'Broken Down Angel.' It was the first big, big hit, and how it came about, I remember the night it all happened. We played at a ballroom in Cardiff. It was a horrible night and we were sitting in the dressing room and our two roadies were taking the gear out and we were just sitting around waiting. Manny was playing the acoustic guitar and we were singing different songs and stuff, and we started doing Marianne Faithfull's 'If You'll Come and Stay with Me.' We used to love that song. And Manny started playing this chord sequence and it developed from that and soon we had the shape of 'Broken Down Angel.'"

Manny Charlton on "Broken Down Angel:"

"We just thought it was a really good tune. We kind of modelled it after Rod Stewart, who was big at that time. I wrote the chorus, and between the rest of the guys in the band we wrote the verses. The two producers we had from previous albums, we didn't really feel were getting things right. We did a lot of dates with Deep Purple, supporting them, and we asked Roger if he would try producing us, for a single. 'Broken Down Angel' was specifically recorded as a single. And he said, 'Sure, I'd love to do it.' And he did a great job on that. And then it was full steam ahead."

"So again, the first thing that we came up with and gave Roger was 'Broken Down Angel.' We went, 'Look, we want to do like The Faces, but make it sound like a Rod Stewart record at the time.' That was kind of how his audition was with us. We went in and did that single and got on so well that it was sort of automatic that we said, 'Yeah, do the album.' 'Woke Up This Morning' we had actually done on our second album, and we were playing it live, totally different from the album version, of course. That was one of the songs right away we knew from the inside out. We had 'Razamanaz' and 'Broken Down Angel' and several other songs."

"You see, even Zeppelin, at that point, weren't making singles; they didn't want any singles. So automatically they didn't go to Top of the Pops and they didn't get airplay during the day on mainstream radio. So that's where the kind of underground connotation came around, because basically they weren't visible, or as visible as, say, T. Rex and other bands that were on Top of the Pops. And in Britain, a band would appear on Top of the Pops and then instantly they'd be headliners. They're the main musical outlet. We didn't get played that much until we came down with 'Broken Down Angel' and they decided that yeah, that fitted the radio format and we were on Top of the Pops and our album nearly went Top Ten."

July 22nd, 1973, Frankfurt, Germany.

May 5, 1973. Nazareth's third album, the Roger Glover-produced *Razamanaz*, is issued in the UK; it reaches #11 on the UK charts.

Dan McCafferty:

"*Razamanaz* I really like a lot, because I think that's the point where we found out what we wanted to do. Because *Nazareth* and *Exercises* before that were kind of varied. But we found out what we liked to do, and we found out what we were good at. We did Exercises and we thought, well, this is not what we like doing very much. So we started writing all this stuff for the stage and went out playing it on the road and it was going down really well with the crowds. Roger had just finished working with Elf, which was Ronnie James Dio, God rest him, and so we said to Roger, would you like to do it? Yeah. So we did *Razamanaz*, *Loud 'n' Proud* and *Rampant* with Roger. But that kind of band had established itself as a rock band anyway. See, *Exercises* was actually the one that was different because Nazareth's original album was a lot heavier as well. So *Razamanaz* was normal for us."

Pete Agnew:

"*Razamanaz* was so much fun to do. We loved playing that music. That was the album where Nazareth became Nazareth. And you've got to remember, that record was recorded in nine days. Same with *Loud 'n' Proud*—it was nine days as well. It's incredible when you think about it. They're almost like live albums, basically a live album with an overdub (laughs). And when we made *Razamanaz*, you know what it's like, Martin, it's a feeling that you get. When we did *Razamanaz*, we went, 'That's a hit. That album is going to make people take notice.' We knew it. You had no doubts about it when you finished it, that you'd done something really good. You just can't wait for it to come out. We were going, 'Release it, release it, release it!' (laughs)."

Manny Charlton:

"Roger was great. If it wasn't for Roger, I don't think we would have gotten anywhere. Because we had done two albums and we didn't know what we were doing. We wanted to be Elton John, we wanted to be Deep Purple, we wanted to be Led Zeppelin, we wanted to be The Band—we went through everything, all our influences, Neil Young. We just wanted to write songs like all our favourites and play them, and we could (laughs) but we found out that wasn't too smart. The albums didn't sell; the albums didn't do any good at all."

"And it was two different producers. The second album was by Roy Thomas Baker; that was his first production, by the way. No, they were just all over the place, basically. And when we went in with Roger, he said, 'Look, your albums aren't selling, but you always get great live reception when you play live.' 'Yeah, we're always going down well.' When we played live, we were something else. We were a hard rock trio, you know? Blues, that's what we were when we played live. And Roger said, 'That's what you do live. You've got to do that on the album.' So fortunately we had a great bunch of songs. And Roger produced it and it was great. Because he knew what he was doing. He was a musician. That's what we needed. We needed a musician to help us translate what we were going to do musically and get it on record."

"But yeah, the first two albums that we did, we were all over the place musically and genre-speaking. But when we played live we went out as a four-piece and basically played hard rock, with Marshall stacks and a lot of drums and stuff and Dan screaming his head off. And that seemed to go over really well. So we were puzzled at the time as to why our records weren't selling but we were doing well live. And so we decided the best thing we could probably do was get a musician that understood what we were trying to do. And we'd been playing dates with Purple in the States and Europe so we knew Roger. And there were these guys that were producing their own bands, and we knew Roger was producing Purple at the time. And Pete Townsend was an influence working with The Who, and Zeppelin and Jimmy Page, so basically we asked the three of them if they would be interested in producing the band, and Roger got back to us first and really wanted to do it. So we went yeah, well we know the guy anyway; we were mates."

July 20, 1973. Nazareth gets on Top of the Pops, with "Bad Bad Boy." The next day they play the Buxton Pop Festival, after initially having withdrawn from the show, followed by a trip to Germany to play the second night of the Summer Rock Festival in Frankfurt.

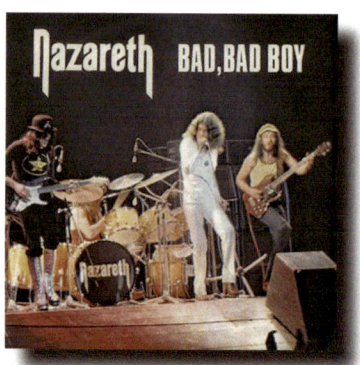
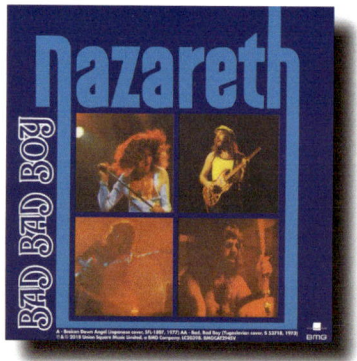

July 1973. Mooncrest float a second single from *Razamanaz*, "Bad Bad Boy," which rises to No.10 on the charts. On the flipside are non-LP heavy rockers "Hard Living" and "Spinning Top."

July 27, 1973. Nazareth play the London Music Festival, at Alexandra Palace, as part of many UK shows throughout 1973.

August 1973. *Razamanaz* gets belated issue in the US and Canada, the latter eventually sending the record to platinum status for sales of over 100,000 copies.

Reviewer Jim Miller:
"Displaying some small flair for contemplating disaster, 'Woke Up This Morning' cheerfully recites a litany of murdered dog, dead cat and crispy burnt homestead. The title tune, nonsense vocals and all, gets the pagan raucous fuzz-zap treatment. 'Sold My Soul,' on the other hand, toys with satanic capitulation, a muddy guitar line accenting McCafferty's earnest confession of sin. And finally 'Broken Down Angel' widens the stylistic spectrum to include Rod Stewart overtones, Purpled C&W passages and a song of lost virtue. As for the band's performances, McCafferty croak-talks rather than sings, and Manuel Charlton's guitar playing proves something less than innovative. But the four Scottish lads rarely avoid an opportunity to turn a stale cliché to their slender advantage. When Nazareth hits snide stride, they turn out enough pop staples to match any modest band: a subdued cheer for Scotch rock."
(Rolling Stone, October 25, 1973)

September 1973. "Broken Down Angel"/"Hard Living" is issued as a single in the US.

September 23, 1973. Nazareth play a gig on the shores of Lake Spivey, just outside of Atlanta, Georgia, with Blue Öyster Cult and hard southern rockers Hydra.

September 29, 1973. In the annual Melody Maker Music Poll, Nazareth take top spot for "Greatest Hope," beating out Wings and Genesis.

October 18 – November 10, 1973. The band mount a short UK tour, just as their new album—and single "This Flight Tonight" (backed with "Called Her Name")—is hitting the shops. The single reaches #11 on the UK charts and #27 as the band's first charting single in Canada.

Dan McCafferty on "This Flight Tonight:"
"You know how you're on the road and everybody's got tapes? Well, that song just kept showing up all the time on somebody's fave-raves tape, off the *Blue* album. So eventually we decided to give it a go. Obviously we wanted to make it as far away from Joni as we possibly could, 'cause you could imagine how it would sound with me trying to sound like Joni Mitchell! It's a good song, and if you start with a good song it should be able to be played any way you want it." *(w/ Steve Newton, Ear of Newt)*

Record and Radio Mirror on "This Flight Tonight:"
"The rhythm on this Joni Mitchell song suggests a galloping Western, with John Wayne or somebody equally stone-faced, in the saddle. Or putting it another way, Nazareth see it as a) a hit and b) some kind of space-age presentation. It's very good indeed, packed with lead-voice power and a lot of galloping. No crash-landing, but a ruddy great hit. Very together, Nazareth."
(Record and Radio Mirror, October 6, 1973)

October 18, 1973. Nazareth get on Top of the Pops with "This Flight Tonight." The guys had great respect for Joni Mitchell, and would play her music on long van rides between gigs. Fortunately, Mitchell was over the moon when she heard Nazareth's heavy metal treatment of the song.

Manny Charlton:
"'This Flight Tonight' was absolutely killer. We were really happy with that. One thing about that one is that Pete asked me when we were recording it, he said, 'Are you going to do the solo on that?' I said, 'The solo is done. That's the solo (laughs). It's that slide solo that I did on it.' And he went, 'That's the solo?!' And I went yeah! (laughs). Basically, I turned my guitar up an octave so all the strings were single note. And I like playing slide a lot, so what was going on was, the guitar was extremely loud and it was feeding back and you were getting these resonances. The feedback would alternate sometimes, and from the high register, sometimes it would drop an octave out of the blue, you know? So I just put a slide on it and I played what I thought were cool notes. I tried to basically imitate a jet, just to give the song some atmosphere, not play a conventional pentatonic scale blues thing. And it sounded great. Roger was knocked out with that."

"The gallop, that was our idea; I liked that rhythm. But Roger helped us a lot in the construction of it, the drumming mainly. He helped out Darrell a lot, pretty much telling him what to play and where to play. That rhythm was familiar to us anyway, because we did 'Morning Dew' like that anyway, on the first album."

October 19, 1973. Nazareth's fourth album, *Loud 'n' Proud*, is issued in the UK, managing a #10 placement on the UK charts.

Pete Agnew:
"Back to the Gangy and the Pye mobile again, which had only 13 of 16 tracks working by this time. I think they scrapped the studio after we finished the album. Anyway, we didn't have enough time to finish recording the album because we had to go on tour so we arranged to do the one remaining track (and all the backing vocals) at Apple studio in London."

"The problem was that we didn't *have* the one remaining track. Here's how things were back in those days. You had two sides on the vinyl record and you aimed at having a total minimum of 36 minutes for the record, or approximately 18 minutes a side. We were about seven-and-a-half minutes short on original

July 22nd, 1973, Frankfurt, Germany.

© Laurens Van Houten / Frank White Photo Agency

July 22nd, 1973, Frankfurt, Germany.

material so we had no idea what to fill this gap with. It was decided that Darrell should go into the studio and lay down eight minutes of a heavy plodding rhythm and we would come up with some ideas to overdub.
I went in after him and stuck down this big fuzzy bass part, and although this was all sounding like fun, we still didn't know what we were going to sing."
"That's when Dan came up with the idea of singing Dylan's 'The Ballad of Hollis Brown.' Not because he loved the song especially, but because it had eight verses and he reckoned he could space it out over the time we needed. It's weird that under the circumstances of how that track was eventually conceived and completed, people still come up to me and tell me that it's their favourite Nazareth track of all time. Go figure."

Dan McCafferty on the *Loud 'n' Proud* cover art:

"That was done by a kid in London. The band was really starting to take off. We had done *Razamanaz* and of course we were doing *Loud 'n' Proud*, so we wanted something that would represent that, and we sent out feelers to see what people could come up with. And they came up with this young artist who did that, and it was perfect for what we were doing at the time. He actually did it the size of the album sleeve. The management company got it, at one point."

Darrell Sweet:

"Individual and collective performances are much better. The numbers are great. Production is also a step forward. ('The Ballad of Hollis Brown') is the biggest thing we've ever covered. For four, it's an achievement. It synthesizes sounds without a synthesizer."
(w/ Steve Clarke, New Musical Express, October 27, 1973)

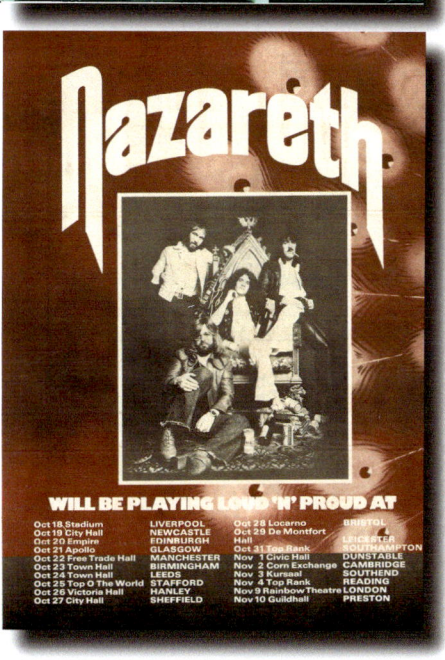

Reviewer Greg Shaw:

"Much as I enjoy the fast numbers, it must be noted that Nazareth are occasionally as monotonous as Status Quo or Uriah Heep, as on 'Not Faking It,' which is all strut and preen, but with none of the substance of their earlier remarkable heavy metal C&W 'Broken Down Angel.' The non-originals provide the best moments. Little Feat's 'Teenage Nervous Breakdown' picks up in power what it loses in subtlety; Joni Mitchell's 'This Flight Tonight' is shocking when heard in a Led Zeppelin arrangement. The clincher comes with a nine-minute version of Bob Dylan's 'The Ballad of Hollis Brown.' An over-long drone of a song to begin with, it's stretched to the limits with every repetitious device known to modern rock, and drowned in a haze of feedback fuzz. Strangely enough it works. And that leads me to the conclusion that Nazareth, in bridging the gap between folk and heavy metal, could easily become the Turtles of the '70s. They are a group worth watching." *(Rolling Stone, May 9, 1974)*

November 1973. "Bad Bad Boy"/"Razamanaz" is issued as a US single.

Dan McCafferty on working with Roger Glover:

"Roger was a great lad, and still is. Pete and I just went to see Purple before Christmas when they were in Glasgow and we went out for something to eat and that was great fun. He's a really nice guy and a dedicated musician. He's a great arranger and knows how to get you to do stuff. He'd say, 'Well, your songs, guys, you know how to do that,' and if there's something he doesn't like, he'll say, 'I don't necessarily like that, but if you guys are crazy about it, fine. It's your stuff, you know I mean?' But he was good at things like, 'Well, there are too many of those bits; you don't need all those.' And as a person, he's a lovely man. He's just a good mate."

Pete Agnew on "Razamanaz."

"Need you ask? Did you ever hear 'Speed King?' (laughs). Actually, when Roger produced the album and we went to them with the album and album cover all done, and they started playing it, all the guys in Deep Purple, Ian Paice said, 'Oh, come on' (laughs). And Roger, 'No, no, no…' I mean, that's obviously what we were thinking about when we did it. Of course it's a different song, but the vibe and the structure, it's practically 'Speed King' part two. But it was Nazareth's 'Speed King.' For us, those kinds of songs came from jams, like Deep Purple did it. They'd jam and then a song would come over the top. We kind of did that with 'Razamanaz.'"

July 22nd, 1973, Frankfurt, Germany.

© Laurens Van Houten / Frank White Photo Agency

1974

February 1974. "This Flight Tonight"/"Go Down Fighting" is issued as a single in the US, concurrent with the belated issue of the source album, *Loud 'n' Proud*, also this month. The record would receive platinum certification in Canada, fuelled by repeated radio spins of "This Flight Tonight," which was classed as Canadian content given that it was written by Joni Mitchell. The "CanCon" rule at the time in Canada was that 30% of what was played on the radio had to be "Canadian content."

Roger Glover:
"I got the Judas Priest job on the basis of Nazareth's 'This Flight Tonight,' which was basically my arrangement. Nazareth had run out of songs. They were going to do 'This Flight Tonight,' but they were going to do it the way, I don't know, Rod Stewart might have done it on a solo album. And I said no, that's kind of boring, let's do something different. So I came up with this whole chugga concept and the arrangement for it. And it was on the strength of that that Judas Priest wanted me to do 'Diamonds and Rust,' which, if you listen to it, you see the similarities."

Pete Agnew on working with Roger Glover:
"When people listen to Deep Purple, they don't realize the arranging and all that stuff—it's all done with Roger. He's the guy that runs the recording sessions, you know? This is how it gets done; he's the man. And when he got with us, he taught us structure of the song, structure of the solo, how to actually record the thing. We learned a lot about recording studios with Roger. Although we'd been in them and used them, this was, 'Do this, do that.' And he's still a great friend. I'm eternally grateful to Roger Glover. He was a big, big influence in making Nazareth believe in themselves as a rock band. Plus he was the first guy in the studio to really spot Dan's potential as a vocalist, a great rock singer."

"It's funny; we learned a lot from him but he learned a lot from us. See, he was all about heavy rock and that was it. He didn't see any farther than that. Deep Purple was 'all.' Well, Deep Purple were never our favourite band. We liked them, but they're not songwriters. They're an instrumental band that's got some vocals over the top of it. So we introduced Roger… and in fact he'll tell people this to this day, that Nazareth introduced him to Little Feat. He'd never listened to them, never heard of them. And we went, 'Roger, this is the best band in the world.' And, 'You've got to listen to them.' And we used to play Little Feat to him every day and every night and he became a huge fan and his actual musical tastes started to spread out a bit. So he kind of thanks us, in a roundabout way. So we helped each other. But no, he was the man that actually put us on the road to success."

"But he could bring everything together; he was a good arranger. And he was a disciplinarian. We would do one track every day, and at the end of the day, when everybody was pretty much tired, he would say, 'Okay, we're going to routine the track for tomorrow.' So we would just start messing around with the track, and we would play for about two hours every night and work out what we were going to do the next day. We wouldn't record it that night, because we were too tired to record it. But he used to go around with his drumstick, you know, like a conductor (laughs). And one of the things that he really loved, when we did the albums, he loved the vocals. Because we have a lot of harmony and he never had that in Deep Purple. Ian was always just singing; Deep Purple wasn't a harmony band. So he had a great time saying, 'Can you do this? Can you do that?' And of course we could. He really enjoyed that."

Darrell Sweet:
"We are fans of Joni Mitchell. I don't care if Joni Mitchell fans like it—Joni Mitchell does and that's the main thing. She thoroughly enjoyed it, especially the phone part." *(w/ Steve Clarke, New Musical Express, October 27, 1973)*

March 1974. "Shanghai'd in Shanghai" reaches #41 in the UK charts; the single issue is backed with "Love, Now You're Gone." Jon Lord is a guest musician on the A-side, playing on "Glad When You're Gone" from the *Rampant* album as well.

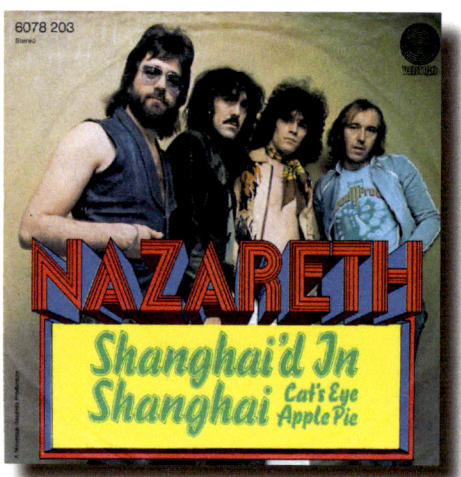

Dan McCafferty, on singing the high ones:
"What I found was, if you can make the notes, fine. Then you can find a way to get your personality into them and make it your own. But if you can't make the notes physically, then that's very odd. Because you get some producers making albums by trying to piece takes together, and I would hate that; I wouldn't know how to handle that very well. So I guess everybody's got to handle it differently. I've had troubles in the studio but I've always overcome them, thankfully, he says, touching wood. But I've got no advice for anybody else how to do it, to be honest."

"I had to go to a specialist in Austria—once—but I just had a terribly sore throat. I got a cold; it was like bad laryngitis. My vocal cords were swelling. He gave me a bunch of really ugly-tasting stuff to take for a couple of days and it was okay. So I've been very lucky. I know some wonderful singers who've had so many problems. But see, I never let it bother me, Martin, because I always figured, if it's gonna go, it's gonna go. I've met so many singers that were paranoid: it's too hot, it's too cold, it's too smoky, it's not smoky enough (laughs), and they just worry themselves into giving themselves a sore throat. But I didn't really worry about it that much, because I figured if it goes, well, it's served me well. It maybe deserves a couple weeks off. What can you say? (laughs)."

Pete Agnew on getting Jon Lord to play on the album:
"We were in Montreux, in Switzerland, and we were recording. Funny enough, we were recording on the Rolling Stones mobile, same as Deep Purple did with 'Smoke On The Water,' down in the Convention Centre. Roger wanted us to go over and do the same thing that they did, so we did that. And it just so happens that Jon was in the area. All of a sudden we needed a piano player. He came

along for a drink with us, and we said, 'Well, since you're here, pal, come down here, we've got a big grand piano, come in and hit it.'"

"But that mobile, the thing was parked in the basement in what's called the Convention Centre. It's still there, I think. And Roger suggested it would be good, because we made a couple of records with him and they were both on mobiles. He liked us working with mobiles, because we didn't like working in studios at that time. We just liked to play our guitars and whenever we felt like it, rather than in a closed-in studio. And he said, 'This will be good for you' and it worked out really, really good; we had a lot of fun."

April 4 – May 26, 1974. The band tour the UK.

Pete Agnew, on stage clothes:
"I tried the jacket and costume stripes when we played at Watford, and I threw a bummer because I was self-conscious about what I got in. I'm used to jeans. You go in jeans and you sweat and you go out and think, 'Yeah, so I'm going to get batteries.' But it's good because you're playing in what you're used to. If Dan imagines himself in a suit, good luck to him, but I feel really stupid. You get guys that go on stage and get really neat—and then they go out and put on a pair of jeans. What's the point? Who are they trying to fool? At least when Dan and Manny started using flashy gear, they used it all the time. Apparently, Elton and the like are the same."
(New Musical Express, June 1974)

April 24, 1974. Nazareth get on Top of the Pops with "Shanghai'd in Shanghai" and then again the following month with "Shape of Things," both *Rampant* tracks. On the record, Roger is credited with synthesizer on the latter, as well as on rousing opening track "Silver Dollar Forger."

Pete Agnew:
"We lost the first place by 40 places—it crossed out at 41. If you don't do Top of the Pops, then forget about it. And why not do it? I care that it doesn't get on the charts. I feel really bad about it. (As for radio) I think the BBC producers are pretty hip guys who get quoted for records and evaluate their merits. But it's the panel that picks the records. Have you seen the guys on the panel? It's quite amazing. They must be the guys who choose people for Coronation Street. They are the ones who really say, 'Yes, this is a good record—it will be played.'" (New Musical Express, June 1974)

April 26, 1974. *Rampant,* Nazareth's fifth album, is issued in the UK, managing a #13 placement in the UK charts and, after a couple years, gold status in Canada.

Dan McCafferty:
"Good album, but it was a transition album for us. It's the last one we did with Roger. He wanted us to do son of *Loud 'n' Proud.* But we were like, 'No Roger, we have this other stuff and we want to move along.' And he was all like, 'Well, Deep Purple do it this way,' and this that and the other. And I don't mean that as nasty toward Deep Purple, but he was more about stick to what people recognise you for. And our attitude was we think that people can think for themselves (laughs). Okay, they like *Razamanaz,* but they might like this as well. But we didn't fall out because of it. Roger was like, 'Okay lads, that's no problem,' and he was a big help on the record. I like it because it was a transition album, but when I look back, I think we were trying to do too many different things too quickly. And again hindsight is an exact science. We were excited about the stuff at the time and it was fun to do. We had the mobile and were in the Swiss mountains and it was a lovely place to work."

"But I love *Rampant*. I mean, I like all our stuff. You look back years later and perhaps for some things, you say, 'Oh that was a bit dumb. Maybe we shouldn't have done that.' But there wasn't an album we didn't like at the time. It's easier in a year's time to go, 'Oh, wrong!' But rock 'n' roll should be spontaneous and instant. Because by the time we get something in the studio that we all agree on, it's been through all the fights. At least we all agree we should record that. And then you do the best job that you can. If it doesn't work, well, you gave it your best shot."

Roger Glover:

"We were always on good terms, but it was definitely the end of the road. They wanted to produce themselves. Manny, I know that every time I made a move in the studio, he was like, 'What are you doing that for?' And you can always tell that when someone is that keen, they really want to be in charge. And eventually it happened, of course, and they did very well with it."

Pete Agnew:

"As I say, the studio was parked in the basement of the convention center and we used a big work/storage room upstairs to actually play most of our parts as overdubs although we had a setup with the drums and some amps next to the mobile. I can't remember exactly how long it took to do my bass parts but I reckon I walked 20 miles up and down those stairs and lost 20 pounds in the process. I also can't remember why we did all that running around because you can overdub in the control room whilst sitting on your ass! Hmm… Anyway, we eventually finished the backing tracks in 14 days, lost weight, got fit, and returned to the UK to do the vocals in Ian Gillan's studio in London. Dan sung all the lead vocals in three days and we did all the backing vocals in one night. When I think back, that album was more of a workout than a recording."

May 14, 1974. Nazareth get on The Old Grey Whistle Test with "Silver Dollar Forger" and "Loved and Lost."

June 7 – August 3, 1974. The band mount a North American tour, supporting Blue Öyster Cult.

July 1974. *Rampant* is issued in the US. Concurrently, "Sunshine," backed with "This Fight Tonight," gets floated as a US single from the album.

July 7, 1974. Nazareth play second on a bill to Blue Öyster Cult, supporting in the third slot is Kiss.

September 14, 1974. In Stockholm, Sweden, the guys are presented with *Loud 'n' Proud* gold record awards for sales of over 30,000 copies.

At the Sheraton Hotel, Stockholm, 1974 receiving gold records.

© Roger Tilberg / Alamy Stock Photo

September – November 1974. The band conduct a twenty-date Canadian tour, with a few of the Ontario dates in late October supported by Rush.

November 8, 1974. Non-LP Everly Brothers cover "Love Hurts," backed with non-LP original "Down" is issued as a single in the UK. On November 30th, the guys present the song on Top of the Pops.

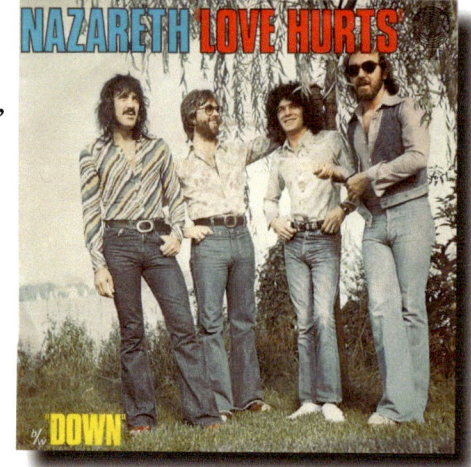

August 30th, 1974, Rotterdam, Netherlands.

© Laurens Van Houten / Frank White Photo Agency

August 30th, 1974, Rotterdam, Netherlands.

© Laurens Van Houten / Frank White Photo Agency

August 31st, 1974, Amsterdam, Netherlands.

"For *Hair of the Dog*, that was a guy who was recommended to us by the people that do the sleeves at Hipgnosis, it was at the time, and he said, 'This guy is great.' And they showed us a kind of rough sketch and we thought, well, that's pretty cool. So he delivered the sleeves (laughs) but he'd drawn it on the wrong size of paper, so that's why there's a black band down the side of the back of the album, right? And we thought, no, we can't ask this guy to do this again, because you never know, it could be worse. So we thought, well, we'll just put that on the back and use it for the titles. Nobody met the guy. He doesn't like to meet people and stuff. You know, you see what he draws through the day—what does he come up with at night, man? (laughs). We called him and said, 'Great job,' and he kinda whispered, 'Thanks very much, man; love your music' and that was that."
Dan McCafferty

1975-1979

April 1st, 1976, London, UK.

The latter half of the 1970s found Nazareth essentially touring in support of their two hits, a song called "Love Hurts," and an album called *Hair of the Dog*. The fact that there were fully four other records released during the multiple national and international legs of the *Hair of the Dog* campaign is neither here nor there.

I'm being facetious, but there is some deep music business truth to that concept. In fact, to take the proposed interpretation further, during this five-year span, the band was touring in support of *Razamanaz*, *Loud 'n' Proud* and "This Flight Tonight" as validly or relevantly or significantly as they were *Close Enough for Rock 'n' Roll*, *Play 'n' the Game*, *Expect No Mercy* and *No Mean City*.

In other words, the impressive platform the band had engineered for themselves in the early '70s, as well as the bona fide hit album they had in 1975's *Hair of the Dog*, had set the band's reputation so profoundly that, although things could have conceivably got better and better, they didn't, which, as a feedback loop, puts even greater emphasis on past glories. As the guys spread their wings fearlessly exploring quite jarringly different music styles across the records of the late '70s, the bloom on this period—most pertinently, the fact that they could headline large venues—in actuality resulted from the evergreen sales of the band's two 1973 albums as well as *Hair of the Dog* and the AM and FM success of their cover of rote ballad "Love Hurts."

Further proof of this proposal is that the guys were able to notch to their belts impressive sales for *Greatest Hits* and *Hot Tracks*, a sure sign that a band had reached the institution stage, en route to being a successful and working heritage act. And even though none of the records of the late '70s yielded that next big hit single, four out of five of them went gold in Canada, meaning that the band could continue to headline all the A-level and B-level hockey barns dotted across the country.

April 20th, 1975, Amsterdam, Netherlands.

1975

March 14, 1975. "Hair of the Dog," backed with "Too Bad, Too Sad" is issued in the UK as a single. On tour dates in support of the new album, the band would be augmented with ex-Tiger keyboard player Tommy Eyre, later of the Ian Gillan Band and The Sensational Alex Harvey Band.

April 30, 1975. Nazareth issue their sixth album, *Hair of the Dog*, produced by Manny Charlton, recorded at Escape Studios in Kent, mixed at AIR London. The US edition switches out Randy Newman's "Guilty" for "Love Hurts," propelling the record to RIAA-certified platinum status, aided by second hit, "Hair of the Dog." The album reached #17 on the Billboard charts and also certified gold in Canada.

Dan McCafferty:

"*Hair of the Dog* was a particularly busy time. We had been working flat-out for three years straight and I think everybody was like needing a break. Maybe that's why it sounds so desperate (laughs). I think also when you tour a lot you start to get a bit more cynical, less trust in people, so maybe the album is a bit cynical. It was the first one that Manny Charlton produced; the three before that, Roger Glover had worked on, which was great fun. But then we decided we wanted to go in this direction and Roger just thought we should stay with what we had. So we said, no, we want to try this. We want it to be really quite raw and quite sort of heavy. Because that's what the music we were writing at the time demanded, you know?"

"And I remember it very well. It was a case of the guys going in and doing the backing tracks. I would do the vocals, and we would say, yes, that's fine but we'll change this a little bit. We had it sort of worked up before we went into the studio, so we knew what we expected to hear. And the main thing for us was getting the sound we were getting in rehearsals, which we managed to get. We recorded it in a studio that's no longer there, and then we finished it off in Air London and it turned out really well. Jeff Beck was there every night, because he just lived around the corner. And Jeff used to drop by and give us his grade, 'Oh, six out of ten, four out of ten; you can do better than that, boys.' And he used to sit and talk about cars 'til four in the morning. We kept saying, 'Come on, Jeff, play something on it.' But he didn't (laughs). Because he's tied up by more record companies than a rodeo cow."

"We did it in somewhere like ten days or something (laughs). It was Manny and a guy named Tony Taverner did it and John Punter worked on the mix as well. So we knew that we would get the sounds that we wanted. We had most of the songs together before we went into the studio so it was a case of just getting the best performance. 'That's the one, guys,' you know? We hadn't played any of those songs live. It was just a case of having rehearsed them up quite a bit at sound checks and little rehearsals."

"When we tried to do the vocals, the studio we were in, they didn't have any compressors (laughs) and you couldn't do any vocals in there. You could only do guide vocals and take them somewhere else to do them because they would just crack up all over the place. So it wasn't all that well equipped for doing voices, which was kind of a hassle. But everything worked out okay."

"'Please Don't Judas Me'... we were going through a bunch of stuff at the time with management companies and record companies and so-called friends. We found ourselves in a lot of trouble, unbeknownst to us, of course. And that was kind of a reflection on that. If you're going to sell me out, just tell me about it, you know? Let's not get a bunch of lawyers to have to work it all out. And then there was 'Changin' Times,' which was a case of, we just loved the riff. Manny and Pete played it so well and we thought, let's get something for this. And it turned out quite nicely with the odd time signature and everything."

Pete Agnew:

"By this time we had had our fill of mobiles for the time being and decided we would use a studio that didn't have wheels. The place we ended up in was on old 'oast house' down in Kent in England. The house was where we lived, and outside there was a barn that these guys had converted into a studio. Problem was, they never told the local authorities that they had converted the barn, so when neighbours complained about the 'noise from the studio,' the local authorities replied, 'What studio?'"

"However, no matter how basic the studio was—and it was basic—we managed to get a great sound on the backing tracks and instrumental overdubs. They were all done in nine days but we had to move up to AIR Studios in London to record the vocals. What I remember most from the AIR sessions was coming into the control room after Dan had just sang 'Miss Misery' for the first time and it was on playback so we could have a listen and see where it needed any fixing. When the track finished, the band members were completely silent having been stunned by this incredible performance. It was at this point that one of our managers broke the silence with, 'That will be great when Dan gets the vocal right!' We never discussed music with that guy again."

May 1975. America sees a single issue for the cheeky title track of the new album, backed with "Love Hurts." At the same time, back home, Mooncrest issues "My White Bicycle" as a single. The non-LP Tomorrow cover (featuring Steve Howe on guitar) manages a No.14 placement on the charts and is backed with metallic *Hair of the Dog* rocker "Miss Misery."

Dan McCafferty:

"We said, 'Who the fuck are Sears?' I had been in the States and I had even heard John Wayne say son of a bitch. So we just changed the meaning behind it to get past the false modesty of Americans. Hair of the dog really means the same thing. But really, the whole band is involved in the lyrics. We do a lot of things like a band. It saves a whole lot of arguing down the road. There were a couple of occasions where Manny wanted to have his name on stuff. We said, fine. Nine times out of ten, when we write something it was credited to everybody. Later on in life, it makes it better."

"But 'Miss Misery,' everybody gets excited during that one. We used to have to use an electric metronome to keep us from going too fast. Some nights we get carried away with it. Some nights it's hard to keep the timing slow enough. Lyrically, it was based on more than one person. Everyone has had their own Miss Misery. If not, then you are a lucky boy."

Pete Agnew:
"We were going to call the album *Son of a Bitch,* because where we come from, 'son of a bitch' is not even a saying. That's just a thing John Wayne said in movies; it's not a British thing. We took it to A&M in California and they said no. So we thought, fair enough, we'd be really smart and we'd call it *Heir of the Dog,* HEIR. And basically, the guys said, 'Oh, we're all Scottish; let's call it *Hair of the Dog.*' So once the dog was mentioned, we went to this guy to draw it and we actually never met the guy. We saw the finished album sleeve and you've got to realise, I'm not really a monster guy; I'm a little more laid-back. They're not my favourite thing (laughs). But I was outvoted and the band loved it. It's a fantastic painting, I've got to admit. Management just showed it to us after the guy did it and the guys thought, 'Yeah, that's punchy.'"

June 19, 1975. Nazareth get on Top of the Pops with "My White Bicycle," with a repeat airing two weeks later.

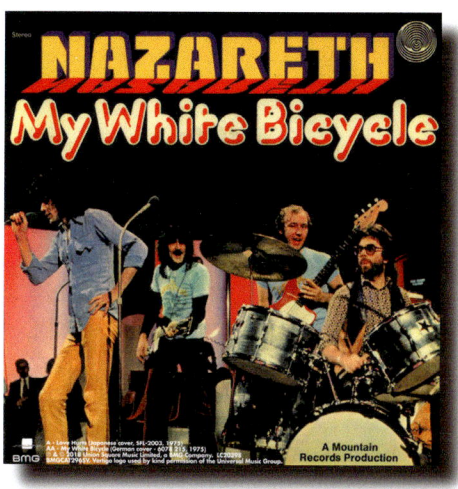

Dan McCafferty, on "My White Bicycle:"
"When it first came out, we were playing on the Scottish circuit of bars and ballrooms. I mean, to stay alive in those places, you just had to play the current hits of the day, you know, all the Beatles and Stones stuff. But what we tried to do was choose songs that we thought would be hits and make them. This satisfied everyone. So we chose 'My White Bicycle' and we have enjoyed it ever since. In fact, it's one of the most requested songs we've ever had."

June 26 – September 26, 1975. Nazareth conduct a cross-Canada tour, many of the dates supported by Rush.

October 1975. Mountain issue "Holy Roller"/"Railroad Boy," both non-LP, as a UK single, with the A-side reaching #36 on the charts.

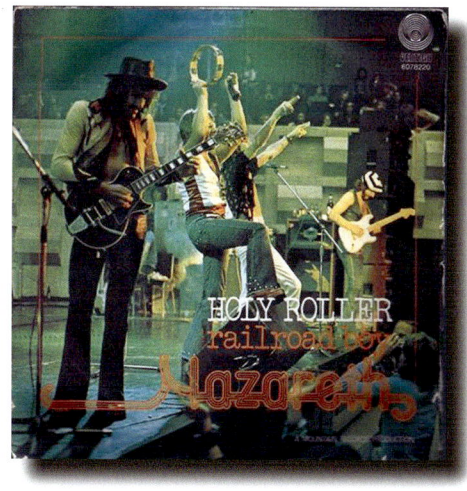

October 1975. Mountain issues *Dan McCafferty*, Dan's first solo album. It's a record of covers, recorded at Basing Street Studios. Five singles are floated from it across a number of years, with only Rolling Stones cover "Out of Time" charting, at #41. Roger Glover plays bass and Manny Charlton plays guitar, as does future Nazareth member Zal Cleminson. Manny also produces the record. The cover art is an early Joe Petagno, renowned for his Motörhead covers.

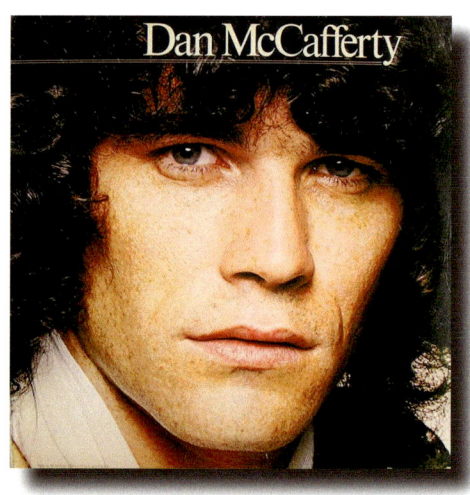

Dan McCafferty, on the guest stars on his record:
"There are three basic reasons for this. I know them all and they are all good companions. What I didn't want was that kind of horrible superstar thing where people just played for a credit up their sleeve. Second, they are all good musicians, and that is very important. And thirdly, they were all available (laughs). (Zal Cleminson) is amazing. When we were here listening to the reproductions, he was writhing and doing all the hand actions and everything. God, he's incredible. What we wanted was to be kind of happy with the album. We didn't want it to sound segmented like, you know, here comes Eric's solo and everyone is quiet. But at the same time we didn't want it to sound like Dan McCafferty and his new band or anything. Yes, we are quite satisfied with it. They're all big numbers and it's just something I've wanted to do for a long time."

"When the band was doing *Loud 'n' Proud*, which was our second successful album, I wanted to do a solo then. But we had to take a tour of the States and then there was Canada and then Germany and then the States again, so you can see that it was a little bit difficult. Then, all of a sudden, there was this month out of nowhere, so I took the chance. That was back in June. While I desperately wanted to do this, I didn't want to be selfish, but the rest of the boys couldn't have been more helpful about it. Manny produced my album and he plays a little bit of rhythm guitar in 'Out of Time.' As a band, we are very much into what the rest of the guys want to do as their own little pet projects And Nazareth is going to do some things from my album on stage. Why not? Because it is another facet for us and it will help to broaden our musical horizons a little." (Melody Maker, 1975)

November 1975. Ballad "Love Hurts" sees success as a single in the US, reaching #9 on the Billboard charts. It is included on *Greatest Hits*, also issued this month. The album is reissued on CD in 1989, 1996 and 2010, each with an increasing number of bonus tracks. Greatest Hits zooms to the #1 spot on the Canadian charts. The album is not issued in the US, with that territory in its stead getting *Hot Tracks* the following year.

Dan McCafferty on "Love Hurts" being added to the US version of *Hair of the Dog*:

"It was only put on the American version. We had a Randy Newman song called 'Guilty' on it in Europe and we did 'Love Hurts' as a B-side (laughs). Shows you what we know. And we sent it to the States, and Jerry Moss from A&M said, 'No, no, no, boys, this is a chance to really get some airplay here.' So he said, 'We'll take off "Guilty" and we'll put on "Love Hurts,"' and God bless him."

"We've always love that song. We used to do it as kids. We covered it when we were in bar bands, like the Everly Brothers version, and Pete and I used to sing it. Emmylou Harris and Gram Parsons did it on the *Pieces of the Sky* album, and we thought, oh, man, that's still a great song, let's do a version of that, so we did! And when we were recording it, Pete and I were at a wedding in Scotland and Manny and Darrell—God bless them—at the time did the guitar part and the drums, and then we came down and Pete did the bass part and I did the vocals and that was kind of that."

"We loved the version. 'That's a really great version of it, guys.' But we had no idea what it was going to do. And it came out in the States and nobody played it. And it was a place down in Texas that just kept playing it and playing it and playing it and eventually it started to spread from there. But it was a year after that song came out that it became a hit. It's an amazing story. And actually, the guy who wrote the song came and saw us in Los Angeles. He told us that the guys had heard it and they thought it was great. It's not like he was going to tell us that he thought it was a load of shit. We also got asked to sing the song at Axl Rose's wedding. We were in Germany so we couldn't do it. I think it was just as well because I think the song lasted longer than the marriage."

"We also covered 'Guilty' and 'Beggars Day' and we just loved those songs too. We still love them today and we're still fans. We just thought that any song we took, we could do our own version of it. The way Nils Lofgren did 'Beggars Day' was different than the way we did it."

November 12, 1975. Nazareth get on Top of the Pops with "Love Hurts."

November 27, 1975. The BBC air a Nazareth set from London's Paris Theatre; the recordings will be included as bonus material on the 2010 Salvo Records reissue of *Hair of the Dog*.

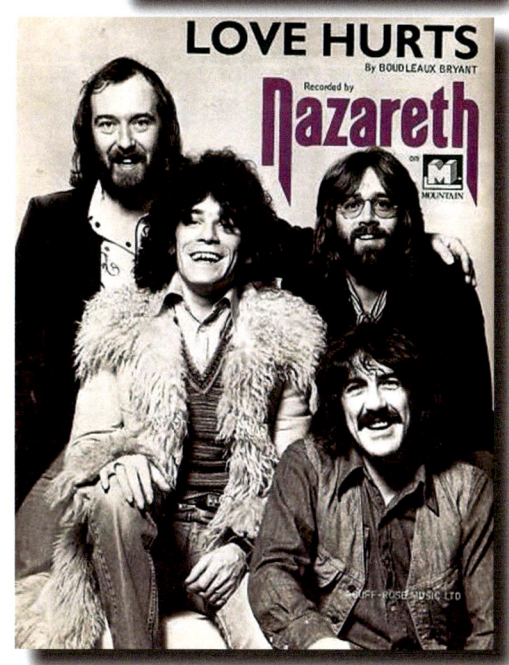

Dan McCafferty, also in 1975:

"It boils down to being a people's band. They have to get off on the music as well as the band. It's spoiled if there's a guy up there on stage preaching about his religion and telling the kids how cosmic it is. That's not where it's at. When we tour, we still keep things like 'This Flight Tonight' and older old numbers because people want to hear them and that's what they pay for. Christ, you can't say, 'Right, we're going to play all new material; forget the old stuff.' We consider ourselves as an old-style band. We play for the people and give them what they want. In doing so, we hit the odd high spot. That's what good rock is all about. I don't think the media is that impressed by what we do because we're not into something outlandish. The music is rock 'n' roll and it doesn't make for good comic books. Nobody is going to call us the saviours of rock 'n' roll." *(Melody Maker 1975)*

Performing on the Austrian TV show Spotlight in 1975.

Pete in Sweden: the epitome of rock 'n' roll.

April, 20th, 1975, Amsterdam, Netherlands.

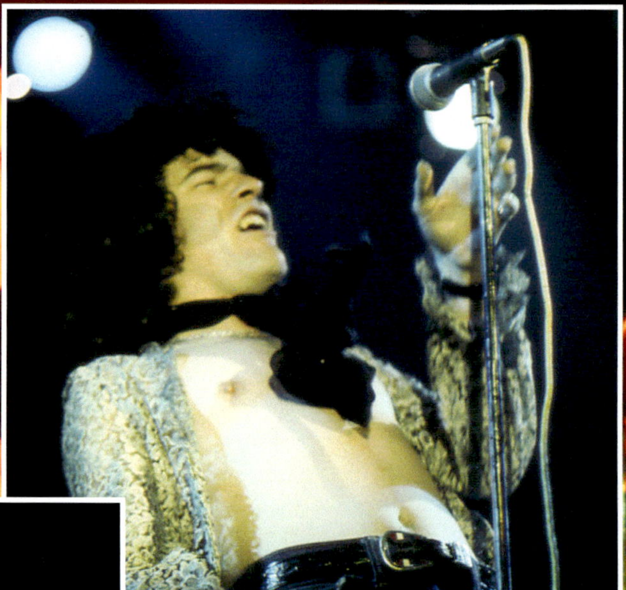

© Laurens Van Houten / Frank White Photo Agency

April, 20th, 1975, Amsterdam, Netherlands.

© Laurens Van Houten / Frank White Photo Agency

1976

January 14 – March 4, 1976. Nazareth tour the States, supporting Deep Purple, followed by UK dates and a return to the US in May.

Glenn Hughes:
"I befriended Nazareth in '72, about a year before I joined Purple, and I befriended Dan McCafferty and the bass player, Pete Agnew. I was living down in London, and we hung out quite a lot together. And then a couple of Purple tours, they opened for Purple. Dan and Pete were very close friends of mine. Dan has an incredible voice. I remember that 'Love Hurts' song, and when were doing Mark IV, that was the No.1 song across America. I have a certain amount of love for a lot of Scottish musicians. There are some amazing Scottish singing/songwriting musicians out there. But Dan, what an incredible, incredible voice. There was a lot of very strong camaraderie with those guys; it was great."

Late February 1976. "Carry Out Feelings," backed with "Lift the Lid," is issued as a single in the UK as well as the US.

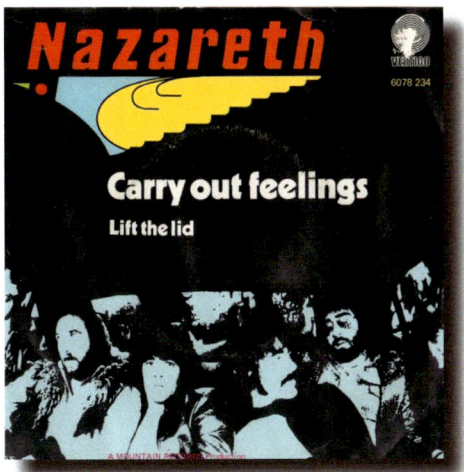

March 25, 1976. Nazareth issues a seventh studio album, entitled *Close Enough for Rock 'n' Roll*. The album would mark the first time the band recorded in Canada, using the legendary Le Studio, Morin Heights, in rural Quebec, north of Montreal. The record would also mark the first time the band didn't reach a certification level in Canada since the pre-*Razamanaz* days (according to official certifier Music Canada, despite other sources citing not only gold but platinum sales).

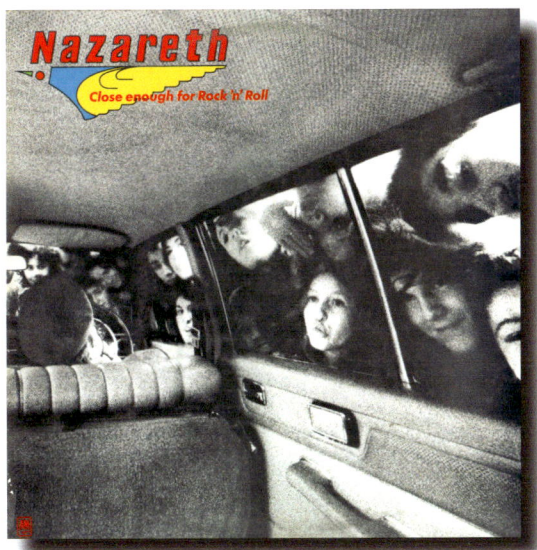
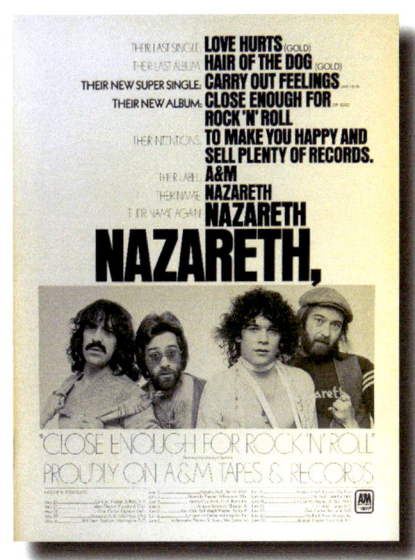

Dan McCafferty:

"I like the covers stuff from *Close Enough for Rock 'n' Roll*. That was another time when we had to make a lot of albums really quickly. Because we were doing really well touring-wise. We were selling out big halls and the record company wanted albums as well. I mean big time. We were doing loads of headlining. We did about three or four years of the halls. 1975 to '77 more or less. It was fine; I liked it. It was no problem. Of course we just got on with it, heads down and let's go! I look back now, and I would have liked to have had a bit more time. But that's the way it was done in those days."

"But Le Studio, that was a great place. See, we always liked recording like that, where you can get away from everything so you can just concentrate on the music. We liked to be in a working environment. And the town was just down the road five miles or something; it was nothing. It was just a lovely place and the people that ran it were cool. It was glass and you were standing in the middle of the Canadian woods with a lake outside. You could plug in near a tree if you wanted and do a guitar solo, if it was a nice day. I didn't sing out there personally, though. I don't think they'd like that, because you'd get bugs twittering and things like that."

"We tried canoeing. They had a wee aluminum canoe and we did try have a go at that. If we would have been the guys trying to find a way across Canada by water, we would've never got past Toronto. We were not canoers, put it that way. The fondest thing for me was playing in places nobody would go and play, but not canoeing there (laughs). We actually played Ulan Bator once, in a football stadium. The capital of Mongolia. That was bizarre, but very, very interesting. It was really good, actually; I enjoyed it. I asked if they'd had anybody play here before. They said, 'We do have a local band; they do "Love Hurts" too.'"

"But no, we always got a good vibe there. I'm sorry to hear that it's gone, but see, the thing is, that's kind of the story internationally. People don't need big rooms to work anymore. Mind you, live drums are coming back. There are a few studios up here that are building a bit on for live drums. But people can make records in their bedroom now. Nobody seems to care about ambience or vibe. I don't know, I'm probably sounding old-fashioned and horrible (laughs)."

Pete Agnew:

"The income tax situation in Britain at that time meant that if you got lucky and your new record was a hit, the government was being so kind that they would save you from having to worry about safeguarding your money by taking it all from you. Most bands found this unhelpful and decided to record anywhere except Britain. We had heard about a studio in the Laurentian mountains not too far from Montreal. Even had an easy name to remember. It was Le Studio and it was beautiful where it sat with its own lake in the woods among the mountains, so quiet it made us wonder if we were actually allowed to cause a disturbance playing rock 'n' roll."

"The studio itself had every latest gizmo that had been invented for recording and was the very opposite of where we had made the last album. We were very well prepared for this album and had written plenty of material so the recording was easy and quite relaxing. We decided that we loved this place and would be back again. Oh, did I mention they had a wonderful little restaurant down in the valley where we ate every night for six weeks? This time I put *on* 20 pounds."

Uncredited record review:
"Finger-in-the-socket rockers Nazareth have arrived again to bring us Gibraltar-solid rock. Side one is preoccupied with the musical diary of a rock band on tour, an inter-blending of their own 'Telegram' and an infectious momentary cover of the Byrds' 'So You Want to Be a Rock 'n' Roll Star.' The clap-along 'Here We Are Again' is a dynamite number with 'short single' potential and the languid tones of the acoustic 'Vicki' are mellow and inviting. Harmonies are dirty-sweet and instruments are clear, giving Close Enough for Rock 'n' Roll vast AM and FM potential. This is certainly the richest and most cohesive outing to date." *(Cashbox, May 1, 1976)*

April 1976. "Love Hurts" is RIAA-certified as a gold single in the US.

Dan McCafferty on the band's predilection for doing covers:
"It was the case of touring so much. We always liked doing covers anyway. We've always liked other people's songs. It was usually just a case of working it out, doing a demo and then putting it away. And then when we get to making a record, we found that we had a whole bunch of these things. And we thought, why the hell not? (laughs). Sometimes we had loads of stuff and other times it was like, 'Oh my God!' Back in the early '70s, putting out a lot of product was the big thing. They had you in the studio like twice a year, and then they wanted you to tour for nine months. So it was difficult to get stuff written. But like everything else, we used to manage it."

May 1, 1976. Nazareth enjoys a blanket certification day in Canada. *Razamanaz*, *Loud 'n' Proud* and *Greatest Hits* are simultaneously certified gold and platinum, while *Rampant* and *Hair of the Dog* are certified gold. As well, "Love Hurts" is certified as a gold single.

June 1976. "You're the Violin"/"Loretta" is issued as a single in the UK. Like "Carry Out Feelings," it fails to chart.

July 1, 1976. The band play a show at the Beacon Theatre in New York, supported by the Ian Gillan Band.

Uncredited reviewer:
"Near the end of the 'Hair of the Dog' segment, Nazareth paid tribute to its Scottish heritage with a bit of showmanship, including the onstage appearance of a kilted dancer, a set of bagpipes and a bottle of scotch. McCafferty teased the audience with a two-minute turn on the bagpipes. He also led the crowd in a round of 'Happy Birthday to Nazareth' before the finale, 'Woke Up This Morning.' The ten-minute encore, which featured the band's own 'Teenage Nervous Breakdown,' Cream's 'Sunshine of Your Love' and ZZ Top's 'Tush,' left the enthusiastic audience wanting more." *(Billboard, July 24, 1976)*

July 27, 1976. The band's beloved manager Bill Fehilly dies in a plane crash, flying in a Piper, en route from Blackpool to Perth, on the way back from a meeting with the band. All six occupants of the plane perished in the crash, caused by engine failure due to an oil leak.

Dan McCafferty:
"Both he and his son were killed. It was horrible. It was very tough to deal with altogether. We had all agreed on everything together. He did really well with us. He was going in the right direction. He had us and he had the Alex Harvey Band. Things were going well for him before his plane hit that mountain. It really took us a few years to get over that. Even business-wise it was tough for us because everything was tied up in court. It got us down for several years but we carried on. With any band, all you have is your talent. If you believe in your talent then keep going. Everyone who has ever been in a band has been ripped off. At some point they have been ripped off or done something stupid themselves. We have been guilty of both. The bottom line is that all we have is our talent. If you don't believe in it then you just go off and say, 'That was fun.' For us it's still fun. We get to see the smiles on people's faces and it really makes you feel wonderful. I know it sounds schmaltzy but it really is true."

August – September 1976. Nazareth work at Le Studio on tracks slated for what will be their eighth studio album.

Dan McCafferty:
"We hadn't seen each other in five weeks before we went into the studio. We decided to just go in and see how our ideas came out. One week we just did little things, changing little bits and just generally messing around. The whole album was actually finished in three weeks. We couldn't believe we'd done it so quick. We kept listening to it to see if there was anything wrong with it, you know? Manny does all the mixing. As far as the instruments are recorded, the band fights it out with him until everybody's happy with it. Seems to work out that way. The new one is much more 'up' than *Close Enough*. The amount of energy that went into *Play 'n' the Game* was incredible. I think it took the band a step forward musically, and communicating with each other as well. There's more energy than *Close Enough*. We've all written from ideas that we've gotten over the last year, from being on the road touring so much. The original songs just came together in the studio pretty much." *(w/ Wesley Strick, Circus, 1976)*

August 1, 1976. "Love Hurts" is certified as a platinum-selling single in Canada.

September 1976. "Lift the Lid"/"Loretta" is issued as a single in the States.

September 24, 1976. Nazareth are presented with a number of Canadian record awards, on a visit to Edmonton, garnering platinum for *Razamanaz* and *Loud 'n' Proud*, gold for *Rampant* and *Hair of the Dog* and double platinum for *Greatest Hits* (plus a platinum single for "Love Hurts"). By this point, the band had sold over 600,000 units across their five albums to date, in Canada. Also on this Canadian tour, at a stop in Vancouver, the front cover image used on *Play 'n' the Game* is shot, courtesy Fin Costello, who captured the band playing poker before the night's performance. The 12-day Canadian tour found the band playing to 100,000 fans, with a ticket gross of $625,000 and Nazareth taking home $250,000.

Dan McCafferty:

"In Canada, almost every album we did was a hit, like a gold record and stuff. And in Europe, we've had ups and downs all over the place. Somebody told me we've sold 70 million records or something crazy like that, but we've had two different managers as well, so who knows how many there really were? (laughs). We've had more court cases than Mickey Rooney. I know *Hair of the Dog* went gold in the States. We even have a gold eight-track for that, if you can believe it. Because that was the format in everybody's truck at the time. And *Greatest Hits* was huge in Canada."

November 1976. Nazareth issue as a single, across a number of territories but not in the US, "I Don't Want to Go on Without You," backed variously with "Good Love" or "L.A. Girls."

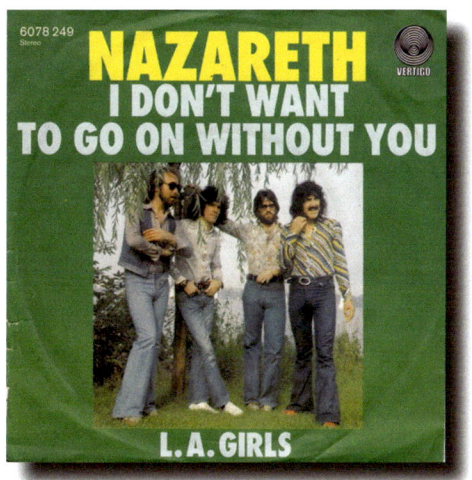

Pete Agnew:

"That's the only time in our career where we did what we said we would never do, which is try to do a single the same as the last one. It was usually, 'No, no, don't give into that pressure.' But we had so little material for that album, we would've welcomed anything, almost, as a suggestion. And that one was to follow 'Love Hurts,' basically; it was to do another 'Love Hurts.'" And Dan did a fabulous job of singing 'I Don't Want to Go on Without You.' I think it's a great record. But it was never going to replace 'Love Hurts.'"

Reviewer Angie Errigo:

The Wexler-Burns tearjerker, 'I Don't Want to Go on Without You' is handled with such unusual restraint that McCafferty for once has plenty of room to lean his powerful, wide-ranging voice on the emotional possibilities. The stab at being classy is a trifle overblown on the vocal echoes and wringing guitar, but the intensity is mighty impressive." *(Melody Maker, December 4, 1976)*

November 13, 1976. Nazareth issue their eighth album, *Play 'n' the Game*, which would certify gold in Canada. The album finds the band back at Le Studio, Manny producing aided by famed engineer, the late Nick Blagona.

Pete Agnew:
"As promised, we went back to Le Studio to record this new one but this time we were nowhere near prepared for it. What happened is this: *Hair of the Dog* had a big hit single with 'Love Hurts.' When *Close Enough* came out there was no hit single on it. Even though 'Telegram' became probably one of the Nazareth's all-time classic tracks, it wasn't a hit single and as we all know record companies just love hit singles (who doesn't?)."

"This meant it was back to the studio for us within six months of finishing the last album. The only problem with that is, because of touring solidly for six months, not only did we not have time to write a hit single, we had no time to write anything! Now picture four guys in a studio with the tape running and countless cases of beer, jamming for all their worth and hoping some sparks will fly in the right direction to create something worth recording. We ended up putting four cover songs on this album but they were cracking cover versions and we enjoyed every minute of recording what we originally thought was a non-starter. I remember when we arrived we said, 'Well we're here and we're nowhere near ready for this but we'll have to play the game.'"

"But yeah, when the engineer said, 'Okay, what are you gonna record for us?' it was, 'Well, we got nothing, absolutely nothing.' So he'd basically run a half-inch tape and we went into the studio and played all day. You know, just play for two or three hours, come down, listen back to all the stuff, play for another couple hours, listen for another couple hours, 'Oh, keep that, and we can do something with that.' That went on for four or five days, and then we started to go in and take bits of that and add it to a piece of that. Sometimes Dan would sing a vocal; like 'Waiting for the Man,' he came in right away for that thing—that happened right on the spot. But other ones, you take little bits of a backing track and you go, 'What can you do for a vocal on that?' It was all very piecemeal."

Manny Charlton:
"Basically, we didn't really have a lot of material for it at that point. We were touring and recording, touring and recording, and when we got… the management, they didn't care. 'You got a break in the tour; go up to Morin

Heights and record a new album.' 'We don't have any songs.' 'Just go anyway. It's booked.' So they booked it for six weeks or whatever. Like I say, we didn't have a lot of original material, so we did a bunch of covers on that album. We were back up to the Laurentian Mountains, outside of Montreal, and it was a great place. We had the studio to ourselves and they had accommodation for us. That album cover was before a show. A photographer came over from the UK to do it, and we were in the hotel in Vancouver. And he just said, 'Set up like you're playing a game of cards.' That was about the only sleeve that had us on the cover."

Reviewer Angie Errigo:
"There's something about Nazareth that makes them more appealing than just any full-volume, full-tilt blasters. Underneath the apparent abandon, they show an enthusiastic taste. And along with having a first-rate singer, they could pick pleasing songs that make them that little bit more spirited than others in the same basic bag. Charlton's production is a little over-clever at times, with guitar lick sliding busily from speaker to speaker more than a few times. But on the whole, it has vibrancy that is almost startling from a band that's been doing what Nazareth have been doing for as long as they now have. They know themselves well and exploit what they have with consistent dynamism." (Melody Maker, December 4, 1976)

December 1976. The band receive a gold record award in Brazil for the single issue of "Love Hurts." The award is accepted by Dan, who flies down to Rio with his wife Mary Ann and son Derek.

Dan McCafferty, speaking in 1999, on the sense of family within the band:
"I've been married for thirty years, so has Pete, so has Darrell. We've all got grown-up kids. I've known Pete since I was five. I've known Darrell since I was in my teens. They're like anybody else in the world who've gone through changes in life. I think what kept us reasonably, well, half-sane, was being brought up in the same area and having the same type of parents, I guess. We got taught the same values. I think that makes it easier for us to communicate with each other. I think if you put one guy from Toronto and one guy from LA and one guy from Edinburgh together, you're looking for trouble here. So I think having the same background and the same kind of education helps."

"We've never had any drug problems in the band, not at all. Although we are fond of a jar or two. It has been known for alcohol to cross our lips (laughs). But drug problems, no. Because I think, again, having families and stuff like that, the little man in the back of your head goes, 'You do it and you die.' It just never appealed to us. It's part of the business. The scariest thing though is that you see more of it outside the business than you do in it."

December 1976. A&M issue "I Want to (Do Everything for You)"/"I Don't Want to Go on Without You" as a single in the States. The single is a featured track on US hits compilation *Hot Tracks*.

April 1st, 1976, London, UK.

February 17th, 1976, Oklahoma City Fairgrounds Arena, Oklahoma City, OK.

© Rich Galbraith

February 17th, 1976,
Oklahoma City Fairgrounds Arena,
Oklahoma City, OK.

October 27th, 1977,
Tulsa Assembly Center,
Tulsa, OK.

1977

1977. The band spend much of the year playing North America, sharing stages with the likes of REO Speedwagon, Point Blank, Head East, Lynyrd Skynyrd, The Outlaws, Ted Nugent, The Dictators, Starz, Riot, Uriah Heep, Foghat, The Michael Stanley Band, Foreigner, Utopia and Aerosmith (quite regularly, in June and July).

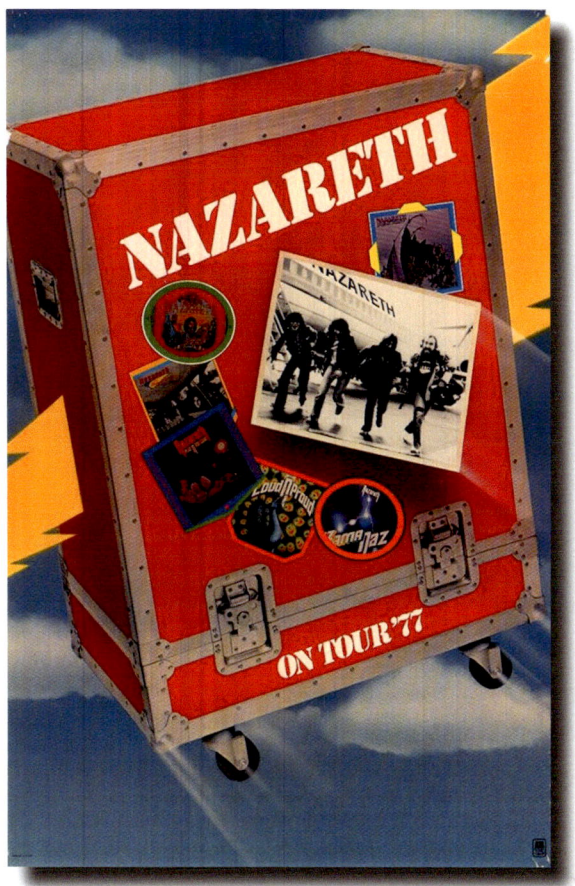

Manny Charlton on British fans shunning bands who spent too much time out of the country:
"That happened; that did happen. Basically right from the Beatles on. You can only go so far in the UK. You can tour around the UK in a month when you're that size. When you're the size of the Beatles or Zeppelin, there isn't the venues that would constitute the tour. So you did your British tour and then what did you do? You sat on your backside and said what else can we do? Where else can we work?"

"So we went to Europe and we played Germany and France and Sweden and all these countries, and then America. That was the big market. Huge market. I mean even the Beatles eventually had to go and do America. And Canada, when we first started coming over to North America, we treated Canada really seriously because it was a great market for us. They really loved us in Canada. We did full-blown tours right across Canada, and we were one of the first bands to do that. So you just had to play and you became a world band as opposed to a British band. And of course people in Britain would go, 'Oh, we never get to see you any more; you're in America all the time.' Well that's where we work."

January 7, 1977. "Vancouver Shakedown" is issued as a belated single, from *Close Enough for Rock 'n' Roll*, backed with "Somebody to Roll."

Dan McCafferty on "Vancouver Shakedown:"

"We got ripped off twice in Vancouver by the same guy. Everybody over here took it as though we were actually slagging Vancouver to death. And we go, 'No, no, we're not slagging Vancouver; we're slagging this guy who lives here.' But there you go—life's a spit and then you die, isn't it? That's all in the past." (w/ Steve Newton, Ear of Newt)

February 1, 1977. *Play 'n' the Game* is certified gold in Canada.

March 1977. Paice Ashton Lord issue an album called *Malice in Wonderland*. Come 1980, Nazareth didn't clue into this until the last minute, and added to the inner sleeve of their record of the same name, a missive reading, "No malice intended, PAL."

April 1977. A&M issue "Somebody to Roll"/"This Flight Tonight" as a single in the States.

September 1977. Mooncrest issue a seven-inch EP version of the *Hot Tracks* hit compilation. The four-tracker reaches #15 in the UK charts.

October 20, 1977. Lynyrd Skynyrd's plane crashes, killing Ronnie Van Zant, Steve Gaines and Cassie Gaines, along with road manager Dean Kilpatrick and both pilots.

Dan McCafferty:
"The guys suggested we go for a barbecue and it sounded like a good idea. But something came up. Our record company wanted us for some promotion thing or something. They were a great bunch of guys though. We did not understand a word any of them said, and they didn't understand us. But we would go out and get drunk and have a great time." (w/ Jack Lloyd, The Dispatch, April 6, 1981)

Pete Agnew:
"We played Greenville Memorial Auditorium that night and Artimus Pyle, Skynyrd's drummer, introduced us onstage before our show. It was his hometown and it was he that invited us to a barbecue they were going to have at his place."

November 19, 1977. Nazareth issue their ninth album, *Expect No Mercy*, the fourth in a row produced by band guitarist Manny Charlton. The cover art is by famed fantasy artist Frank Frazetta, with the classic image reproduced a second time without text on the inner sleeve.

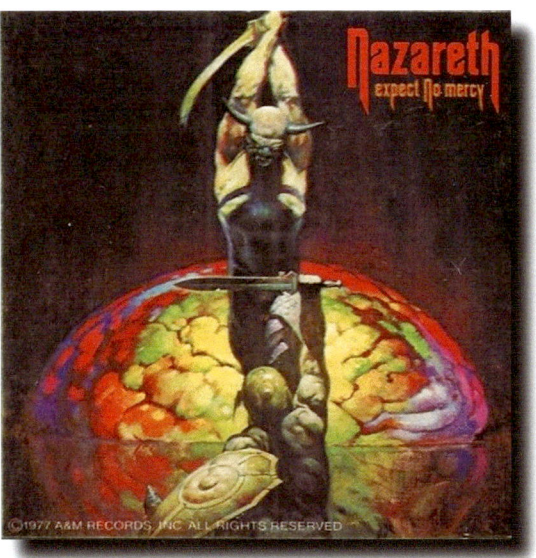

Dan McCafferty:

"At the time we were the first to use Frank Frazetta, who we used for *Expect No Mercy*. We were in the studio in Montreal, and they had a coffee table book of Frank Frazetta's art, and we were flipping through it and we thought that would be perfect for our album. We phoned him up and we said, 'Could we speak to Frank?' And his wife said, 'This is his wife; Frank doesn't like phones. What is it that you want?' We asked him if we could use the sleeve. 'Right, give me a number and we'll get back to you.'"

"So she got back to us and said, 'Yes, sure you can use it, no problem. Thanks for asking.' Obviously there was a fee involved, but fair enough, you know? Still, it cost us practically nothing. Which I'm sure changed rapidly after that, because there were a whole bunch of people using his stuff. But he was cool about it. It just seemed to go with the music: *Expect No Mercy,* you know? The guy's getting his head chopped off (laughs). That sort of said it simply, really. Actually, if you look at it again, he can't chop off his head because his arms would never get past his horns. It's true. We thought that was quite ironic. That's why we picked it, really."

Pete Agnew on tough bass parts:

"The ones that are killer for me are things like 'Morning Dew' and 'Expect No Mercy.' I mean, I was stupid on those, and that's what the guys all tell me. When I come offstage complaining that my hand is going to fall off, they say, 'Well, you were stupid enough to write that part in the first place. You shouldn't have done that.' Those are just really hard work. I like playing them all, really, but I like the more mid-tempo things. I like 'Whiskey Drinkin' Woman' and I like 'Heart's Grown Cold' and 'Beggars Day.' I like playing all the songs, but it's just that some of them are harder to play than others."

"But yes, as Dan says, that album cover, that painting—it's called *The Brain*—it was very funny because the big devil guy that is standing with the sword, and is trying to kill the guys in front of him, he's going to take his own arms off, with his horns (laughs). Of course, after that, people like Molly Hatchet and a whole bunch of people used Frank Frazetta stuff."

"For *Expect No Mercy,* the love affair with Le Studio continued. We were prepared for the studio this time with a bunch of songs that sounded like they were going to work but we were not prepared for a Canadian winter! Anyone who has experienced winter in Canada will know what I mean. We get snow at home and as we all know, Europe gets its fair whack of snow (we hadn't toured Russia at this point in our career) but Canada gets big *giant* snow. We spent most of our money paying tow trucks to pull our cars out of snow drifts and spent most of our time stuck in the studio with snow half way up to the roof. I think we had more playbacks of *Expect No Mercy* than any other album we made simply because of the time we spent as prisoners."

October 27th, 1977,
Tulsa Assembly Center,
Tulsa, OK.

© Rich Galbraith

October 27th, 1977, Tulsa Assembly Center, Tulsa, OK.

© Rich Galbraith

October 27th, 1977,
Tulsa Assembly Center,
Tulsa, OK.

© Rich Galbraith

© Rich Galbraith

October 27th, 1977,
Tulsa Assembly Center,
Tulsa, OK.

© Rich Galbraith

October 27th, 1977,
Tulsa Assembly Center,
Tulsa, OK.

© Rich Galbraith

1978

January 1978. Issued as a single in the UK is "Gone Dead Train" along with the non-LP "Greens" and "Desolation Road." The Expect No Mercy song gets to #49 on the UK charts.

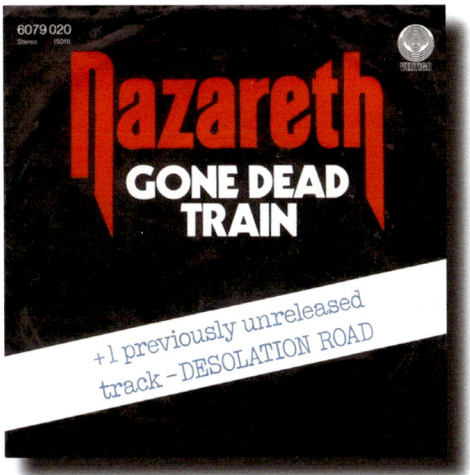

Pete Agnew:
"'Gone Dead Train,' well, we loved the *Crazy Horse* album. I mean, that was a phenomenal album; we loved it so much and played it so much. We did 'Beggars Day,' from that album and 'Gone Dead Train' and it was every intention… you know, Rod Stewart was always a guy that could pick a good song, and he did 'I Don't Want to Talk About It' from that album. We would've done that, but we didn't get to do it because he beat us to it (laughs). In fact at one point we thought about 'Dance, Dance, Dance' and 'I Don't Want to Talk About It,' and 'Dirty Dirty' was another song on that album—we used to play that at sound checks and things like that. But 'Gone Dead Train,' what a great rock song—we just loved the whole vibe of that."

Late January – Late March 1978. The band tour the States, supported mostly by Head East, Frank Marino & Mahogany Rush and Sammy Hagar.

April 1978. Issued as a single in the UK is "A Place in Your Heart" backed with "Kentucky Fried Blues" while the US gets "Shot Me Down"/"Kentucky Fried Blues." The US single doesn't chart but the UK offering reaches #70.

April 25 – May 23, 1978. Following German dates in mid-April, the band mount a cross-Canada tour, mostly supported by The Guess Who.

1979

January 1979. Issued as a single in the UK is ballad "May the Sunshine" backed with "Expect No Mercy," with the A-side notching a #22 placement on the home country chart.

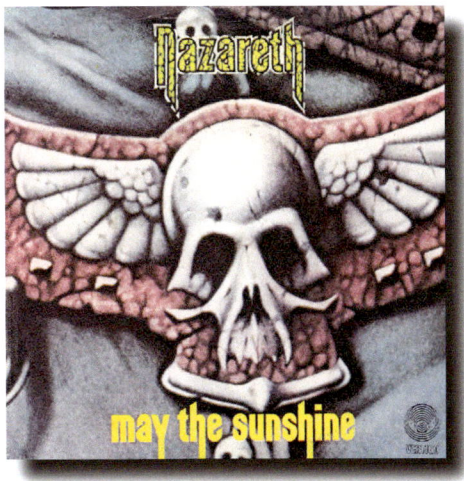

Mid-January – February 20, 1979. Following UK dates in January and into February, the band play Luxembourg en route to a German leg, supported by Whitesnake, commencing February 9th until the 20th.

Pete Agnew:

"We took them on a big long European tour. That was when Jon Lord and Ian Paice were in that band, and they had other people as well, mates of mine, actually. And they had David Coverdale. So we took them out kind of repaying the favours that they did for us.

Same with the Ian Gillan Band. When Ian first put his band together, we actually did a big long US tour, and we took Ian out with us, to break his band, hopefully. Because they did us a big favour in taking us there, we took Ian out with us in the States for quite a long tour, five or six weeks."

January 13, 1979. Manny Charlton is back in the producer's chair for the fifth time, as Nazareth issue their tenth album, *No Mean City*. Cover art is by famed fantasy illustrator Rodney Matthews. It is the first of two albums for Zal Cleminson as part of Nazareth.

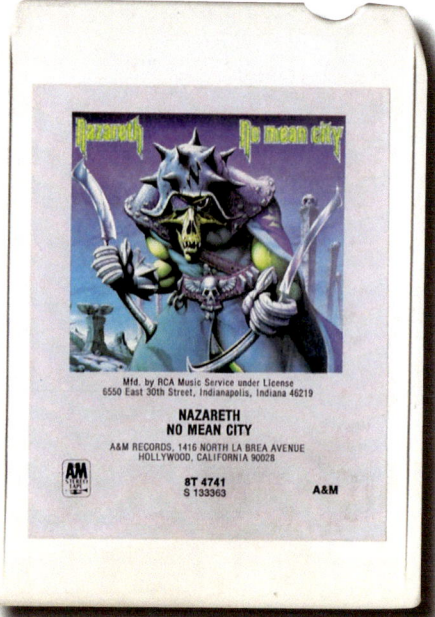

Dan McCafferty:

"We had known Zal since we were kids in Glasgow. He had always been around; he was in a lot of bands, and the Alex Harvey Band split up and Zal was driving a car and we said, 'That's stupid. Why don't you come and be in Nazareth for a bit?' So he did (laughs). He's a great player, so it was obviously easy to bring Zal into the band. It was good to have him for a couple of albums."

"*No Mean City* is actually based on a book that every Scottish student has to read in school. It was about gangs in the '20s and the Depression and stuff. It was standard school reading for children at that time, all about the gangs in Glasgow. And it was after that one being so heavy, and the subject matter being as heavy as it was, we decided subconsciously that we better lighten up a little bit. Looking back on it now, I think that's what we must have thought. Plus at the time we had Manny and Zal in the band, and we got a lot of guitar-oriented stuff because the two of them were playing together. We had evolved, we changed, we go left and right and go off on it, and that's the kind of music we were writing at the time, so that's what we did. And it had to be heavier because the basis of *No Mean City* is the song about razor gangs and they were nasty characters. So we couldn't really make a light album around that (laughs)."

"We were recording on the Isle of Man at the time, so the cover artist, Rodney Matthews, came up there and had a word with us. We gave him a rough tape of the music and that's what he came up with. We were there because we used to like to use mobiles. And at the time, Pete and I and Darrell were staying on the Isle of Man, so it seemed like an appropriate place. We did it at an old farmhouse and just put the mobile outside and did it there. With those things always something goes wrong—a track goes out that takes away all the effects and stuff like that. But generally speaking it was okay."

"The funny part, everybody grew beards. And they sent a photographer out to take these pictures of us and our manager at the time freaked out. He's like, 'No, y'alls have to shave your beards off!'"

Zal Cleminson:

"The Nazareth guys were just friends of ours. We had sort of grown up almost together in Scotland. We started about the same time, in music, and when Sensational Alex Harvey band split up, I was driving a taxi cab in London for a couple of months. I was doing all sorts of things trying to pay the bills. And then I got a call from Manny Charlton and he said do you want to come down and get involved in the *No Mean City* album they were recording at that time. I think what they were looking for, really, was a lot of input and musical songs, some writing contribution. They were looking for songs, basically. I just said yeah, this is cool, okay, let's just see where it goes, and I spent a couple of years with them, touring, recording a couple of albums, and they're good guys. We just worked together. We had the same management company, for example. So, we were like old pals."

"But they were never really my cup of tea, Nazareth, to be perfectly honest. They were never really a band that I would associate myself with musically, which sounds like a contradiction in terms as they're a pretty basic rock band. They just play that stuff and it's great. At that time, as a musician, I had a broad… I was more into the sort of Frank Zappa jazz-fusion thing, all that kind of stuff, compositions and creating soundtrack type music and whatever else. So, the basic rock thing for me was going back to a very, very basic style of playing, and I thought, okay, that's fine. It was good. The albums were okay."
(w/ Marko Syrjala, MetalRules)

Pete Agnew:

"Our manager at the time phoned and was thinking we needed a change. We needed someone new. And Zal was driving a taxi. 'What do you think of Zal?' And I remember thinking, hey, that's a great idea. We were at Manny's house that night mucking about, and we said, 'Give him a ring; give Zal a ring.' So it was Manny that made the call—'Phone him and see.'"

"As for the album, there's a book called No Mean City, written way back in the '30s, about the razor gangs. It was a rough place to be at that time. And we all read the book when we were younger. The guy in the book that is the main man, he was The Razor King, and he had two razors, and that's why you've got Fred, as we call him, on the front cover, with his two razors. The song itself was about that, but the rest of the album was… I suppose it does fit because it was a hard rock album. It harkens back to those days. But we didn't really go into the idea with a concept. Zal had just joined, and he came in with a couple of songs and we all had some songs and we just decided to make them into an album. We didn't really say that we were going to do a concept but I suppose when you look at it from a fan's point of view, it does sound a little like that."

"To record it, we got Jethro Tull's mobile and we brought that up. We had a big farmhouse up there. We were all living on the Isle of Man at the time, all the band. And we'd got this farmhouse where we were rehearsing and writing, and it was decided that we loved the place and were very relaxed there, loved the atmosphere. Actually, if you saw where it was, it was so idyllic, and you see the kind of music we were actually playing there, it was actually very funny. Because the place isn't like that (laughs)."

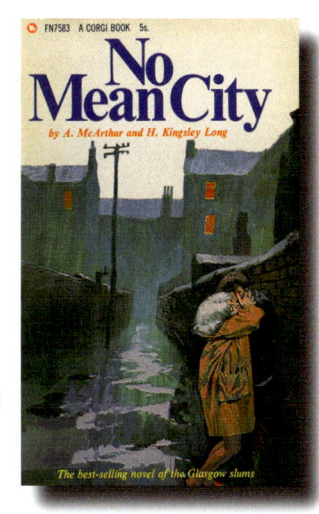

"We didn't record all of it there. We did all the backing tracks and stuff there, but the vocals, you can't do a lot. You can get the tracks down, so we did that there, and then we went to Queen's studio in Montreux, Switzerland and that's where we did all the vocals. Over there at the casino, when Queen owned the studio there. I think we did one or two guitar overdubs there too but most of the album was done in Isle of Man."

Manny Charlton:
"We produced a killer album. I was producing and we had the songs, and we had Zal helping out, and helping out quite a lot, filling out the sound. It's a great record. Zal was a good friend of all of the guys in Nazareth, and myself, and I admired the hell out of him. I thought Zal was a great guitar player, and with his writing and helping out with the guitar playing, I could sit back and concentrate more on the production. We didn't try to make him play anything different. It was just a great team, and *No Mean City*, to me, is one of the best Nazareth albums, a great rock record. Zal played his heart out on it."

Late February – early April 1979. Nazareth tour the States, playing most regularly with Thin Lizzy, who bow out after the March 25th show in Saginaw, Michigan.

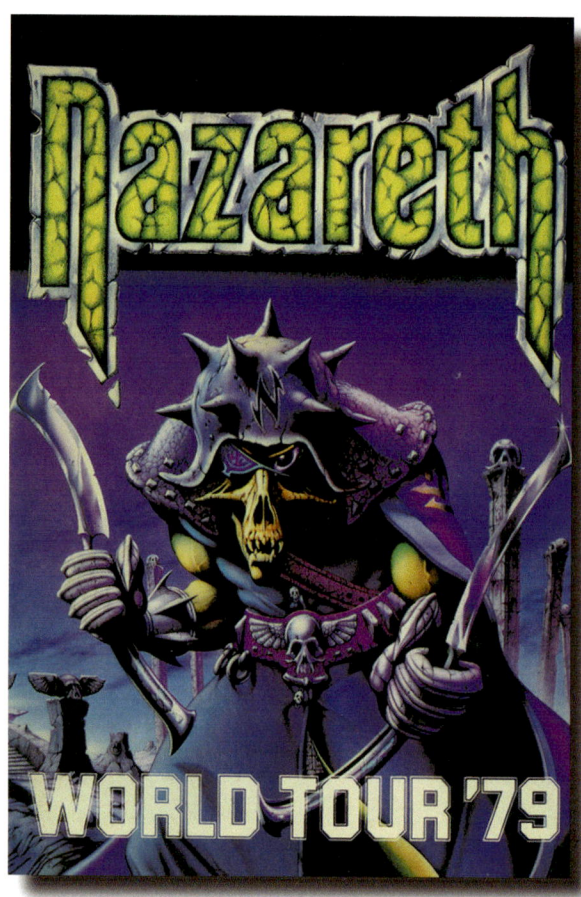

Uncredited record review:
"This could probably be the first Nazareth album that incorporates texture and subtlety into the musical proceedings. The addition of erstwhile Sensational Alex Harvey Band lead guitarist Zal Cleminson might have something to do with why the total sound and feel of *No Mean City* is less heavy-duty industrial strength rock 'n' roll and even less uni-leveled metallic drone. A natch for AOR acceptance, with at least three possible singles lurking around to boot."
(Cashbox, January 27, 1979)

April 1979. Issued in the UK is a picture sleeve single pairing "Whatever You Want Babe" with "Telegram."

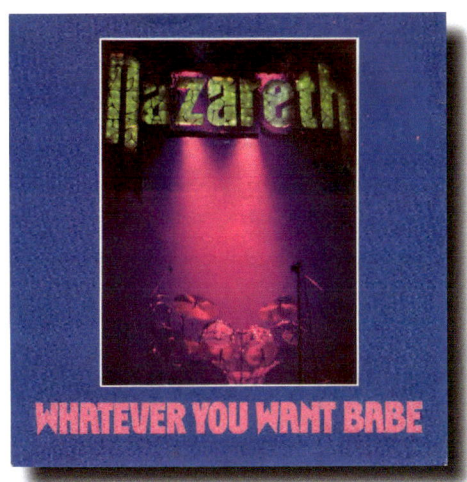

Pete Agnew on "Telegram:"

"When we did *Hair of the Dog*, we started to build a studio here in Scotland. We got a hold of this premises. This wasn't the Ganghut, that we had ourselves in the early days. We never used it as a recording studio, but we used it as a rehearsal place; it was really nice. And when we got there, we were talking about getting this new album done. We'd been touring ourselves stupid on *Hair of the Dog* because of 'Love Hurts' and never really had that much time to think about writing."

"So the first thing we did, in the preparation, was just playing a chug—we just started chugging away, like we used to do. Just chug, chug, chug. And then it developed, as things do—there's no explanation. And the lyric, it was, here we are, you've been on the road, you get your record done and get back on the road again. We were just thinking about the busyness of the whole thing. You're recording, touring, recording—it was all in our heads at that point. We were very, very busy. The whole thing became a song about touring. And once we started, it was one of these where everybody's going, 'What about this bit?, you could say this, oh, and you can say that, you can say this, and what about this line, what about that line?' It was like a complaint almost (laughs), a complaint to your manager and record company. It ended up being a story about touring. And then once we decided what it was going to be, then it became a real fun song to make. Mind you, the times I've had to play it since then… but it became a major favourite for the fans. It's one of those ones where every now and again, you think let's give this thing a rest. In fact, at the moment, it's getting a rest (laughs). But it was an opener for years on end."

May 15 – May 17, 1979. The band play Japan, with all dates in Tokyo, followed by a long North American tour leg into July, including a number of festival dates. Main support is Frank Marino & Mahogany Rush.

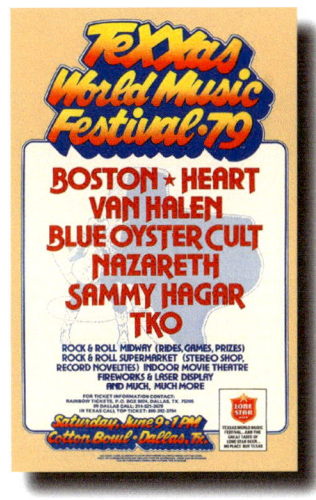

Pete Agnew on the band's new two-guitar team:
"They got on well together but they were totally different players. Manny was into the rough sound thing—he goes for the noise and likes creating noise. Zal is an amazing technician, and a good songwriter as well. The guy is mind-blowing, one of the best guitar players on the planet. It was quite an honour, actually, to play with the guy for a couple of years."

June 1, 1979. *Expect No Mercy* is certified gold in Canada.

Mid-1979: Manny Charlton produces *Under Heaven Over Hell*, the second album from Canadian band Streetheart. The record goes platinum in Canada, for sales of over 100,000 copies.

Matt Frenette:
"You know what? The coolest thing that Manny did was that he let everybody play. Because, he was a producer that came from a band where their sound was vital. With Nazareth, you had the screaming vocals but you had the really raunchy guitar and the straight-ahead drums. Darrell wasn't a flashy drummer but he was very punchy and straightforward. Everybody had their sound, right? The rhythm and bass and drums were very strong, but not complicated. I mean, we played way more chops than Nazareth. But that was their sound, right? You feature the vocal and the guitar in that band, and the catchy hook lines. And McCafferty's vocal was so distinct—it's still distinct today. And he wanted Streetheart to sound the way we sounded live, on vinyl—he wanted to catch the energy. But the cool thing he did was cut us all live on the floor, and do as few overdubs as possible, and erasing as possible, so he caught the energy of the band all playing live together."

July 1979. Issued as a picture sleeve single in the UK is "Star" backed with "Born to Love." The US version (non-picture sleeve) gets "Expect No Mercy" as its B-side.

July 4, 1979. Nazareth play one of Bill Graham's Day on the Green shows, in Oakland, California. Alternately called The 4th of July All American Rock 'n' Roll Show, that package included Journey, The J. Geils Band, UFO and Thin Lizzy.

Pete Agnew on the *No Mean City* tour campaign:
"We did a whole world tour, really, played with Thin Lizzy, Blackfoot. We had the backdrop with Fred on it and everything. It used to drive the road crew mad, putting this thing up every night. It was huge. I mean, you wouldn't do that nowadays. You would do it with a very light fabric. But at that time, the record company had this made up and it was the size of a house and it was made out of cloth and it was almost velvet and weighed a ton, maybe two tons. And we had to suspend this thing every night, off of light rigs and things that we used to bring. We made the crew work for their money."

"Nothing in the '80s was really that much of a big success. It was a pretty bad time for us. Not so bad in the early '80s, but it wasn't until *Move Me* that we even started to get the airplay again. The whole system seemed to be geared towards dance and MTV at the time, and in Europe anyway, rock 'n' roll was on a few obscure shows, late at night. In the States, everything rock was classic rock, so they were playing your old stuff but not your new stuff. Very strange time not just for us, but for a lot of rock bands."
Dan McCafferty

The 1980s

July 5th, 1986, Out in the Green, Dinkelsbuhl, Germany.
© Wolfgang Gurster

Hey, all of our favourite '70s bands, if they made records through the '80s, they were confronted with the results of what they had forged in the '70s through the phenomena of the New Wave of British Heavy Metal—its brief and regional flash—followed by a long golden period for heavy metal in general, juiced by the success of a subgenre called hair metal. Some of these bands embraced it wholeheartedly or to considerable degree, while others ran screaming, arms waving wildly, in the other direction. I'd say foremost in the latter camp would be Rush and Nazareth, both successes in Canada and tour mates, Rush supporting Nazareth in the beginning and then eventually, Nazareth supporting Rush.

I remember quite distinctly when *Malice in Wonderland* came out, and there was indeed some excitement about the new non-hard rock direction. Even myself and my usually uncompromising buddies weren't completely averse to the new sound. Why? Well, through the previous handful of albums, there wasn't much metal anyway, and the new record seemed to mark an uptick in songwriting quality, in sophistication, in all 'round smarts and maturity that even we, as boneheaded metalheads, could appreciate in our teens.

The bloom of novelty quickly wore off, along with any confidence in the band's songwriting abilities, through the following clutch of records. As it turns out, the record-buying public agreed and Nazareth fell out of the public consciousness precipitously. As it turns out, the lack of creative and commercial success would begin to cause squabbles within the band dynamic as well, with Manny Charlton flaming out after the last record of the '80s, the pretty much disastrous *Snakes 'n' Ladders*. Along the way there had been Zal Cleminson and Billy Rankin, as well as keyboard player John Locke. The youth and pop of Billy, along with the very fact that John Locke was a keyboard player, arguably served as gateway drugs toward too much '80s technology being used. Then again, a bunch of that could be blamed on Manny, who was the band's producer as well as a natural gear-head, not to mention just curious about new music.

In any event, it might've gone well, but it didn't. We might have been calling these rock-lite Nazareth records the greatest artistic documents of their career, but we aren't. I know it's 20/20 hindsight, but man, imagine if this band would have seized upon and amplified their heavy metal hobby from the '70s (I say "hobby" because it wasn't all they did, nor particularly deliberate) and hit twice as hard, inspired to riff madly by the NWOBHM. Sabbath and Priest and Scorpions stayed heavy, Kiss got heavy again, Deep Purple came back doing what they did in the '70s, Aerosmith stuck around and did essentially what they did on *Rocks* and *Draw the Line*, and even Alice Cooper came back from the crack years to become a hair metal sensation. And what of Uriah Heep? Fact is, they were closer to their heavier early '70s sound throughout the '80s than they were to their Nazareth-scattered late '70s sound.

So yes, it boggles the mind, given the records we actually got, but Nazareth is certainly a case where nothing much would have been lost had they headbanged their way through the '80s, with potentially vast payoffs to be gained.

May 1980, The Spectrum, Philadelphia, PA.

1980

January 1980. Issued across a number of territories is "Holiday" backed with "Ship of Dreams." The single reaches #87 on the US charts.

February 8, 1980. Nazareth mark the new decade with a change in musical direction, issuing *Malice in Wonderland*, produced by Jeff "Skunk" Baxter, working with the band at Compass Point in Nassau, Bahamas. The album would reach #41 on the Billboard charts, and #43 on the German charts.

Dan McCafferty:
"Jeff was introduced to us by an executive at the record company who thought it might be interesting if we worked together. Jeff had a reputation as a very inventive musician, and even though he had never produced before, his knowledge of the recording studio and his musical background just made him perfect for us. We had always relied on our own ability to produce records before, with Manny handling the controls and the rest of us just playing as hard and as loud as we could, but that just naturally tends to restrict your thinking a little. When Jeff started to work with us, it was like a whole new musical area opened up. We gave him a lot of freedom to work with, and he really helped us. I think it's safe to say that the partnership between Mr. Baxter and these 'nice' Scottish boys has not yet come to an end."

"The songs on the new album show a lot more taste and style than any of our earlier things. We're not scared to try and express a little feeling and emotion in our music anymore. Before, we tried to either just blow everyone away with our energy or slow down completely for a ballad like 'Love Hurts.' Now, we found that we can also have a middle ground where we can still rock, but with a little more subtlety. And honestly, it's nice to really sing for a change instead of just yell as loud as I can. Also, I think that we've become more cohesive as a band on this album and the reason is that we're back to really playing music again."

"I guess we changed as a matter of necessity. We knew we couldn't change so much that we'd lose the long-time fans, yet we knew we had to change enough to make the music exciting again. It wasn't easy, but I think the results speak for themselves." *(w/ Andy Secher, Sacramento Bee, November 22, 1980)*

Zal Cleminson:

"The production wasn't really my cup of tea, the second album particularly. *Malice in Wonderland* I thought was very peculiar from Nazareth as a band. It was like a complete departure in some way. I don't know what happened there. Manny got his head around this idea that his favourite band at the time was Fleetwood Mac, with the *Rumours* album. And Fleetwood Mac, you know what that's like; it's very melodic, a nice rhythmic album, beautiful, lovely musicians, etc. It's full of amazing, classic songs, of course, but it's much more in that vein than Nazareth wanted to be—or that's what I thought. I think he got carried away with the idea of those types of songs and that kind of production that he wanted to try maybe create an album that was a bit more mainstream, let's call it, mainstream commercial." *(w/ Marko Syrjala, MetalRules)*

Pete Agnew:

"Our record company suggested we get Jeff 'Skunk' Baxter. You can imagine, we were a bit sceptical but at the time we met him, Jeff was also playing session guitar on 18 hits that were in the Billboard Top 40 that month so we figured he must know a thing or two about making records. We decided to record in the Bahamas at Compass Point studio which turned out to be a bad choice. Although the country is a lovely place with lovely weather, that was not the reason for us being there. We were trying to make a record, and almost every day something or other broke down in the studio and all we did was play pool on the two big tables they had, passing the time while they flew in engineers from Miami to repair the recording machines."

"After a month of this going on, we became almost competition-standard pool players but the record was going nowhere fast. At this point Jeff phoned his friends who owned Cherokee Studios in Hollywood and they fitted us in there to finish the rest of the album. This place had four separate first-class studios and while we were in one of them, they had Neil Sedaka, Harry Nilsson and—Lord save us—the Blues Brothers in the other three studios. As you can imagine, things got pretty mental at times but we ended up with a classic album that sounded nothing like anything we had done before but still appealed to fans who had always favoured the heavier side of the band. It's still one of my favourite Naz records of all time."

Darrell Sweet, on working with Skunk Baxter:

"On paper it was probably the biggest mismatch of all time, but it worked out really well. We'll always be that adventurous, and try to be that melodic, but I think a few of the rough edges were smoothed off just maybe too much on *Malice*." *(w/ Cameron Cohick, Fort Lauderdale News, June 15, 1980)*

Jeff Baxter:

"I was really impressed with the band after I heard the songs they had ready and their live playing. My job was just to give them an album that was technically state-of-the-art. We set out to make the first '80s album, and I think we came as close as anybody could." *(Cashbox, January 19, 1980)*

Uncredited Record Review:

"*Malice in Wonderland* is such a radical departure from this band's musical norm that not until Dan McCafferty's distinctive lead vocals click in do you realise that this is indeed the group Nazareth. It's all very deceptive though, because Nazareth has never sounded better. Their bicep-bursting energy has a crystal-clear focus now that totally excludes the word boredom. The chances taken are nearly shocking in their brilliance. An AOR must." *(Cashbox, February 2, 1980)*

March 16, 1980. The BBC record a Nazareth set at the Hammersmith Odeon in London; these performances would be included on the 2010 reissue of *Malice in Wonderland*.

Pete Agnew on the Malice in Wonderland album cover:

"Kind of a freaky cover, isn't it? It gives me goose bumps, having all these mannequins, and it's mainly really, really young people. Creepy, that one. I was never very relaxed with it."

April 1980. A&M in the US and Canada issue "Heart's Grown Cold" as a single, backed with "Ship of Dreams."

Zal Cleminson:

"We're just trying to take the band in another direction. We must progress. You've got to develop. You listen to what's getting written nowadays, and what is being played by the young groups and you'll see what I mean. You've got to know what you're doing. Jeff is an excellent technician and a very good musician. He was a great help with the arrangements. Obviously he preferred some things and other people preferred other things, so it was always a compromise. The two of us really got off on each other from a musical point of view." *(w/ Zach Dunkin, Indianapolis News, June 6, 1980)*

Dan McCafferty:

"Jeff's smoothed things over a little, but there's still our basic aggression. You should've seen some of the things that went on. Like one day when we were recording, Neil Diamond put his head 'round the door and said, 'I need a guitar solo.' So off popped Jeff. Then the next day, Harry Nilsson suddenly arrived: 'Got a moment, Jeff?' And off he disappears for another five minutes. I'm telling you, I came running home screaming after three weeks there (in LA, mixing the album). It's just that he demands high standards. 'Feel is real but time is right' is his motto. But at least we know why all those albums by LA acts sound the same. They all use the same musicians, whether it's the Doobie Brothers, Donna Summer or Linda Ronstadt. Jeff's worked with 'em all!" (w/ Mike Nicholls, Record Mirror, March 22, 1980)

May – June 1980. Following a UK tour and a mainland European campaign, the band transitions to the States, for a series of shows supported by Blackfoot.

May 25, 1980. The band play Saginaw, Michigan, as one of the stops on the *Malice in Wonderland* campaign. A performance of J.J. Cale song "Cocaine" would be recorded and added to the band's next studio album, *The Fool Circle*.

Darrell Sweet:
"It was a unanimous decision to become more melodic. We had been going the same way for more than a decade, and it was time for us to move on. Hopefully it still has the rock feel, and the melodies add more to the songs. We're too old to be punks" (w/ Kim McAuliffe, Detroit Free Press, May 23, 1980)

June 1, 1980. *Malice in Wonderland* is certified gold in Canada.

Dan McCafferty:
I like *Malice in Wonderland*, because it was different, you know? It showed a more melodic side of the band. That cover was by a French artist. At the time we had done quite a bit of the monster-y ones. It was just a photographer really, who wanted to do these art photographs. But we really liked his stuff and I think that worked really well."

Mid-1980. Canadian hard rockers Streetheart issue their Manny Charlton-produced third album, *Quicksand Shoes*.

Daryl Gutheil:
"Manny produced our second album too, and this one. He came in immediately and suggested that we record 'Here Comes the Night,' and we worked on an arrangement for it, and we recorded probably in an evening or something, and we still do that song. So I've always liked that. I think there's a bit more sophistication and style on that second album than there is on the first one. Manny also produced 'Under My Thumb,' later in the year, when we went back for a couple days and recorded that."

"There was a bit of a thing going on with Nazareth at that time. I mean, they were traditionally a hard rock band, and they had a couple of personnel changes, added another guitarist, and they just came off recording an album and it was kind of light rock for them, and it seemed to be getting a lot of attention. I remember they were on the cover of Cashbox magazine, and I think in his mind Manny was thinking, for some of the bands that were playing hard rock, lightening up was the way to go. That was the way he was directing us on that third album, *Quicksand Shoes*, which, you know, in hindsight, I think it was a mistake for him and for us."

December 1980. NEMS issue a double-seven-inch EP called *Live*, featuring "Heart's Grown Cold," "Razamanaz," "Hair of the Dog" and "Talkin' to One of the Boys" recorded at the Hammersmith.

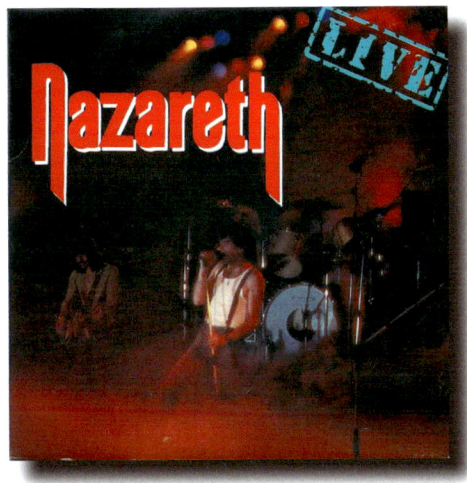

December 17, 1980. The band, introducing new members Billy Rankin (new after the recording of *The Fool Circle*) and John Locke (on the forthcoming album but not as an official member), perform a five-song set for Scottish TV's In Concert. The performance airs the following month.

Dan McCafferty:
"A few years ago, we just felt the need for a change. The rock style was still selling records fairly well, but we felt that we were getting a little stale with it. When the music starts to bore the people who are playing it, well, then it's time for a change. We had no desire to become another Fleetwood Mac, but we had always been viewed as a band that only knew three chords and we just wanted to show off a few of the skills that we had kept hidden over the years."
(w/ Andy Secher, Asbury Park Press, October 11, 1981)

May 1980, The Spectrum, Philadelphia, PA.
© Rudy Childs

May 1980, The Spectrum, Philadelphia, PA.

1981

February 14, 1981. Nazareth issue *The Fool Circle*, their 12th album. It is the first for ex-Spirit keyboard player John Locke, although he is listed as an "additional musician." The album was recorded in Montserrat, with Jeff Baxter producing the band for a second time. Engineering is Beatles associate Geoff Emerick. The album peaks at #70 on the Billboard charts and achieves a #60 placement in the UK. It is the band's first album since *Close Enough for Rock 'n' Roll* not to go gold in Canada.

Dan McCafferty, at the time, on the band's new political stance:
"We are not into flower power or anything like that. But the whole thing is scary. We talk to people. It's not just our opinion. It's what people on the street are talking about. They're scared. And I don't feel too secure about it myself. I live in the country, 40 miles from Glasgow, which is very close to where the US has the largest Polaris missile base in the world. So there we are in Scotland, watching what's going on in the world. All we can do is say, 'Excuse me, why don't you talk all this over and work something out?' It's scary."
(w/ Jack Lloyd, The Dispatch, April 6, 1981)

Pete Agnew:
"By the time we got 'round to writing the songs for this one, our management company had gone bankrupt leaving us in a real mess, having to pick up the pieces and put everything back together again. Zal had left because he had had enough of all this crap and I can't say that I blamed him. Hostages in the American Embassy in Iran had been held for more than a year. Russia had invaded Afghanistan and the Cold War was getting hot. The world in general was going to hell and I can say, it *did* have an effect on the way we were writing. Because of this, *The Fool Circle* became a kind of social commentary but we tried to do it with tongue-in-cheek humour so as to not come across as pain-in-the-ass preachers. I think we were successful in that."

"Anyway, just to cheer ourselves up we picked Air Studios on Montserrat to record. What a place that was and what a studio! Jeff was producing again but this time we had Geoff Emerick as our engineer. Geoff is one of the world's most famous studio engineers. He recorded *Sgt. Pepper* and all the Beatles albums, so say no more. He actually designed the studio in Montserrat with George Martin, the studio owner and Beatles producer. We had worked with Geoff many times in the past at AIR London and knew we were in good hands."

"While recording, we mentioned at one point that it would be good to have piano on a couple of tracks and wondered who we should fly in to play it. The studio manager then told us that a guy named John Locke was living on the island and would probably love to play piano for us. We couldn't believe it: John Locke from Spirit, one of our favourite groups, who made *Dr. Sardonicus*, one of the best albums of all time, and here he was on this tiny island. 'Bring him in immediately' we cried, and in he came and proceeded to blow our minds with some of the best piano playing we had ever heard. John ended up playing on five tracks and before we left to go home, we asked him to join the band. That album had many happy moments but finding John was the happiest. Reagan was elected President of the United States during the recording of the album, so obviously the world was still fucked up when we left Montserrat."

Uncredited record review:
"This is the second time in a row that Nazareth has enlisted the help of Jeffrey (nee "Jeff 'Skunk'") Baxter as their producer. Consequently this album continues a musical trend that finds the band diving even deeper in Doobie Bros. waters. A denuded Nazareth still sounds okay enough for AOR, but several mid-tempo ballads liberally sprinkled throughout the album (plus a token reggae cut) could conceivably find them on A/C playlists." *(Cashbox, February 7, 1981)*

February 16 – May 26, 1981. The band conduct a major North American campaign, supported at first, mostly by Donnie Iris, followed by April Wine and then finally Krokus in May.

Mark Faris, in 1981, in a live review:
"Dan McCafferty's singing is hard to describe. Sometimes it resembles the howling squeal of new tires on hot asphalt. Other times it sounds like a tomcat being garrotted over an inexpensive public address system or a large chimpanzee undergoing a heavy session on the thumb screws. Basically it is a series of guttural, ear-shattering, agonizing shrieks that, more than anything else, evoke utter amazement in listeners."
(Akron Beacon Journal, March 13, 1981)

March 1981. Issued as a single is "Dressed to Kill"/"Pop the Silo," picture sleeve in the UK, non-picture sleeve in the US and Canada.

Dan McCafferty:
"The social commentary and the timing of the Reagan election were coincidental. We wrote the album before Reagan got elected. Iran was holding the hostages and the Russians were in Afghanistan. All Carter said was, 'Boo, hiss, you guys can't do that.' So we wrote that album to say that soon people are going to get fed up and could everybody please try and communicate?"
(w/ Bruce Britt, Detroit Free Press, October 30, 1981)

Pete Agnew:
"*The Fool Circle* was the nearest we came to making a concept album, trying to inject a bit of humour into a pretty heavy subject. I think the fact that we recorded it on the island of Montserrat might account for a teeny bit of reggae poking its way through." (w/ Dmitry Epstein, dmme.net)

May 23, 1981. Nazareth play the Pacific Coliseum in Vancouver, BC. The show is recorded and issued as the '*Snaz* live album later in the year. Or at least that's what the liner notes say (see September 17, 1981 entry).

August 1, 1981. MTV launches. ZZ Top is on board. Nazareth isn't.

Dan McCafferty:
"I hate doing videos. I like doing live concert-type videos, but I've hated the ones where I'm trying to be an actor. I'm not an actor, you know; I'm a rock 'n' roll singer. I suppose we'll eventually have to do another one, but I'm trying to avoid it. I'm hoping that I can make it on the music alone. Remember when music used to sell records?" *(w/ Steve Newton, Ear of Newt, 1984)*

August 7, 1981. The two-LP soundtrack album to the movie *Heavy Metal* is issued. Among a number of non-LP tracks from big bands is Nazareth's "Crazy (A Suitable Case for Treatment)." As well, at his juncture, the UK is in the throes of the New Wave of British Heavy Metal.

Dan McCafferty on the heavy metal genre:
"I liked it when we first started getting into it. But back then it was just rock 'n' roll. Then they changed it to heavy rock, and then they changed it to heavy metal. And it had this image. You had to have long hair and wear spiky metal things and play thrash and make funny faces and stuff, and we didn't fancy any of that. I mean, there was a lot of good, but there was also a lot of poor stuff that came out, just because it had that image, and that got you signed. A lot of it was great, bands like Metallica and stuff; they're the gods of heavy metal sort of thing. But they always had good tunes and they could play."

"But eventually we thought, well this is going a bit farther than we would like to take it. Because we had tried to avoid having anything other than a basic rock image. We've never gone in for a big flash image or anything like that. And heavy metal was definitely going for that, and we decided, no I don't think so. We played a few festivals, and the bands were good and stuff, but unfortunately they all looked the same to me (laughs). I don't know, like with other forms of music, there's good stuff and then there is some absolute crap."

"You see, I'll explain it this way. When we started, we were a band. And then we were a rock band, and then we were a hard rock band, and then we were a heavy metal band. So this wasn't us that was making up these titles. This was journalists that were making up these titles (laughs). Because in the '70s, when I first started, we were signed to the same label as Genesis. You could like Genesis, Jethro Tull, Nazareth, Led Zeppelin, Deep Purple, Uriah Heep— you could like all of them and nobody cared. But then they had to put you into a box. All of a sudden the press became quite large, in a way. And they had to put you into pigeonholes. So I always just thought of us as a rock band, to be quite honest. But then the other thing in my life that I've been is the new guys in the club, the most promising newcomers, and then I was a dinosaur for a while. And then I was a legend. A legend was a lot easier than being a dinosaur."

September 17, 1981. Nazareth issue a double live album called 'Snaz (or It'Snaz if the carry-over text from the back cover is included). It is Scottish "boy wonder" guitarist Billy Rankin's first record with the band. The album reaches No.83 on the Billboard charts and #78 back home in the UK. Issued as a single from the live album is the band's cover of "Morning Dew" backed with a studio track (which was also included on 'Snaz) called "Juicy Lucy."

Zal Cleminson:

"Billy. Baby Billy Rankin. Yeah, he was a lovely musician and a good writer. I don't recall recommending him, but I might have. Somebody probably did. He seemed to be like the next in line (laughs). He was a substitute sitting on the bench, waiting to get called on. 'Get your tracksuit off, Billy. You're on next.' He was completely shell-shocked to be involved in the Nazareth thing. He was just like, 'What the fuck's happened to me?' and he had to go on and play. But he was talented. He's a talented musician." (w/ Marko Syrjala, MetalRules)

Dan McCafferty:

"The time's right for us to finally release a live album. People have been asking us for years, 'When are you guys gonna finally release a live album?' And quite honestly, I was getting pretty sick of it. The band just really seemed to be happening during our 1981 Spring tour, so we recorded a number of shows and said to ourselves that if everything sounds as good on tape as it does on stage, then this would be the time we finally do that live album. Needless to say, those tapes sounded mighty good."

"We wanted to spread our sound out a bit. We saw the opportunity to do something a little different on our tour, so we added keyboards and an extra guitar. Both Billy and John have added a new dimension to our sound. They've revitalized some of the older songs and given a more expansive feel to some of the more recent stuff. I guess we're always looking for some way to be a little different, and a little unusual. That's what's kept Nazareth healthy for so long, and I sure don't see any reason to change now."

"Getting on stage is still the greatest feeling in the world. Those two hours in concert make up for all the time you have to spend sitting around your hotel room or in airport lobbies. Every time we play, we feel we have to reward our fans, because they're the greatest in the world. They stuck with us over the years, and most of them have accepted all the changes we've gone through.

This album is for them. It's a way of saying thanks and that we love them. The two studio cuts are included as a bonus for those people, 'cause they're the ones who really kept us going over the years, and this is our opportunity to show our appreciation."
(w/ Andy Secher, Asbury Park Press, October 11, 1981)

Pete Agnew:
"After we returned from Montserrat we decided to go all the way and add another guitarist to the band. After having Zal, we had kind of got used to hearing two guitars so a pal of ours who had worked with our management at one time suggested a young man named Billy Rankin. Billy was not only an extremely accomplished guitarist and excellent singer, he was a cracking songwriter who could knock out a new tune in the time it took to boil a kettle. At 21, he was the baby of the group, but only in age. In all other aspects he was a seasoned rocker who had been performing live since he could tie his own shoe laces."

"Now having a six-piece band (including John on piano) this lineup became affectionately referred to by our road crew as the Nazareth Orchestra. Our record company and the people around us had been bitching at us for a while to make a live album and now seemed like the perfect time to do that. With this lineup and instrumentation there wasn't a song we couldn't do live. The band had toured a lot that year and we were playing tighter than a gnat's ass so we lined up the recording to take place on a US/Canadian tour in the cities of Houston and Vancouver. The Orchestra hit it on the button both nights and we have an album that every member of the band is proud of. Our good friend John Punter (another AIR Studios man who we worked with many times, even on our first album) was the sound engineer and ultimately the producer of 'Snaz.'"

September 17 – October 2, 1981. The band conduct a short UK campaign.

October 15 – November 29, 1981. The guys tour North America, supported at first mostly by The Joe Perry Project and later by Billy Thorpe.

November 28, 1981. The band play Houston, Texas, supported by Trapeze and Krokus. The show is filmed and would be released on DVD in 2005 and again in 2007.

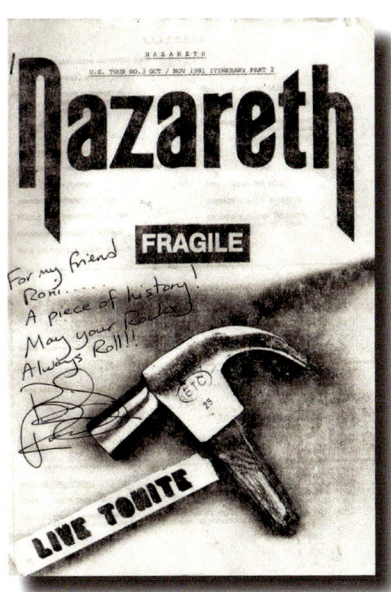
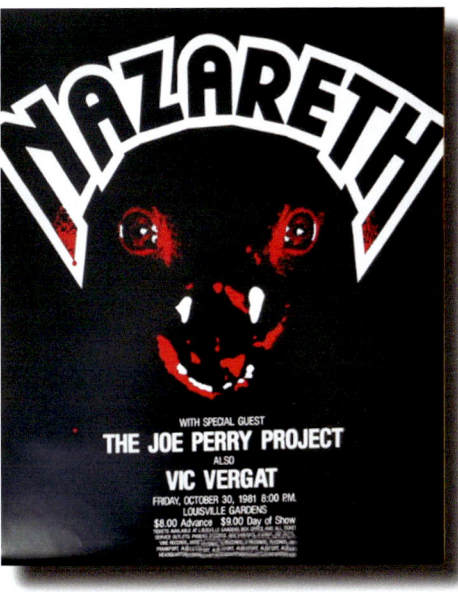

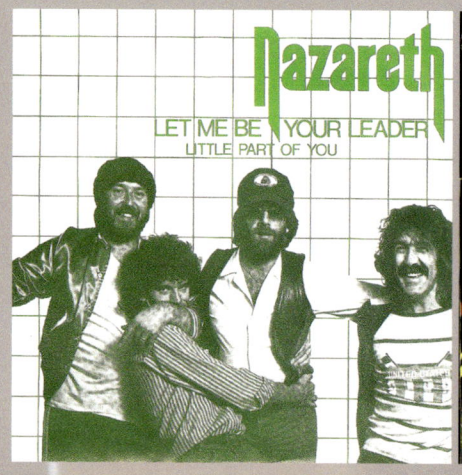

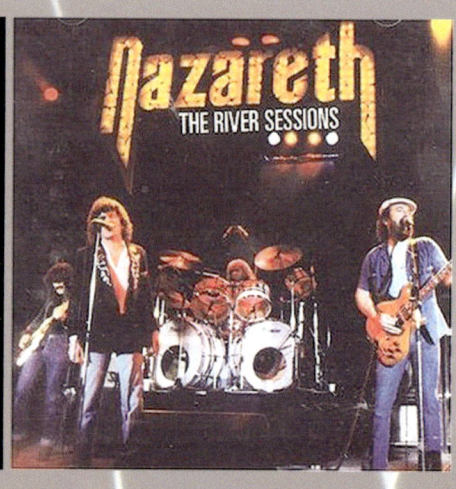
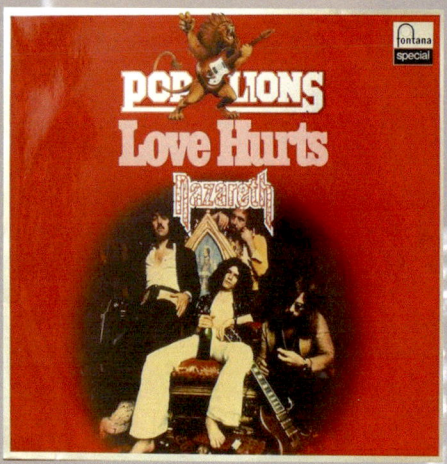
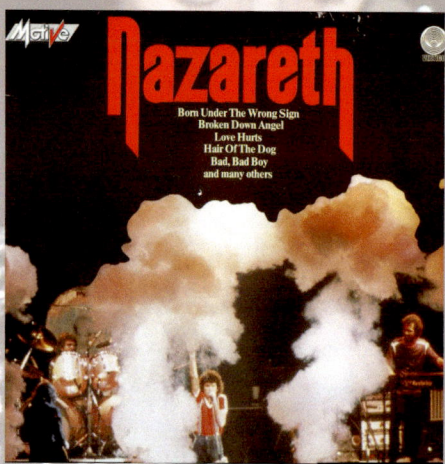

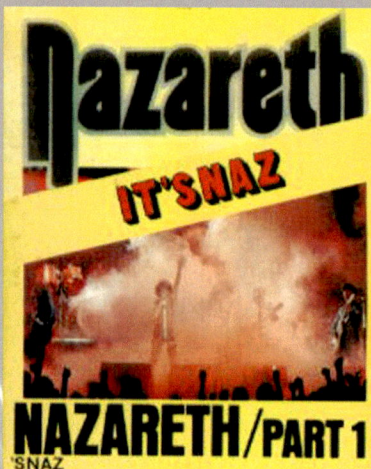

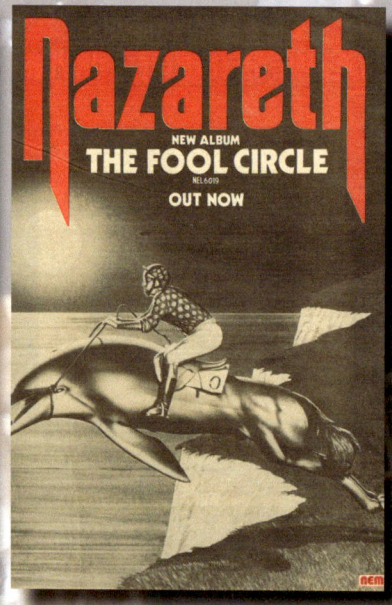
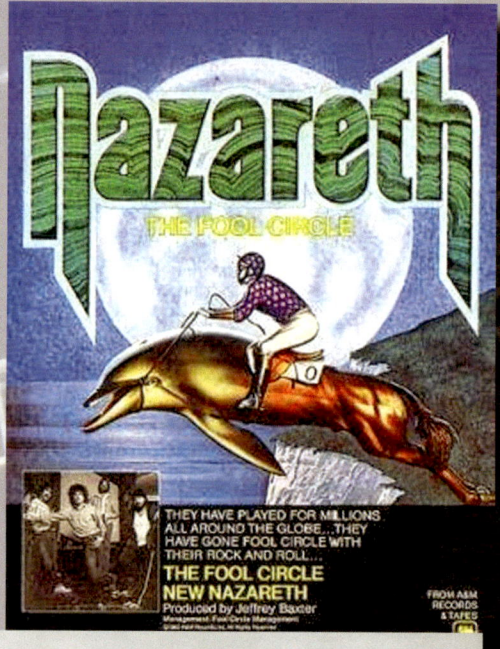

1982

May 1982. Nazareth work at AIR Studios in Montserrat on material slated for the follow-up to *The Fool Circle*. Producing is John Punter, who comes to the band from sessions with Roxy Music, Sad Café and Japan.

May 1, 1982. *No Mean City* is certified gold in Canada.

July 1982. Nazareth issue, on Vertigo, their 13th album, *2XS*, which stalls at #122 on the Billboard charts and #74 on Canada's RPM chart. The band is presented as a six-piece, the original four plus Billy Rankin and John Locke.

Dan McCafferty:
"I think what's going on is that we've already done 15 albums now, we've survived, and rather than get respect for that kind of longevity from radio programmers, we're simply being ignored by them. They go, 'Oh, it's just another Nazareth album. Who cares? Give us something fresh and new and young.' The programmers probably don't even listen to our albums anymore. They probably don't even know there are six of us in the band now, instead of just the original four. What I think it comes down to for Nazareth today is that radio's never really been on our side, except for 'Love Hurts.' But then again, it didn't exactly take a genius to figure out that one was a great car radio song."

"We've always just played the music we wanted to play, and carried on with it. Who knows? Maybe we have too much melody for heavy metal and too much heavy metal for people into melody. But it's simply the kind of rock music we like to play, and we're not about to change and become dedicated followers of fashion or jump on the latest synthesizer bandwagon to make it. That would really be the death knell of this band."
(w/ Jon Marlowe, Miami News, September 10, 1982) for us." *(billyrankin.com)*

Pete Agnew:
"And were we ever sorry for naming this album! We thought it was pretty obvious that it meant 'to excess' but we couldn't believe some of the

pronunciations we heard, 'two times five' being the favourite. Nowadays there would be no problem with everyone doing SMS/text speak but back in 1982 the drugs must have been stronger."

"We went back to Montserrat with the Orchestra and this time we had so many songs written we didn't know where to start. The album was so much fun to make and it's personally one of the highlights of my career. I remember the first time we went to Montserrat in 1980; we walked down inside the volcano which was close to the studio. The smell of burning sulphur made our eyes sting and heated water popped out in little streams all around the walls of the cone. It's hard to believe now that the studio no longer exists since it was completely destroyed in a hurricane not long after we were there, and the main town of Plymouth where we spent many a happy evening, was totally buried in ash when the volcano erupted. I don't think pronouncing our album title wrongly is such a big deal after all."

Reviewer Steve Futterman:

"The spectre of REO Speedwagon's belated superstardom must hang heavy over a band like Nazareth. After flirting with hard rock success during a 12-year, 14-album career, the Scottish sextet can almost taste that long-awaited breakthrough. Unfortunately, 2XS will not be Nazareth's *Hi Infidelity*. Identity rather than inspiration seems to be the problem here. Though it unwisely relies on decibel roar, the group actually sounds more soulful and relaxed on the ballad 'Dream On' and the reggae-tinged 'You Love Another.' When acoustic guitars and keyboards dominate producer and engineer John Punter's precise mix on 'Love Leads to Madness' and 'Games,' Nazareth sound almost inspired. These cuts prove that restraint rather than excess is where Nazareth's talent lies."
(Rolling Stone, September 2, 1982)

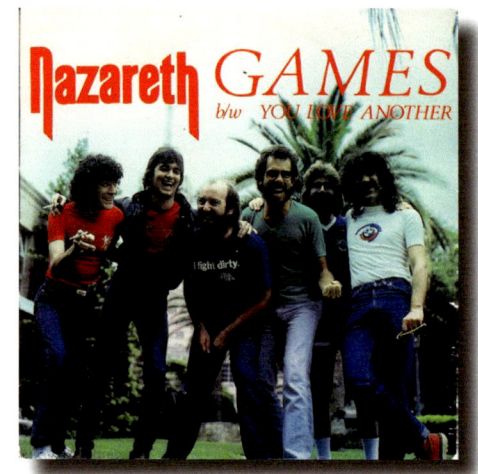

Uncredited record review:

"On their 15th album, veteran Scottish rockers Nazareth have come up with a surprise. The album begins with an obligatory AOR tune, and then goes into a hard rocker, but the next song, 'You Love Another' contains a slinky bass line that sounds like it came over from a Police album. This is followed by a Dave Edmunds-type of rockabilly song and then a big ballad. That is only side one. It is good that Nazareth is willing to take chances and even more heartening that they get away with it so well. This LP is one to cheer for." *(Billboard, July 3, 1982)*

July 1982. "Love Leads to Madness" is issued as a single across a variety of territories, backed with "Take the Rap," followed the next month by "Dream On" with varying B-sides. "Dream On" hits No.1 in Germany.

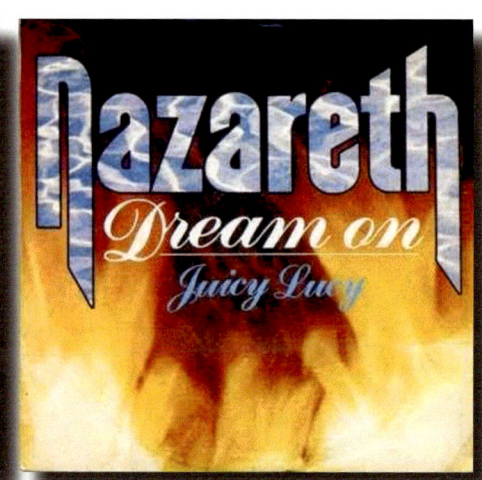

Pete Agnew, on the hiring of Billy Rankin, composer of "Dream On:"
"Years later, we were actually doing a live album, a DVD thing, in Brazil. One of our biggest songs there is 'Love Leads to Madness,' and it's one of the songs that is so, so big in Brazil, it's almost like an anthem. And of course we forget. We were starting to play this thing, and were recording it for a live album, and then the crowd started singing and it was, 'Scrub it; you can't use this track' (laughs). Because you can't hear the band. So sometimes songs are just that popular, where we were doing it and you just couldn't hear the band."

Mid-September to early December 1982. Nazareth play North America, most dates supporting Billy Squier. As the tour is ending, the band split with A&M, possibly due to the demands manager Jim White had been putting on the label as they negotiated a new contract.

November 1982, Brooklyn Zoo, Brooklyn, NY.

November 1982, Brooklyn Zoo, Brooklyn, NY.

1983

1983. Keyboard player John Locke leaves Nazareth to reform Spirit.

January 17, 1983. "Games" is issued as a single in the UK, backed with "You Love Another."

February 14, 1983. Nazareth play a charity gig at Coasters in Edinburgh, marking the first time back for a show on home turf in a year-and-a-half. The band was now a five-piece, after the departure of John Locke back to his old band, Spirit.

February 22 – April 6, 1983. The band work at Little Mountain in Vancouver, on tracks to comprise their forthcoming album. While in Vancouver, Billy Rankin befriends Bryan Adams who signed to A&M just as Nazareth were leaving.

May 1983. Blackfoot issue their sixth album, *Siogo*, which includes a cover of Nazareth's "Heart's Grown Cold."

May 1983. Nazareth log a few German dates supporting Rush.

June 1983. "Dream On" is issued in the UK as the third and final single from the *2XS* album. The Billy Rankin song goes to No.1 in Poland and charts well in other European countries as well.

Pete Agnew, on Billy:

"There were umpteen suggestions. You know, 'Get this guy, get that guy.' But we wanted someone that would fit into the band. Billy was perfect because he's still impressionable. Yes, we've fixed him there. He was 21 when he joined the band; he's 45 now (laughs). He just gets battered if he doesn't agree with us. Seriously, we didn't want to have an ever-changing band. Generally, you find that guys that go from band to band are going to do that to you as well. You just get the thing to how you like it, and they're leaving."

"Even though Billy and John have been with us one-and-a-half years, there's no way they're going to know us like the four of us know one another. They see us fighting and they think it's the end of the group. But the next morning it's all blown over. For a few days after the fight, they keep asking if everything is alright. They've now developed the good sense so that when a fight starts, they just leave." (w/ Barbara Jaeger, The Record, August 22, 1982)

June 30, 1983. Vertigo issues a second Nazareth album for the label—and the 14th for the band—called *Sound Elixir*. Producing is Manny Charlton, who shares guitar duties with Billy Rankin—this is Billy's second and last studio album with the band before returning in 1990. "Where Are You Now" is issued as a single but it fails to improve the poor sales of the record.

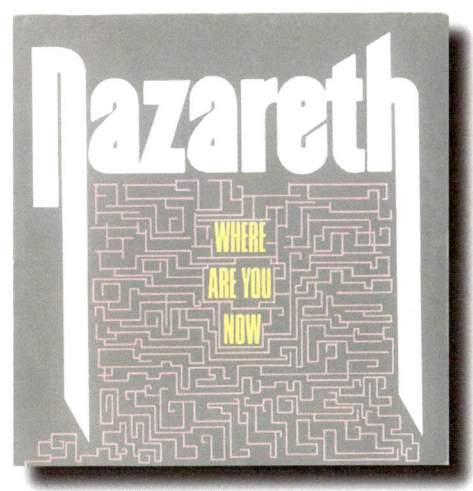

Pete Agnew:

"John left after having had enough of the manager we had at the time—we fired him soon afterward—and he met up again with his old mates in Spirit when they put the band back together after all those years. We wished him well. So now we were a five-piece again and it was time to do another album. Again, as in Montserrat, we had so many songs that it was hard choosing what

May 17th, 1983, Eishalle Liebenau, Graz, Austria.

© Isabella Seefriedt

should be recorded and what should be left out. The problem here is this that when a song is passed over (and I only speak for Nazareth) it is unlikely to pop up at a later date because the writer will probably be tired of it by then and have written other songs to be considered. Okay, enough of that."

"This time we went to another mountain studio but this one was in Vancouver. It was a very nice studio and right in the middle of the city. We did some crazy stuff there experimenting with different noises that weren't created on musical instruments. My personal favourite is when we recorded the studio pinball machine and built the whole track around the pulse that it made."

"Being in the middle of the city, and since we knew a lot of people in Vancouver, we tended to get more visitors than normal at our sessions. I especially remember one young guy who our record company sent along to meet us. They said he was a good songwriter and they wanted to put him and Billy together to write as they thought the two of them would make a good team. Billy and him met at the studio a few times, had a few drinks and promises were made to get in touch. But like most of these things, nothing ever came of it and we never heard from him again. We did, however hear of him quite a lot in the years to come and it seems Bryan Adams managed to write one or two hits without Billy's help. Shortly after the album's release, young Billy left to have a stab at a solo career. As with John, we wished him well."

Dan McCafferty:
"*Sound Elixir,* that's the one from the '80s I'm not really sure about. At that time we were going through yet another record company and yet another management and we were in court at the time trying to get an album done. And again, that was a bad time for us, because we trusted our manager and he screwed us, or tried to anyway. A lot of the material on that album deserves better than it got, to be honest, really."

Uncredited record review:
"Big Country may be Scotland's entry into this year's charts but the band owes a great deal to such relentless and enduring pub rockers as Nazareth, who have kept the fire burning in the land where the guitar plays second fiddle to the bagpipe. Nazareth's latest release is yet another blues scorcher which pays considerable attention to melody as well as energy. One of the band's many noteworthy attributes is its ability to compose inspiring ballads and this record is no exception. 'Where Are You Now' and 'Rain in the Window' highlight Dan McCafferty's ragged yet warm and soulful voice as well as the band's folk influences often not heard on the band's boogie rockers like 'Why Don't You Read the Book' and 'Rags to Riches.'" *(Cashbox December 3, 1983)*

October – December 1983. The band tour Canada in October, followed by American shows to close out the year. Some of the Canadian dates are in support of an Ian Gillan-fronted Black Sabbath.

May 6th, 1985, Sporthalle, Böblingen, Germany.

© Wolfgang Gurster

© Wolfgang Gurster

1984

1984. A&M in Canada issue the two-LP *The Very Very Best of Nazareth*.

Early 1984. Billy Rankin issues a solo album called *Growin' Up Too Fast*, which generates a minor US hit called "Baby Come Back." Also included is a version of "Where Are You Now" last heard on *Sound Elixir*. He's quickly back into the studio to record a second album, *Crankin'*, which is issued the following year, but only in Japan.

Mid-1984. Nazareth work at home in Scotland on tracks to comprise their forthcoming album. It's the first time they've recorded an album in Scotland in eight years. Producing is John Eden. Billy Rankin is now out of the band, due to a maelstrom of legal issues pertaining to publishing, management and his solo career.

Dan McCafferty:
"When you record in, say, Montserrat or Vancouver or France or somewhere, you tend to pick up the vibes that are happening in the street of that particular country. Basically, what we wanted to do was see what was happening at home. Because things are pretty tough at home at the moment. There are millions unemployed, lots of kids just hanging around with nothing to do. Musically, because of that, there's a bunch of things happening. Years ago, these kids could've come to Canada, but no more."
(w/ Ted Shaw, Windsor Star, January 19, 1985)

July 4 – July 14, 1984. The band conduct an extensive tour of Sweden, playing Finland as well.

September 1984. "Ruby Tuesday" (banjo part included!) is issued as a single in the UK and Germany backed with "Sweetheart Tree." In Canada the B-side is "This Flight Tonight." For the home territory, Vertigo offers an expanded four-track version.

September 22, 1984. Nazareth sees the release of their 15th album, *The Catch*. The record consists of seven originals assigned a simple full band credit, plus a cover of the Rolling Stones' "Ruby Tuesday" and a version of 1966 Carole King/Gerry Goffin number "Road to Nowhere."

Dan McCafferty:
"A lot of our earlier albums were made in studios that had an on/off switch, and we didn't know any better either. Plus we were younger and we only knew four-and-a-half chords. I don't think we've ever consciously thought, 'Right, let's change, let's do this.' The reason we've been together so long is because we've always done what we like to do at the time. We just went along with how we felt. It was the only way to go. We like to try other things and we have tried other things. But we like the original four-piece. I think the energy level of the band comes up when it's just the four of us, because everybody's busy, you know. We're back to the real deal." *(w/ Steve Newton, Ear of Newt, 1984)*

Manny Charlton:
"We were now back to the original lineup, and this time, unlike the last four or five albums, we didn't have a surplus of songs to choose from. Except for one song in particular (two at the most) we struggled with the material for this album and I'm sorry to say that it's not an album I would hold up to represent Nazareth at its best. We recorded it back in Scotland in a wee place called Pencaitland whose old schoolhouse had been converted into a studio. It's a great studio and is still in operation, but now with different owners. We recorded several things there other than *The Catch*. For instance, we recorded 'Crazy (A Suitable Case for Treatment)' for the movie *Heavy Metal* and also 'Cinema,' the title track for the album we recorded next."

October 2 – 29, 1984. The band tour the UK, winding up not successful in their quest to get the album to chart. Germany however grants the band a No.60 placement.

November 12, 1984. The band appear on famed German live music show Rockpalast, performing twenty numbers in Bochum, albeit offering only two selections from *The Catch*. Another filming for TV takes place on the 19th in Munich.

1985

1985. The band is forced to take legal action when their ex-manager Jim White issues a spate of Nazareth records on his own Sahara imprint.

1985. A compilation called *The Ballad Album* is issued by Vertigo in a number of territories, foremost being Germany.

1985 – 1988. Future Nazareth guitarist Jimmy Murrison attends the Perth Rock School. He will become a guitar teacher, with his connection to Nazareth coming when he plays with Lee Agnew in the band Trouble in Doggieland.

February 13, 14, 1985. Following scattered Canadian and US shows, the band play two nights at the Viña del Mar International Song Festival in Chile.

February 22 – March 11, 1985. The band conduct an extensive German campaign.

Dan McCafferty:
"Nothing in the '80s was really that much of a big success. It was a pretty bad time for us. Not so bad in the early '80s, but it wasn't until *Move Me* that we even started to get the airplay again. The whole system seemed to be geared towards dance and MTV at the time, and in Europe anyway, rock 'n' roll was on a few obscure shows, late at night. In the States, everything rock was classic rock, so they were playing your old stuff but not your new stuff. Very strange time not just for us, but for a lot of rock bands."

September 14, 1985. The band play a metal fest put on by Metal Hammer magazine. Also on the bill are Metallica, Venom, Heavy Pettin', Wishbone Ash and Warlock. How big Nazareth might have become had they gone the heavy metal route in the '80s is thrown into high relief. Wishbone Ash as well.

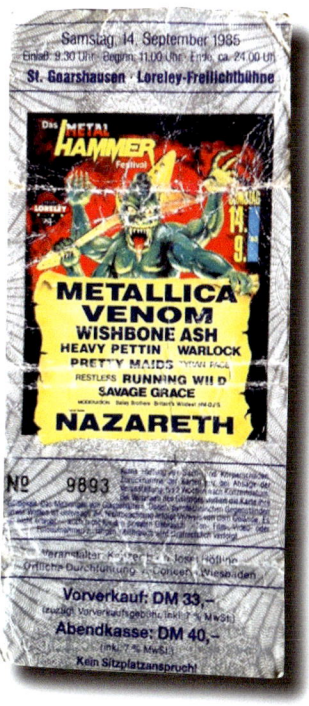

February 23rd, 1985, Biberach, Germany.

© Wolfgang Gurster

November 14 – November 25, 1985. The band tour Eastern Europe.

Dan McCafferty, on close calls in the Baltics and around the world:
"There was the time in Yugoslavia. Oh, that was wonderful. A guy rips us off at the hotel and we call the police. The next thing we know, the police are chattering about hash and sticking the muzzles of their machine guns up our noses. We said, 'Hey, you don't understand. *We* called *you*."

"Then there's Italy. If you don't end up in a communist riot, you'll end up in a fascist riot. When you play Sicily, they shoot the tires off your truck because you haven't paid the 10%. When you ask, 'What 10%?,' they answer you with guns and you suddenly realize you could disappear over there. You realize it's not Scotland anymore."

"And there was Iceland. Procol Harum, Led Zeppelin, Deep Purple and Nazareth are the only bands ever to go there as far as I know. At the end of the night, you discover that the Chief Justice, who's supposed to pay you, doesn't want to turn over any cash. Finally at 4 AM, we held him up against the wall and threatened to pack his head in a suitcase. We got what he owed us."

"We went to #1 in Guatemala and our manager is saying, 'Look, now you gotta go there to support the record.' Somehow we didn't fancy giving target practice to a bunch of guerrillas and turned him down."
(w/ Jack Lloyd, The Dispatch, April 6, 1981)

July 21st, 1985, Sporthalle, Linz, Austria.

© Isabella Seefriedt

1986

February 22, 1986. Nazareth issue the Eddie Delana-produced *Cinema* album, recorded (during a freezing winter) at Pearl Sound Studios in Canton, Michigan, except for the title track, which was recorded in Scotland. The album is issued in Canada and various countries in Europe but not in the UK or the US.

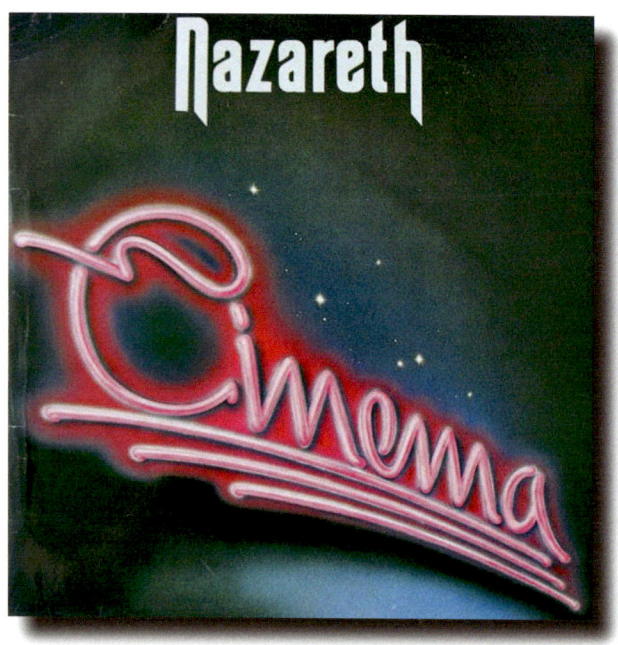 

Pete Agnew:
"This was a great Nazareth album but what I remember most about it is the place we made it. Our manager at the time (a really nice guy) had Nazareth and Ted Nugent as his acts. He and Ted lived near Ann Arbor in Michigan and he told us to come over and that he had a nice studio for us to work in. The studio he had for us belonged to one of the guys in Grand Funk Railroad and it was a nice enough place but it was all carpeted—on the floor, up the walls—and the ceiling was heavy with acoustic tiles. This place was deader than your grandma's great aunt, so we said, 'No thanks.'"

"Now our manager (poor guy) had to find a place quick since we were all here and ready to go. He found one. The studio was infested with these crawling bugs, the likes of we had never seen before. It was a dump beyond description. The control room was okay, and so as long as you stayed in there you were fine. But when you weren't playing, they only had this little area—I won't call it a room because that would be a gross exaggeration—with a two-seater couch, which was infested with these bugs, and a Space Invaders machine, and that was your lot, mate! We couldn't wait to get out of the place every night and I have no idea to this day how we managed to make such a belter of an album in there. I won't bother telling you where it is because the local health and safety people have probably burnt it to the ground by now."

Manny Charlton:
"At that point we were looking for management, and we knew of a guy called Doug Banker, from Michigan, who managed Ted Nugent. We were friends with him and he suggested that we come over to America and record in a studio in Michigan. So that's what we did. Cinema was a return to form for us. It's a good

Nazareth rock 'n' roll record, you know? Eddie Delana was basically an engineer, more an engineer than a producer, but he got the band to sound good. Plus we were back to the original four-piece by that time too, just the original four of us. There's a few good songs on that record and like I say, for me, it was a return to form for the band. We were back writing rock 'n' roll and playing in the right pocket."

Dan McCafferty on the '80s album that was the most work:
"*Cinema* actually, because we had to keep changing studios and stuff. There were a lot of technical problems and breakdowns, major repairs in the studio, so we had to go somewhere else for a few days and then come back. We started to lose that continuity. You get in the studio, and then you go, 'God, there's no bottom end here. It sounds different than the last one we were in.' You make little tapes and take it out into the car to see if it sounded good. Probably stress-wise, that was the worst. But I like the song 'Cinema' a lot."

June 4, 1986. After Axl Rose expressed interest in having Manny Charlton produce the first Guns N' Roses album, Charlton records some early sessions for the band at Sound City in LA. Scheduled work with Nazareth had Manny bowing out of the project, with Mike Clink taking over the production duties on what was to become *Appetite for Destruction*.

October 30 – November 28, 1986. The band tour mainland Europe, concentrating as usual on Germany.

July 5th, 1986, Out in the Green, Dinkelsbühl, Germany.

© Wolfgang Gurster

November 20th, 1986, Kammersaal, Austria.

1987

1987. Live album 'Snaz is issued on CD for the first time, however it is pared down by five tracks to fit on a single disc.

1987. Dan sees the release of a second solo album, *Into the Ring*, recorded at Chameleon Studios in Hamburg and issued by Mercury in Germany. Floated as a single is "Starry Eyes"/"Sunny Island." Pete co-writes with Dan on six tracks.

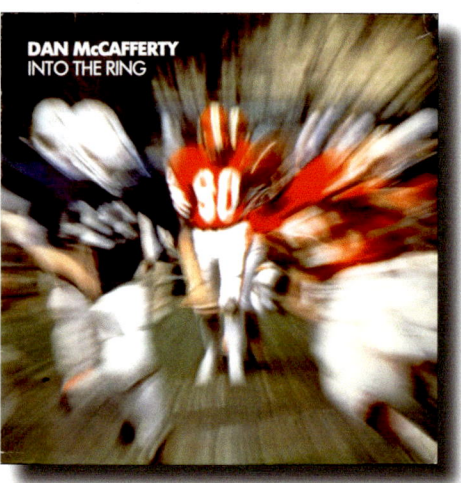

Dan McCafferty:
"Half of it was stuff Pete and I wrote and the other side was a soundtrack for a German movie. There's no reason how you would have known about it. It's one of these obscure things. I think it actually sold one copy in Tokyo or whatever the hell it was (laughs)."

February – May, 1987. The band tour North America, followed by Europe and then a few more North American dates later in the year.

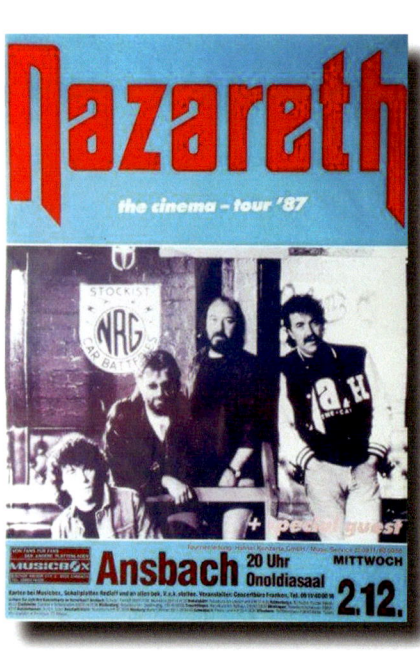

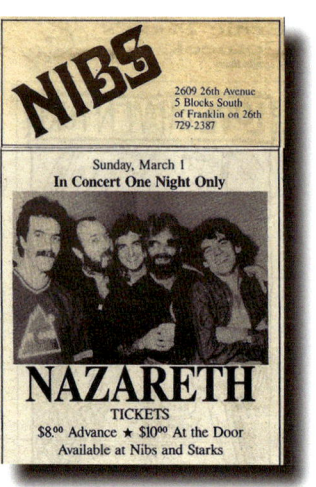

Dan McCafferty on the '80s:
"MTV and all these things started, so it became less of an audio form than a visual form. So we just had to stick with the music. Because we're British, we were very aware of let's do what we do and stick with that. Because Britain changed its mind every three seconds. It was very fashion-motivated and very aesthetic, visual, that kind of thing. So we just stuck to our guns and played rock 'n' roll and survived through all those times."

June 21, 1987. Canadian heavy metal band Helix issue their sixth album, *Wild in the Streets*. On it is a cover of Nazareth's "Dream On," from *2XS*.

July 21, 1987. Guns N' Roses issue their seminal debut, *Appetite for Destruction*, which goes on to sell thirty million copies worldwide. As discussed, Manny Charlton almost produced it.

1988

February – June 1988. The band tour North America, kicking off with a Canadian leg before transitioning to the States.

© Wolfgang Gurster

1989

January 23, 1989. Nazareth issue what will be their last album with Manny Charlton in the ranks, entitled *Snakes 'n' Ladders*. Producing is Joey Balin, with the team working at Comforts Place Studio in Surrey, England. Vertigo issues the album in Europe and Japan but not in the UK or North America.

Pete Agnew:
"This was the Nazareth album that Nazareth never made! How's that? It went like this: all of our recording contracts had expired by this time so our German record company (who had us for the world excluding America) offered us a new deal on the condition that we used an American producer who was a big favourite of theirs at the time. No problem. After meeting this guy a few times I get the distinct impression that what he really wants is to do a solo album with Dan, whose voice he absolutely loves."

"Anyway, in the weeks before we go to the studio, him and Manny have become good buddies and they've decided that we will have 'programmed drums' instead of a live kit. Everyone including Darrell—actually *especially* Darrell—is quite happy to go along with this so they arrange a session programmer to handle this. Unknown to myself, and for whatever reason, they have also decided to replace me with a session bass player, but I don't find this out until I have played on a couple of tracks in the studio. By the way, the studio was a beautiful big old manor house near Lingfield in England."

"So that's two of us not playing on the album now. I'm still hanging out at the studio because I have all the backing vocals to do, when three or four days later I'm told that Manny has now been replaced with a session guitar player. Oops, he didn't see that coming! But dear me, can we still call this a Nazareth album? Apparently we can, because the session keeps rolling on. However, after getting the backing vocals out of the way, I don't need to hang around so I hop on a plane home. The album eventually gets finished and at least it has Dan doing the vocals, so we had *one* Nazareth guy that managed to finish the course. I've often wondered what would have happened if this guy had decided he didn't like Dan's voice either. Funny thing is, one track from the album, 'We Are Animals,' became a massive hit in Russia and all the surrounding countries.

This is one of the only two tracks that we—Manny and me—play guitar and bass on together. I guess the Russians must have wanted to hear 'Nazareth!'"

Dan McCafferty, on the record being issued only in Europe and Japan:
"We do quite good in Japan. They think some albums are great and others they think are crap. In Japan, a lot of that is down to promotion. If the record company decides that this is going to be hot, it's going to be hot. That's how the country is geared. They just blast things at people."

July – October 1989. The band tour Europe, with most dates taking place in Germany, supported by Canada's Lee Aaron.

September 1989. Hanoi Rocks singer Michael Monroe issues his second solo album—*Not Fakin' It* contains a cover of the Nazareth song of the same name.

November 9, 1989. The fall of the Berlin Wall.

Pete Agnew:
"When the wall came down, I mean, so much happened. People don't realize that it was a different career, '89 to '90, when that wall came down. That changed rock 'n' roll for the planet. You don't notice it so much in the US and Canada, but over here in Europe, there used to be a big chunk of concrete there and that just disappeared. That opened up the biggest market in the world to us, all these Eastern European countries. What an incredible difference to us that made, and many other bands. I mean, you could write a book on that alone."

December 17, 1989. Hair metal band Britny Fox issue, on Columbia, their second album *Boys in Heat*, which includes a cover of "Hair of the Dog."

July 27th, 1989,
1.Radio Rock Nacht,
Illertissen, Germany.

July 27th, 1989, 1.Radio Rock Nacht, Illertissen, Germany.

July 27th, 1989, 1.Radio Rock Nacht, Illertissen, Germany.

© Wolfgang Gurster

October 11th, 1989,
Longhorn Club,
Stuttgart-Wangen,
Germany.

"In the '90s, you could always sell tickets. You could always go out and work. It's just that you couldn't get arrested on the airwaves at all. But the end of the '80s, when Guns N' Roses came along, for instance, all those bands, and they started talking about us and Queen and the other influences growing up, that didn't hurt us at all. And then the boys covered 'Hair of the Dog,' which didn't hurt either. In my experience, I've been doing this for 40-odd years now and it tends to go in circles anyway, music. Fashion as well, oddly enough, seems to go in circles. If you just wait long enough it will come around."
Dan McCafferty

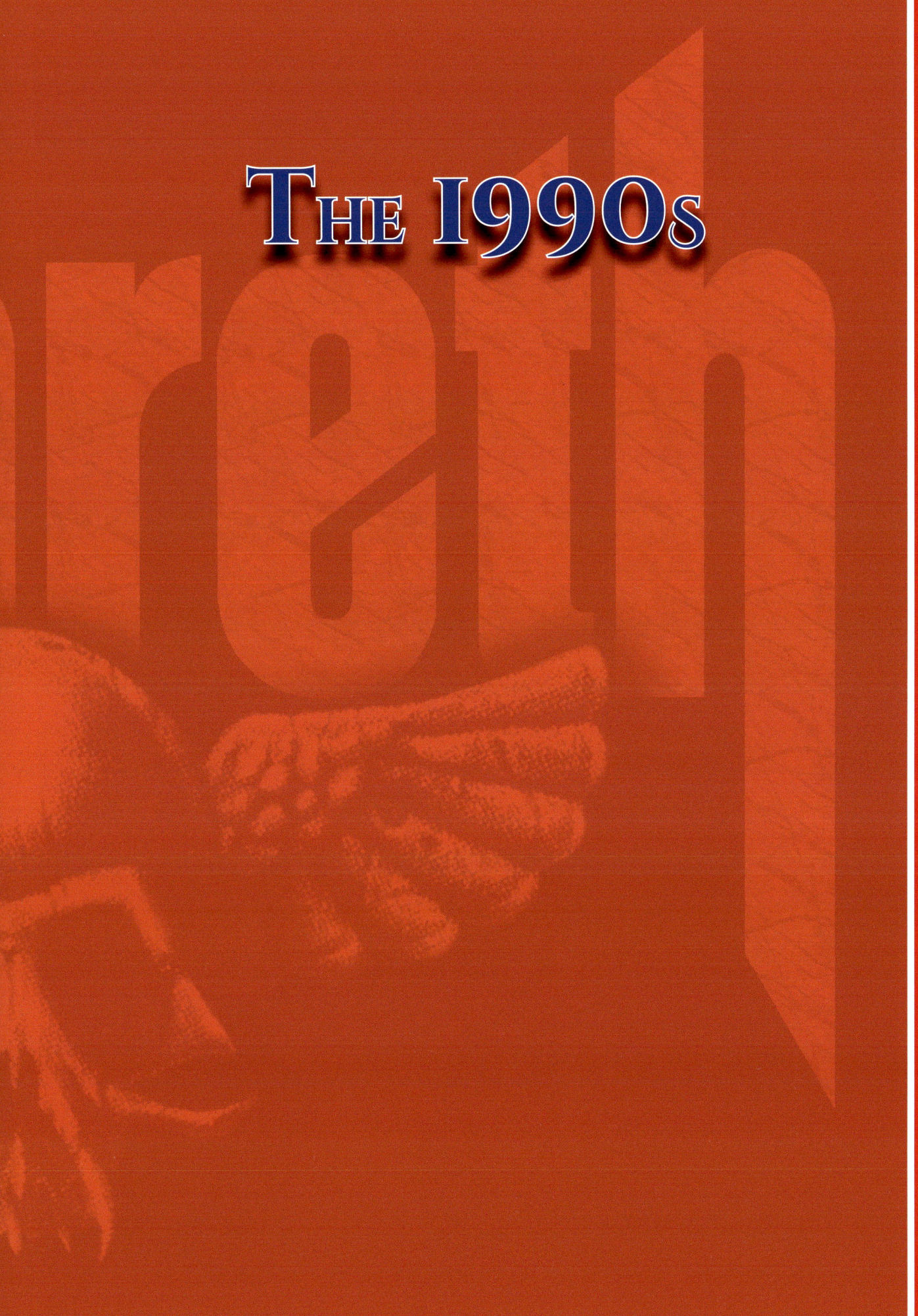

THE 1990s

In the 1990s, Nazareth makes the shift away from the record/tour cycle to a band that has touring as its identity, showing up, punching the clock, and then making the odd record not because they're particularly inspired, but because it's about time, or because a record deal with a decent advance happened to materialise.

Still, there's an exciting dimension to each of the records that we got. For the first two, in 1991 and 1994, Billy Rankin returns to the band despite ongoing financial disputes. And not only does he rejoin, but his writing sort of defines the band, with *No Jive* and *Move Me* being a sort of up-tempo pop metal (if you allow the generality), with glossy late-'80s production values making everything behave.

For the third of the three records we got this decade, 1998's *Boogaloo*, Billy is out of the picture again, replaced by Jimmy Murrison. And despite the fact that we are about to embark on the longest gap between Nazareth albums, ending with 2008's *The Newz*, *Boogaloo* is essentially the first of a quartet of bold, swaggering, creatively very much successful Nazareth albums that would serve as a nice surprise this late in the band's career. Ronnie Leahy is brought back as keyboard player after a five-year "retirement," but he's more so emphasizing the band's old school, rock 'n' roll values, much appreciated after years of Nazareth trying to look youthful.

Unfortunately, *Boogaloo* would be the last record for original drummer Darrell Sweet, who would die in 1999, quite unexpectedly from a heart attack while the band was out touring America, in fact. Still, if we are to stress the positive, Darrell was there for the entire decade, clutching his lunch box as Nazareth went to work, at this point more or less delivering a hits-heavy set, but one that nonetheless stressed how rich a history this most famous of Scottish bands very loudly professed night after night from stages all over the world.

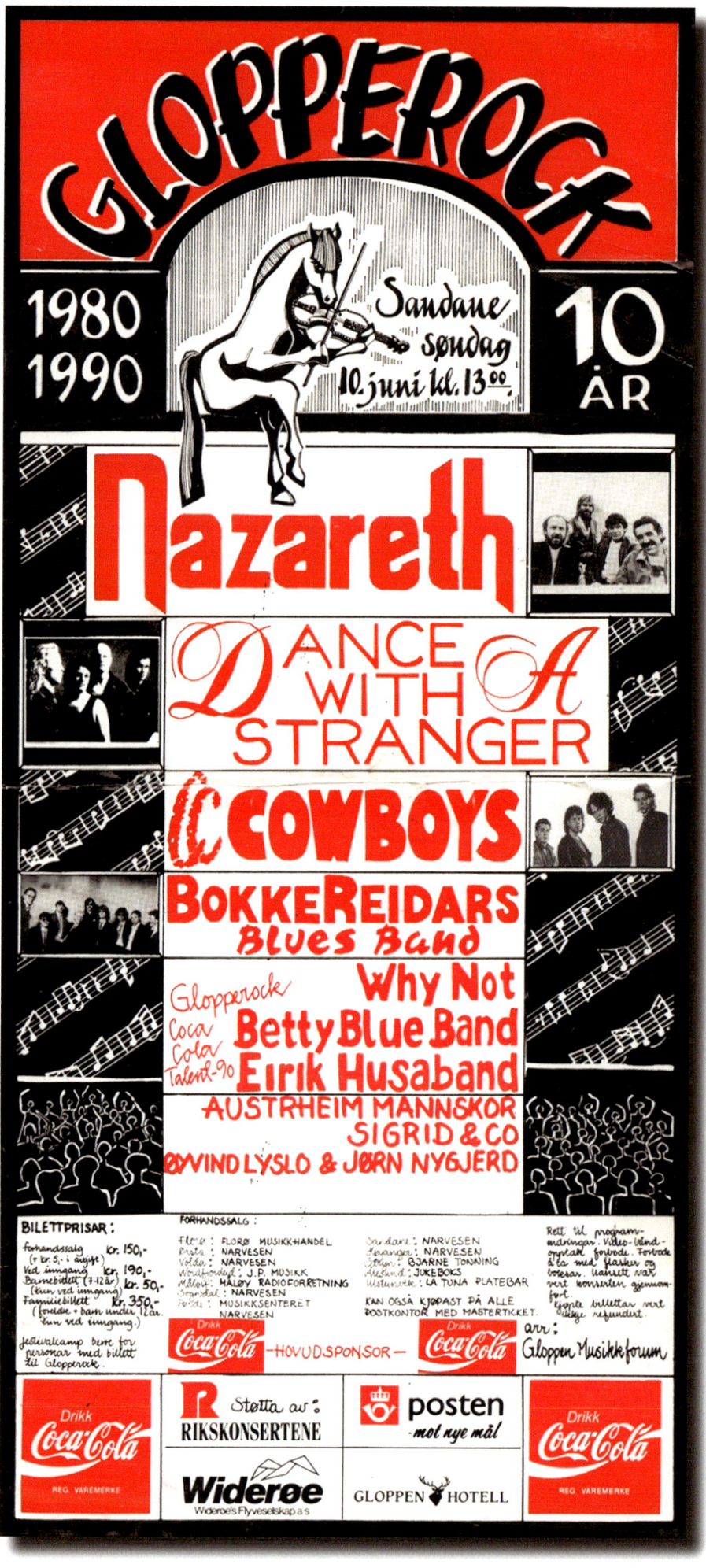

1990

1990. *Hair of the Dog* is issued for the first time on CD.

May 13, 1990. After twenty-two years faithful service, guitarist and sometimes producer Manny Charlton leaves Nazareth, playing his last show in Nazareth's hometown of Dunfermline, Scotland, at a benefit for wheelchair sports. Opening on the night is Fish, ex-Marillion, with the prog legend also joining the band for a rendition of The Sensational Alex Harvey Band classic, "The Faith Healer."

Dan McCafferty, in 1999:
"We had been together for twenty-six years, and basically we wanted to do what we do and he wanted to do something else. And eventually that starts to get in the way. I mean, break-ups are never pleasant at all, really. Unless the whole band just decides to call it quits. After the band, he was in production for a while and he did a couple things in Europe, and then he was running a studio for this guy and doing a lot of stuff on the side. I think he got bored with that and I believe he has an album that is either out or it's coming out."

Pete Agnew, in 2017:
"We had disagreements—that's it. We totally disagreed with some stuff and that was it. There was no point in staying together. Since then we haven't spoken to each other. We have agreed to be apart. We were doing our own paths, and we never had big fights. So it was just a goodbye and just, 'Go do your thing. We'll do ours.' I've never seen the man for 18 years, since Darrell Sweet died. I've only seen him maybe four to five times in all those years, after he quit with the band. But the last time I saw him was way back when Darrell died."
(w/ Marko Syrjala, MetalRules)

June – July 1990. Nazareth tour the US in a package with Blackfoot and Ten Years After. Manny has been replaced by a returning Billy Rankin.

November 3 – 16, 1990. Nazareth mount a German tour, as part of a package with Saga and Kansas.

November 9th, 1990, Deutsches Museum, Munich, Germany.

© Wolfgang Gurster

1991

Mid-1991. Nazareth work at Cas Studios, Inbert-Schüren, Germany, on tracks to slated for their 18th album.

Dan McCafferty:
"We produced ourselves and did it with as few overdubs as possible, because we wanted it to sound like us live. Mike Ging is a big fan of the band and so he knew our sound really well. It was like having the album mixed from a fan's perspective. *(w/ Tom Harrison, The Province, July 14, 1993)*

November 1, 1991. Nazareth issue—through Mausoleum in German, Griffin in the US and Attic in Canada—*No Jive*.

Dan McCafferty:
"It's the best record we've done in a long time. I had a good feel about it. Rock was having a bit of a comeback and it's like everything else in this business: you get the right tune in the right three minutes at the right time, then you are lucky. And if you don't, well, you've just got to keep trying. We still have fun with it. We enjoyed playing and the only way you can do that is if you go on the road. And we enjoy each other's company, and having fun, basically."
(w/ David Howell, Edmonton Journal, July 9, 1993)

Pete Agnew:
"After the dust had settled from Snakes, Manny was no longer in the band and we had Billy back, so this album was always going to be fun and games. Of course with Billy's return we had more songs than you could shake a stick at, and some really great ones at that. We went to a studio in a tiny village (well, not even a village, more a street) near Saarbrücken in Germany. The place had been a restaurant until Frank Farian bought it and made it into a studio. He was the guy who made all the Boney M and Milli Vanilli records. It was a great studio but the resident sound engineer kept disappearing for hours on end so we—well, Billy actually—ended up engineering the sessions. We had such a good time making this record that we were sad when we finished it after six weeks.

The German newspaper, Bild, were following the recordings and doing stories about it every other week as a sort of serialization of the making of an album. This coverage led to all sorts of nutters turning up at the studio with all sorts of instruments, wanting to jam with us. As you can see on the album, we resisted the temptation."

December 21, 1991. Nazareth play a charity gig at home in Dunfermline, upstairs at a bar called Sinky's. The gig was in support of the Darrell Sweet Memorial Fund.

1992

February 1992. The band begin the year playing Germany with Uriah Heep followed by UK dates in April, followed by more European shows and then more UK concerts in October.

February 18th, 1992, Neu-Ulm, Gorki Park, Germany.

© Wolfgang Gurster

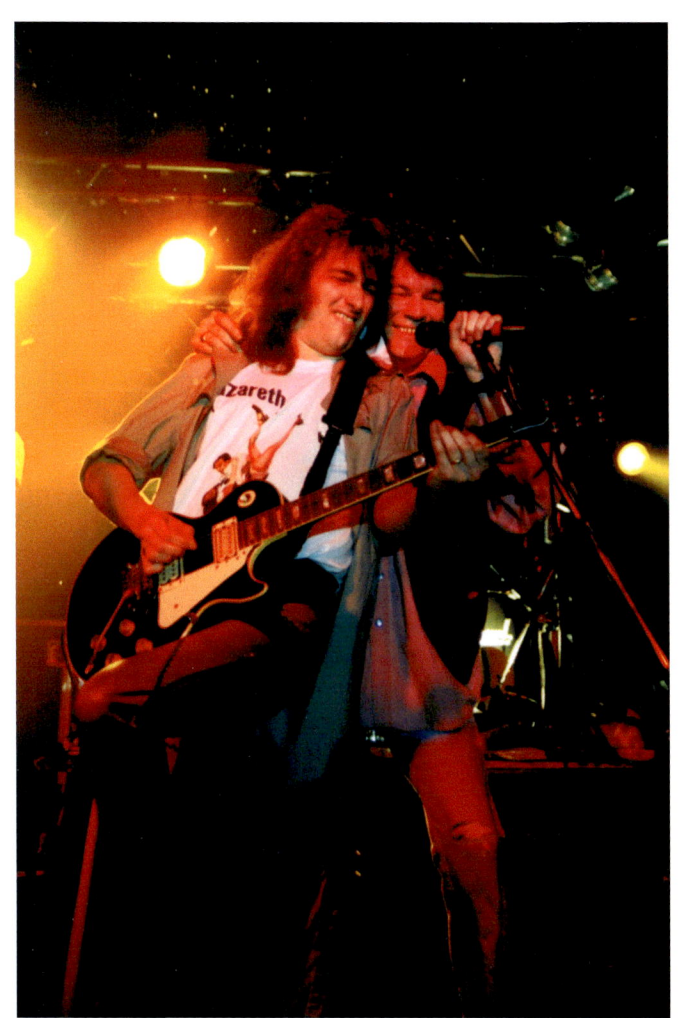

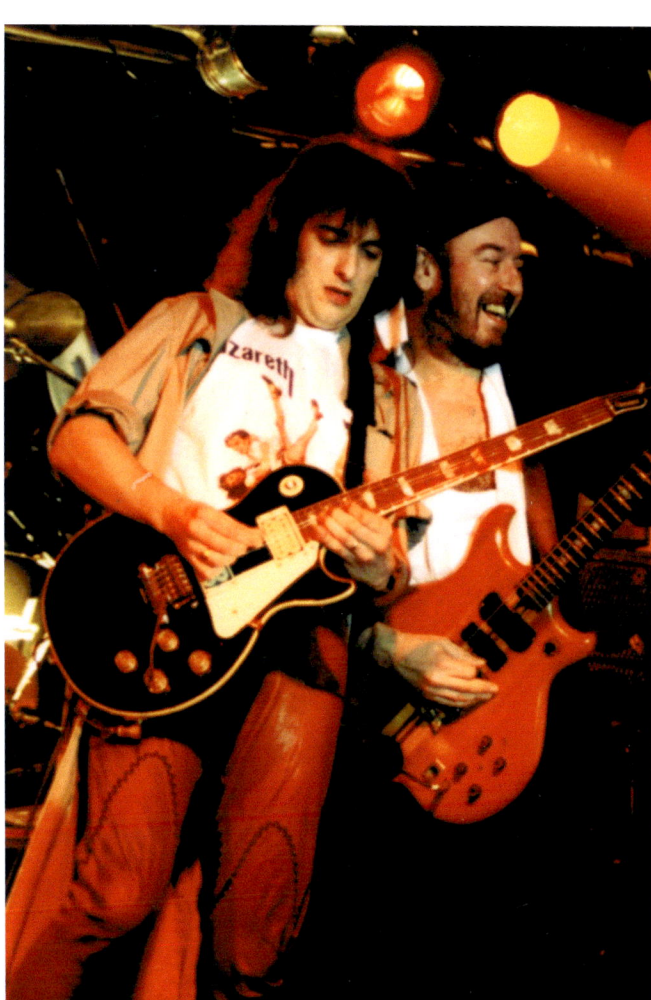

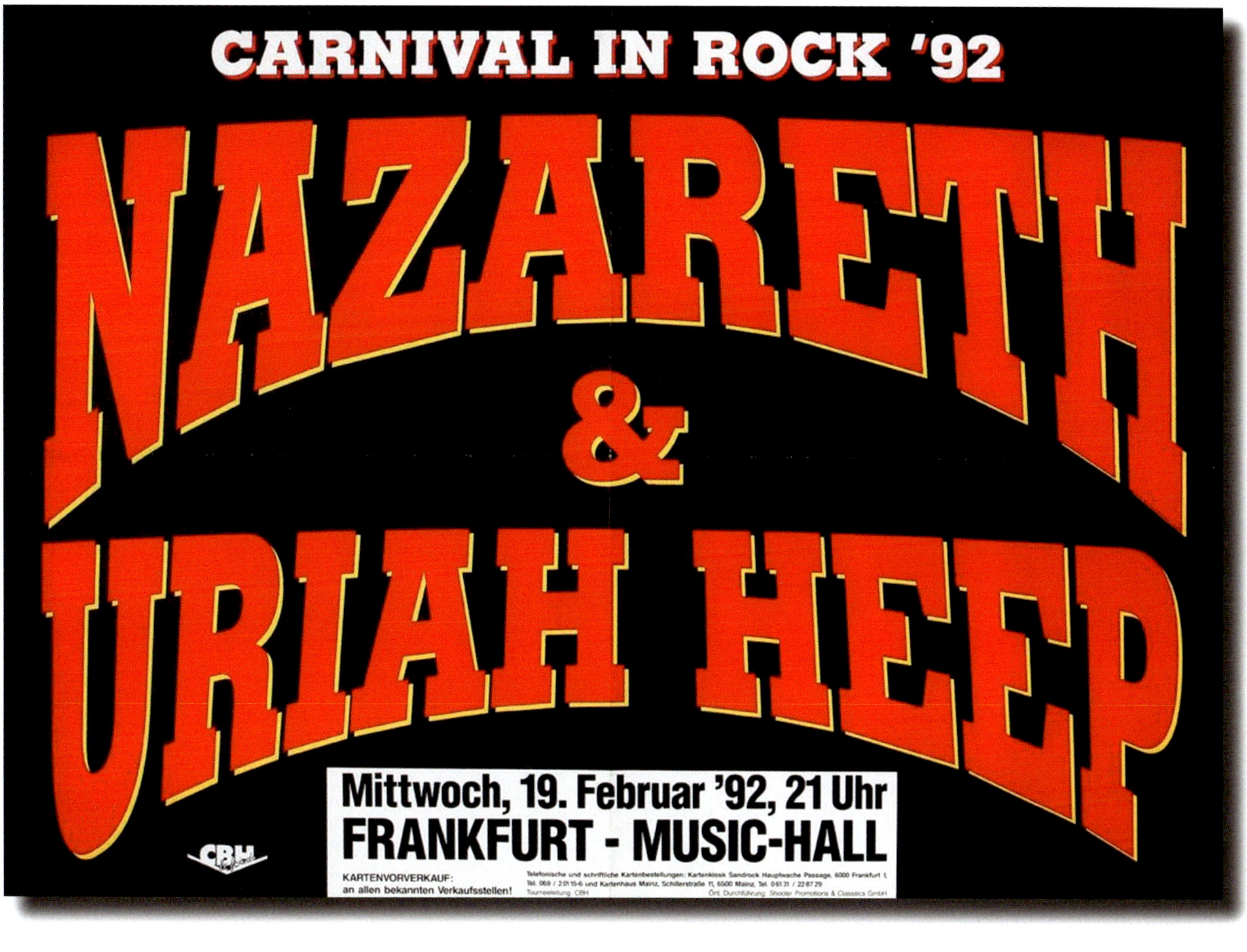
CARNIVAL IN ROCK '92
NAZARETH
&
URIAH HEEP
Mittwoch, 19. Februar '92, 21 Uhr
FRANKFURT - MUSIC-HALL
KARTENVORVERKAUF:
an allen bekannten Verkaufsstellen!
Telefonische und schriftliche Kartenbestellungen: Kartenkiosk Sandrock Hauptwache Passage, 6000 Frankfurt 1,
Tel. 069 / 2 01 15-6 und Kartenhaus Mainz, Schillerstraße 11, 6500 Mainz, Tel. 0 61 31 / 22 87 29
Tourneeleitung: CBH
Örtl. Durchführung: Shooter Promotions & Classics GmbH

March 1st, 1992, Orpheum, Graz, Austria.

© Isabella Seefriedt

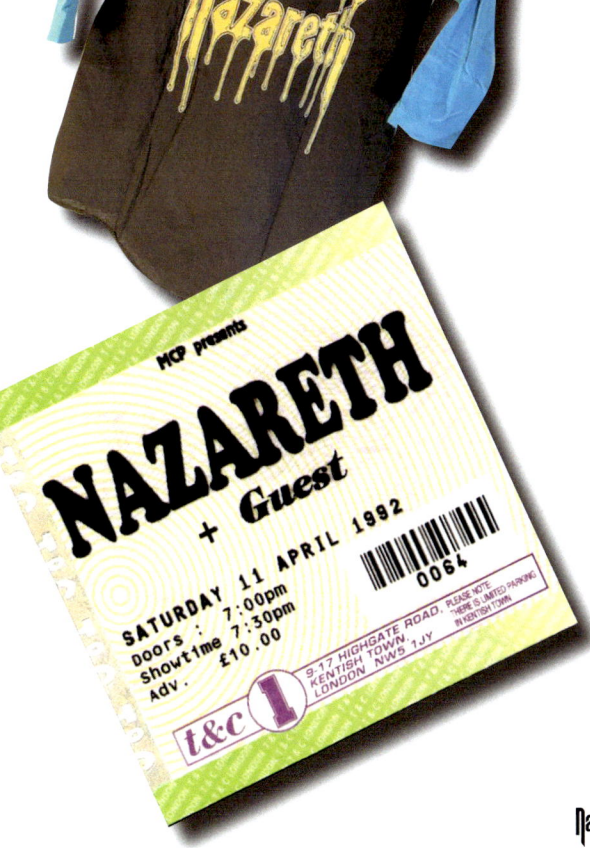

© Isabella Seefriedt

June 26th, 1992, Knittelfeld, Austria.

1993

1993. Sequel Records issues a Nazareth compilation called *From the Vaults*.

February 1993. Once again Nazareth tour Germany with Uriah Heep.

April 30 – December 4, 1993. Nazareth spend much of the year touring North America, including their usual spate of Canadian dates. Much of the campaign is conducted as a package with Uriah Heep and Wishbone Ash.

November 23, 1993. Guns N' Roses issue a covers album called *The Spaghetti Incident?*. Included is a rendition of Nazareth's "Hair of the Dog."

September 13th, 1993, Graz, Austria.

September 15th, 1993, Oberwart, Austria.

1994

June 3, 1994. Lemmy from Motörhead joins the band onstage, at a biker festival in Wiesen, Austria.

Pete Agnew:
"What happened is, we were on the road and we were starting a European tour that was going to last about five weeks. Our agent told us there was this tour that was out there, and it was weird, with Suzi Quatro, Bay City Rollers, Marmalade, The New Seekers, light bands. And the headliner cancelled and there were six shows to go. And they said 'Would you guys go out and play?' Strange bill, but then we thought, well, it was in Austria, Germany, and we only had to play for 40 minutes or something. We said, yeah, we'll go and have some fun."

"We got there and after the second or third date, one of the guys who worked with us turned up at the hotel with Lemmy. And Lemmy was having some fun—Lem had come around to see his pals in Naz. So he came along to the gig and we were doing 'Tush' as an encore type of thing. We did it as a sort of last number of the set and we got Suzi Quatro up and the girls did dance steps and all this and Lemmy had come up and played bass and I was just doing handclaps or something stupid like that. But it wasn't just the playing the bass. After that, Lemmy stayed with us for about three days on that tour, just coming around with us, and I don't think he ever went to bed. I really don't. On one occasion, at 4:30 in the morning, after a gig, I'm saying, 'I've got to go to bed.' And he's going, 'Wimp!' (laughs). But yeah, he hung about for a couple of days with us and stayed at the same hotel. It was fun."

October 17, 1994. Polydor are the label of choice for Nazareth's 19th album, *Move Me*. Producing is engineer Tony Taverner in conjunction with the band, the team laying down tracks in Germany. Chief writer of the material on the record is Billy Rankin.

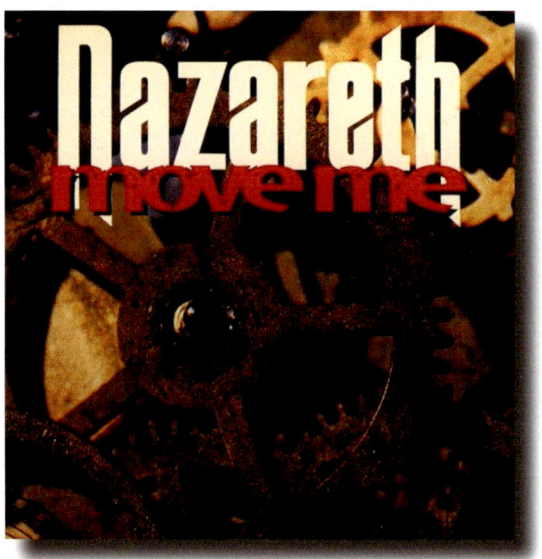

Pete Agnew:
"*Move Me* was great fun. We decided to program the drums—again—and we got Steve Pigott, who actually had his own recording studio in England. It was great; he wrote a lot of songs, great songwriter and stuff, but he was

a great programmer and he had quite a reputation for it, and he was a pal of Tony Taverner, the engineer/producer on that one. And it was absolutely amazing because it does not sound like programmed drums. I mean, guys that know programmed drums and guys that had recorded a lot, you can tell right away, even if the general public can't pick it up, but with Steve, it's absolutely impossible. It sounds so much like real drums, a real human being playing. And of course Darrell sat with him and they discussed, 'Let's do this, I like that, I like that.'"

"But he was so good that when he finished working for us on that album, the guy who had the studio, they had done reams of these disco dance music records, and when he heard what was going on, he said, 'This guy's amazing.' So he says, 'When he's finished working with you, can he come and work with me?' And what happened was Steve spent the next six months in Germany (laughs), working up in this other control room on these other records with him. Anyway, the actual record itself was good fun to make."

"What's funny, we weren't really sure about what we were going to call the album. In fact, the first idea was *Steamroller*, which was one of the tracks we did. We didn't have any management at the time, we were just doing it ourselves, and we thought maybe we would go for somebody. So we were actually approached by Deep Purple's management—I won't name any names here, but we all know who they are—and he said he was quite fancy managing Nazareth because he heard the album and everything and could hear what was going on and he'd like to manage us. We said, we'll give it a shot. And when he was listening to the album, what happened is, we had done a photo shoot for the front of it. You know, the old Mercury car that's on the front of it? It was a next-door neighbour of mine who had that. He was into cars and stuff and he had this thing all in pieces. And it was Deep Purple's manager who actually suggested we should call it *Move Me*, with the car, which we thought was pretty funny."

November – December 1994. The band conduct a UK tour, playing a number of home base Scotland shows.

Late December 1994. Jimmy Murrison and Ronnie Leahy join Nazareth, more than making up for the departure of Billy Rankin, due to a big dust-up over the divvying of the £50,000 advance on *Move Me* from Polydor.

Pete Agnew:
"Around that time there was a spate of so called 'unplugged' concerts being done by bands that were traditionally loud electric outfits, so Dan, Billy and myself decided we'd like to have a shot at this (Darrell was unavailable at the time) and got together at our rehearsal studio to try it out. Billy was on acoustic guitar and had a 'stamping board,' a raised wooden board with a little instrument mic underneath, so that was guitar and drums taken care of, and I used my acoustic bass."

"We completely rearranged all our songs and did them using three-part harmony vocals wherever possible—yes, even 'Razamanaz.' We thought the combination of this instrumentation and vocal approach sounded wonderful and as it turned out, so did the fans. I think we played about 15 shows, all in the UK, and it was one of the most fun things we ever did."

"It was billed as 'An Acoustic Evening with Nazareth,' a title which suggests a cozy night by the fire listening to tinkling melodies. But it was in fact a couple of acoustic guitars and a stamping board cranked up through a PA system.

It was acoustic, but we still tripped the decibel meters in a couple of clubs we played. You can actually hear it on YouTube under 'NAZARETH - Live in Scotland 1994.' The recording is taken straight from the sound desk so the audience is very quiet. Great fun, and we finished with a concert in our home town just before Christmas, which turned out to be Billy's last show with the band."

1995

February 15, 1995. The new Nazareth lineup begins touring, playing throughout Europe and into festival season. This is followed by US and Canadian dates with shows in the UK and more German festival dates rounding out the year.

March 1995. Jimmy Murrison joins Nazareth, with Ronnie Leahy to follow two months later, more than making up for the departure of Billy Rankin.

Pete Agnew:
"We knew Ronnie back in the day, when he was with The Pathfinders, when we were a part-time band and just young guys. And then we got to know him pretty well, when he was playing with Maggie Bell and that. We were in London at the same time. And then after he played with Jack Bruce and we used to meet up with Ronnie then. The thing is, he was another Scotsman as well. And this was a good thing: we'd never had just one guitar and piano, never had it like that. When Billy was gone, we got Jimmy and we actually thought of having two guitars but it didn't really work. We had brought in Bruce Watson from Big Country, because he's a good pal and he lives in the town with us. So we thought we would try with two guitars. So Bruce came in and he was playing with us at rehearsals for about two weeks and it looked as if that was going to be the lineup. And then Big Country had some legal things happen at the time and he had to go back and do some tours. Long story short, Bruce couldn't do it."

"Then we thought, okay, he's gone, and we already had our mind on having somebody in again, so what about a piano player? And what happened was, when we were off the road, Dan had been doing this fun thing in Glasgow on a Friday and Saturday night. He'd got this band together called The Party Boys. It was the old Alex Harvey Band, basically, with Dan singing. It was Zal on guitar, Ted on drums, Chris on the bass, and they didn't have Hugh on the keyboards—they had Ronnie on keyboards. And this band, The Party Boys, with Dan singing, was a brilliant band, fabulous. So I used to go off on a Friday or Saturday night and I used to go have a jam with them. Great fun."

"By the way, we'd never played any gigs with Jimmy at this point, but we were sitting and having a drink at some point, and we were talking about how much fun that Party Boys thing was. So we thought, what about Ronnie? Ask Ronnie and see if he would fancy it. So we asked Ronnie and he was up for it. It was the first time we'd had just one guitar and keyboards. Any time we had the keyboards before, it was with Billy, so it was two guitars. I mean, I loved the sound. The stuff we did on *Boogaloo*… 'When the Light Comes Down' is one of best songs we ever did. It's a fabulous record and the keyboard playing on that album is just amazing. So I loved playing with Ronnie; Ronnie was such a nice guy, and a really funny guy too."

"As for Jimmy, well, at the beginning of 1995 we were looking to replace Billy and there was a unanimous decision that Jimmy Murrison was the man. I had first met Jimmy in 1988 when he was a student at Perth Rock College playing in Trouble in Doggieland, that he had asked Lee to join. They actually played on a bill with Nazareth at East End Park in Dunfermline, which was Manny's last show with the band. We saw Jimmy playing many times after that and now we all agreed he was not only a brilliant guitarist but a very good songwriter and an all-around very nice guy, so that was that. So there yo go: Jimmy joined us in March and eventually Ronnie joined in May.

May 21st, 1995, Koeflach, Austria.

© Isabella Seefriedt

May 8th, 1995, Longhorn Club, Stuttgart-Wangen, Germany.

September 16th, 1995, Aeroanta Curitiba, Brazil.

1996

1996. *Razamanaz* is reissued by Castle Communications, highlight being two non-LP bonus tracks, "Hard Living" and "Spinning Top."

February – March 1996. The band tour Russia, returning for another leg in late September through October.

> **Dan McCafferty:**
> "We've played all over Russia, out in Siberia and stuff, which is interesting. The people are great; it's just that getting around there is difficult. Like, with roads just stopping (laughs). 'The road stops, but don't worry about it—it starts again in a couple hours.' 'Okay.' And I remember travelling once in the airplane, and the woman said, 'Fasten your seat belts!' And I said, 'I haven't got one.' 'Well, that's okay then!' I suppose the fans are little more staid than Western fans, because of the years of looking over their shoulders. But nowadays, since 1990, things have changed a lot there. They get MTV and all the rest of it too."

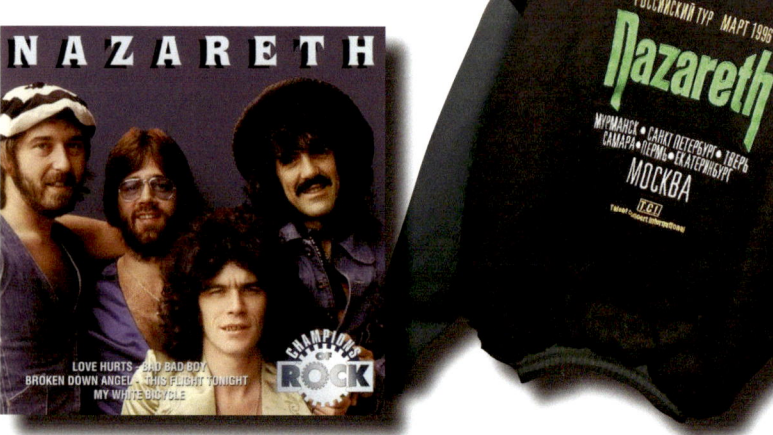

April – July 1996. The band tour the US, taking a break for festival season in Europe.

1997

1997. Manny Charlton issues *Drool*, his first solo album and the only one he assembled when living in Scotland, before he moved to the US.

1997. '*Snaz* is issued on CD for a second time (through Castle Communications), adding "Let Me Be Your Leader" over and above the 1987 issue but leaving four tracks off versus the original vinyl issue from 1981.

Late 1997. Manny Charlton moves to Fort Worth, Texas.

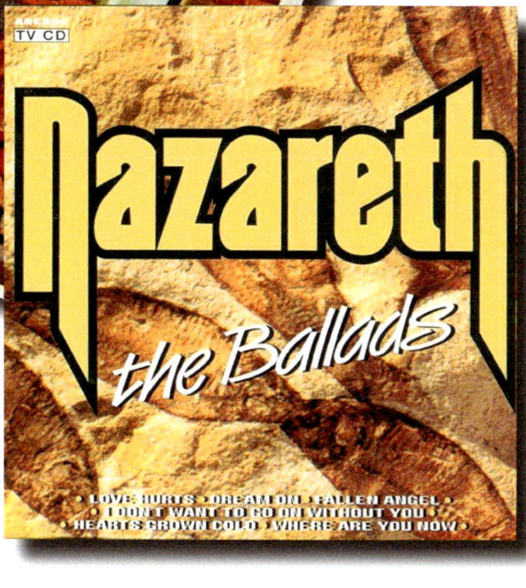

1998

1998. Essential issues *Greatest Hits Volume 2*, offering 20 tracks from 1979's *No Mean City* through to 1994's *Move Me*. Also this year comes the two-CD *At the Beeb*, issued by Snapper.

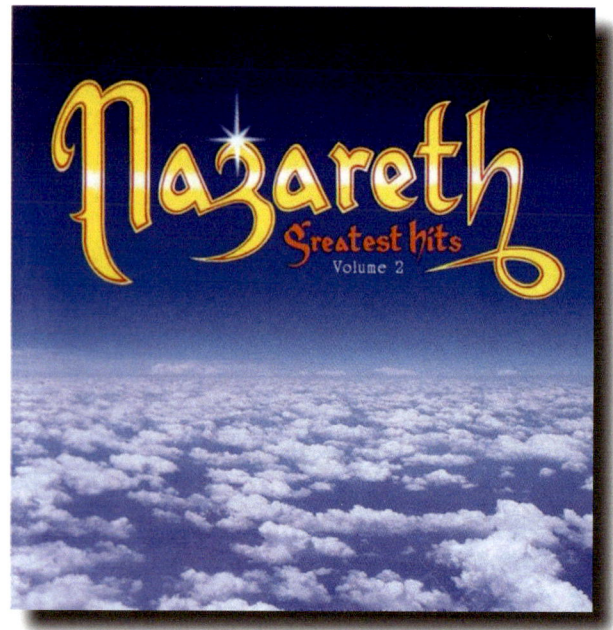

1998. *The Fool Circle* is reissued on CD by Castle Communications, including as bonus tracks the four tracks from the original *'Snaz* album left off the label's 1997 reissue of that record.

February 14 – March 9, 1998. The band tour Russia, also taking in the Ukraine, Latvia and Kazakhstan.

July 25, 1998. Nazareth issue their twentieth album, *Boogaloo*. As noted, by this point guitarist Billy Rankin has been replaced by Jimmy Murrison and Ronnie Leahy is added to the lineup on keyboards.

Dan McCafferty:

"I like it. What we did with it is that we didn't use any tricks, more or less. We went in and recorded it live off the studio floor. All of us playing at the same time. I think it has more feel than a lot of the albums we've done recently. The material is quite natural as well. We wrote most of it together, so it has a band thing going for it. At the moment there are very few albums like that out. Everything is electronic-ised, you know, affected in some way. Not that we haven't done that ourselves at times, but we decided to go au naturel this time (laughs). I really like this one because it's got a modern edge to it, but at the same time it really has a rock and bluesy feel to it. It has the best of both worlds."

"What happened was when *Move Me* came out, Billy had left the band and then we got together with Ronnie and Jimmy, and we had a whole bunch of work lined up, so we went and did that. And in the meantime we were getting stuff together for *Boogaloo*. Then the five of us got into the studio, did the record, and we didn't like the mix. So by the time it came out, we had another bunch of touring, so this went on for months and months and months. That's why it took so long. There was no rush for the album, and while we were making it, we had to keep doing these tours. It was just the mix we didn't like. So we went back in and fixed it, but because of work commitments, that's why it took so long."

Pete Agnew:

"*Boogaloo* is very much more rhythm-and-blues-based, and more of a band effort. On the next album, for example, *The Newz*, everybody in the band wrote songs individually a lot more than they did with *Boogaloo*. By the time this was recorded we had Jimmy on guitar and Ronnie on piano. The studio was another old country house near a place called Battle. This was the site of the Battle of Hastings back in 1066 and I'm pretty sure that was the last bit of excitement they'd had down there."

"We had rooms at the studio and as it turned out, it was a very relaxing and peaceful place to record. If we needed someone and he wasn't in his room, then we would find him in the village pub because that was the only other place to go. It was the first time we had recorded with this lineup but the band had been touring for more than two years and by then we were very familiar with each other's style of playing so there were no surprises in that department."

"However, there was one thing we weren't aware of and it was soon to cause much amusement. We were to discover that Jimmy and Ronnie were ardent fans of the two biggest TV soap operas in Britain, and any time these things came on the telly, recording stopped immediately. Sometimes they would discuss the ongoing plots of these soaps during dinner, causing much hilarity amongst the rest of us. And you wonder what your rock 'n' roll heroes get up to in their spare time…"

July – September, 1998. The band tour the US, with many of the dates in a package with Blue Öyster Cult and April Wine.

October 27 – December 6, 1998. The band tour Europe with most of the dates in Germany, and many of the shows with Uriah Heep.

European Tour, October-December 1998.

185

1999

April 30, 1999. Darrell Sweet dies of a heart attack, aged 51, before a concert in New Albany, Indiana on the second leg of the band's tour supporting *Boogaloo*. He is survived by a son, a daughter, and his wife Marion.

Dan McCafferty:
"Darrell was loud, and he liked huge monitors—he really did (laughs). No, Darrell was just loud, in life, as well as a drummer. And he was a very bright guy. He was an accountant, so I guess numbers and drummers... timing and all that. But he was a super guy. He had all these terrible sayings and terrible jokes he used to crack all the time, and people used to just crack up with them. Me, if I tried, 'That's not funny, man.' But when he did it, it was funny. So he was a good lad. Good boy. I miss him."

Pete Agnew:
"Darrell was a great drummer. I've played with Darrell since he was 16, when he joined us, as The Shadettes, so we go way, way back. We got on very, very well together and we played together so much that when you started into any song, we just automatically locked in without even thinking about it. We saw the thing getting played the same way."

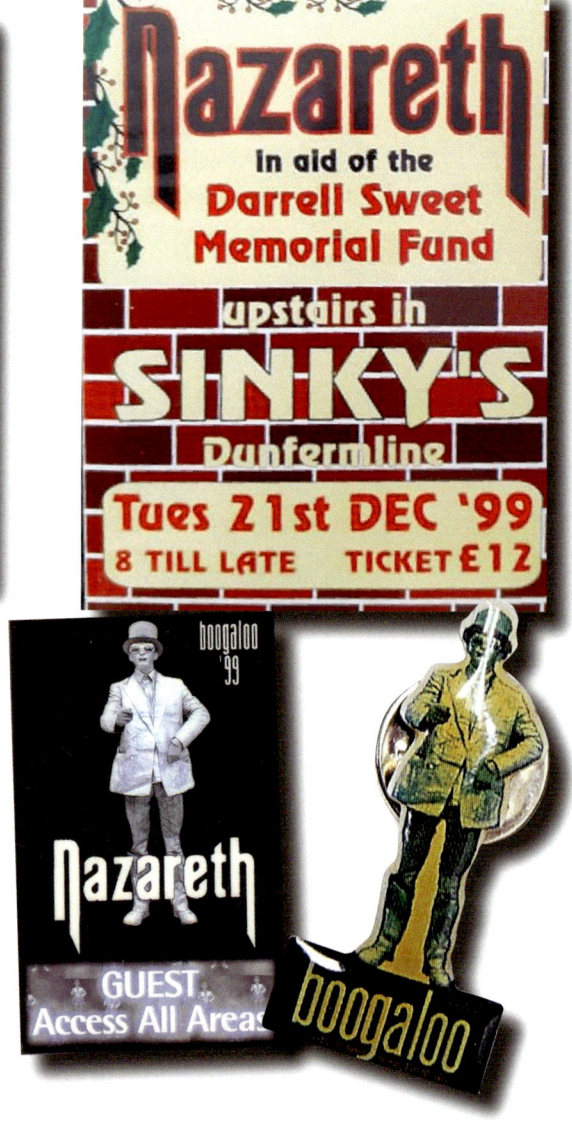

October 8, 1999. Swiss legends Krokus issue *Round 13*, the band's only album to feature future Nazareth singer Carl Sentance on vocals.

"I have five sons, Lee, Stevie, Chris, Blair and Stewart. Lee you already know. Stevie's a singer, guitarist and songwriter who has a couple of albums on release. Chris is a bass player, singer and songwriter who has played on many albums as a session player and is also bass player for the Rezillos. Stewart's a pianist, singer and actor. Blair, although he isn't a musician, can play a wee bit guitar but actually works with Nazareth in our road crew. So you see, when we have a family gathering, we don't need to hire a band!"

"Lee went to college and he met up with Jimmy, our guitar player, and they played in the same band for a few years, called Trouble in Doggieland. And Lee also used to come out with us when we were touring, when Darrell was still alive. And actually Lee was one of Darrell's favourite drummers. He used to go along and watch Lee playing; they had a sort of mutual admiration society. So if he had six weeks where he wasn't working, Lee would come out and be our drum tech and play percussion with the band, over the years, long before Darrell died. So when Darrell died it was the obvious choice, to bring on Lee as the drummer. And when we're on stage, and when we're touring, these days, I mean, you know, I'm going on 65 and he's 40 years old. It's not like, 'Hello dad,' 'Hello son.' It's really, we're on a tour and we're a drummer and a bass player. The only time it's still, 'Hello dad,' 'Hello son,' is when he needs money (laughs)."

Pete Agnew

The 2000s

To put it politely, the 2000s marked a period of reflection for Nazareth, first upon the death of drummer Darrell Sweet, but then watching on as all manner of reissues and compilations and video and audio live sets saw the light of day (sometimes dubiously), to keep the guys on the road throughout the decade, despite the band only delivering one new studio record throughout the entire ten years. But *The Newz* turned out to be worth the wait, being the first record of what would become a solid and successful lineup, consisting of Dan, Pete, guitarist Jimmy Murrison and now Pete's son Lee on drums—and actually so much more. In fact, both Lee and Jimmy would pull their weight in the reinvigorated version of the band, writing and injecting youth into the style and arrangements of the impressive records to come.

Otherwise the decade found the band playing to their strengths, hitting Germany, embarking on expected return visits to Brazil and, just as expected, return visits to Western Canada. The guys at this point would play anywhere, resigned to this life on the road they'd known so long, indeed making peace with the fact that this is who they are, town-to-town troubadours presenting songs bigger than the people playing them.

Another happy circumstance of the decade would come with the guys making the acquaintance of producer Yann Rouiller, who would both toughen the band's sound as well as add to it a certain type of Mack Reinhold smack, last heard on Queen albums like *The Game* and *Hot Space* as well as hit records from old Nazareth tour mate Billy Squier. Really, it would be Yann, Lee and Jimmy combined that would help the old warhorses of the band make the following decade so purposeful. Still, Nazareth spent the 2000s essentially celebrating its past, in a bit of a holding pattern until 2008, when a bright future beckoned, if not particularly commercially, most definitely creatively.

2000

2000. Manny Charlton issues *Bravado* while his old band continues to hit the road.

2001

2001. '*Snaz* finally sees reissue of the complete original vinyl album, through Eagle, as a 30th Anniversary Edition. A Salvo Records reissue ten years later expands the set further.

March 2001. The band tour the UK, with Stray and old friends Uriah Heep.

Dan McCafferty, on the new guys on stage:
"We've known Lee all his life. The guy's been around the band for a long time. He was the drum tech for us when he wasn't playing himself. He's part of the family and an excellent drummer. (As for Ronnie Leahy), a rock 'n' roll piano player is what he is. We can do different things now that we couldn't do before, and we're quite happy with the way the band sounds. We've always stuck by the rule that if we like what we play, then there's a good chance the public will like it too." *(w/ Blair S. Watson, Calgary Herald, June 6, 2000)*

Pete Agnew, further on Darrell's replacement on drums, namely his son Lee:
"Lee and I have been jamming now for close on twenty-three years. Lee has played in a lot of bands but none more so than with his brothers, Stevie and Chris, who he still plays and records with in-between Nazareth tours—they go by the name Satellite Falls. We have a studio at home, and the boys and myself would play together a lot when I was at home."
(w/ Dmitry Epstein, dmme.net)

May 22, 2001. Receiver issues the two-CD *Back to the Trenches: Live 1972 – 1984*.

October 18, 2001. Manny Charlton Band issue *Stonkin'*.

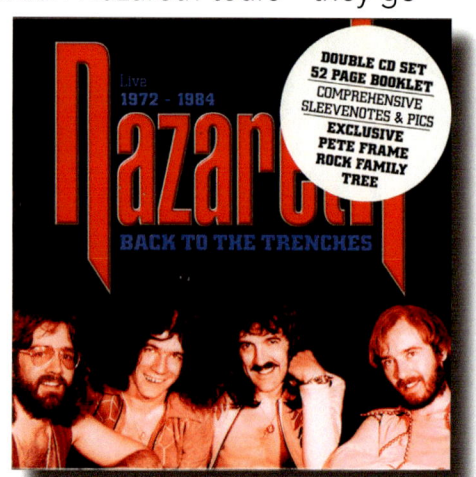

March 23rd, Astoria, London.

2002

2002. The year finds the band concentrating their live performances in Germany and Russia.

2002. Zebra Records issues a star-studded album called *Another Hair of the Dog: A Tribute to Nazareth*.

Pete Agnew:
"Nobody takes part in a tribute unless they like or respect—sometimes both even—the artist or the band. For that alone we thank the guys who took time to work on those albums. It's nice to see what other people do with your songs, but most of all it's a great compliment and we appreciate it very much."
(w/ Dmitry Epstein, dmme.net)

April 23, 2002. Eagle issues a live album called *Homecoming*, which captures the band live in Glasgow from the previous year. The set is also issued on DVD. A pared-down version of the album would be reissued the following year as *Alive & Kicking*.

Pete Agnew:
"This live CD and DVD almost didn't happen. We had a new lineup, with Lee on drums, and as there were no plans to do a studio album in the near future, it was decided that maybe it was time for another live one. The venue was The Garage in Glasgow and we had a sell-out crowd. During the second song there was a feeling onstage that something wasn't quite right but we couldn't place what it was. It was much later in the set that we realized there were no spotlights and this is what had made things feel odd. In the dressing room after the show it was explained that up in the balcony, where all the power was being drawn to feed the mobile studio truck and the stage lighting setup, one of the main cables had burst into flames. By the time our lighting crew had got the fire under control, the balcony and stairs leading to the auditorium were filled with smoke and it looked as if the show would have to be stopped. Meanwhile our crew (who were choking in the fumes) managed to redirect the smoke through a fire door using the electric fans that they have for cooling themselves while operating the spotlights. By this time all the cables to the spotlights had been destroyed, but at least they didn't have to stop the show. Quite a few people have mentioned to us that the DVD seems a bit flat as regards to lighting—well, that's the reason."

May 6th, 2002, Bad Aussee, Kurhaus, Austria.

© Isabella Seefriedt

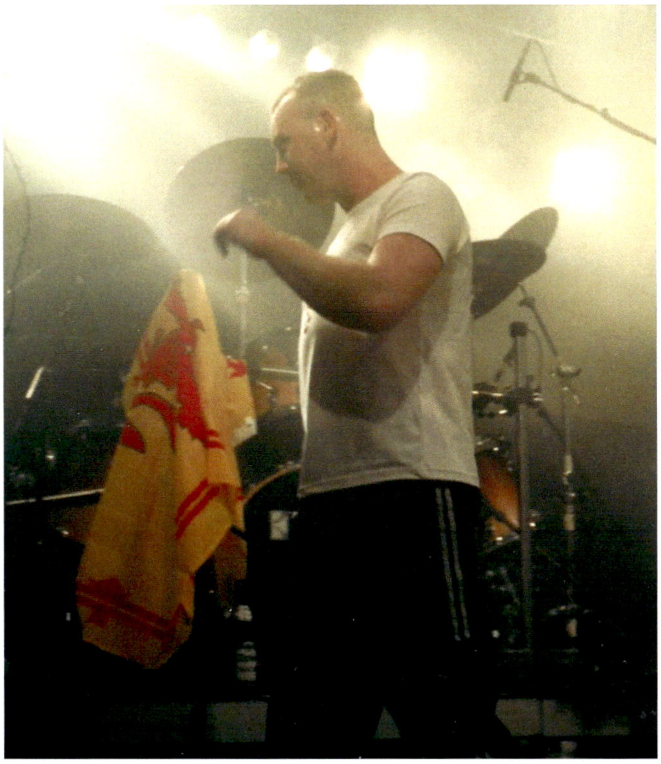

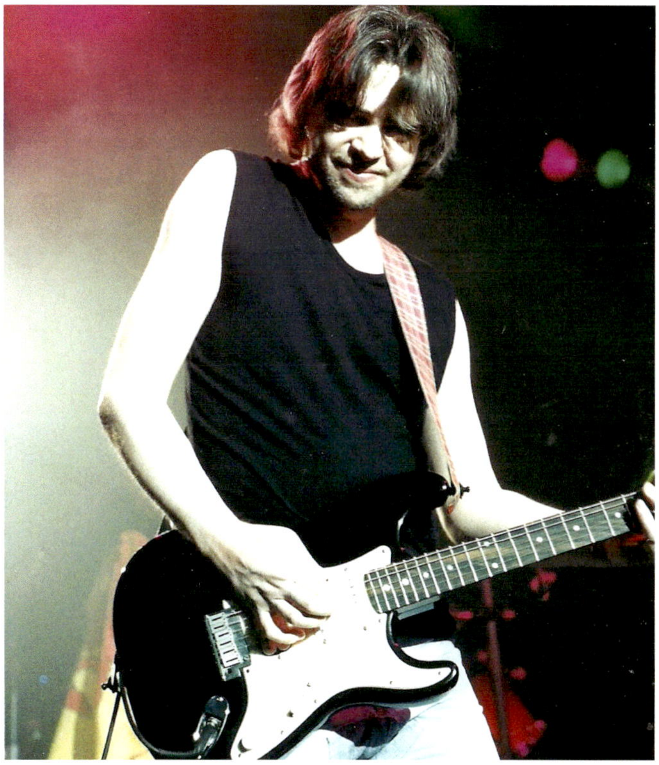

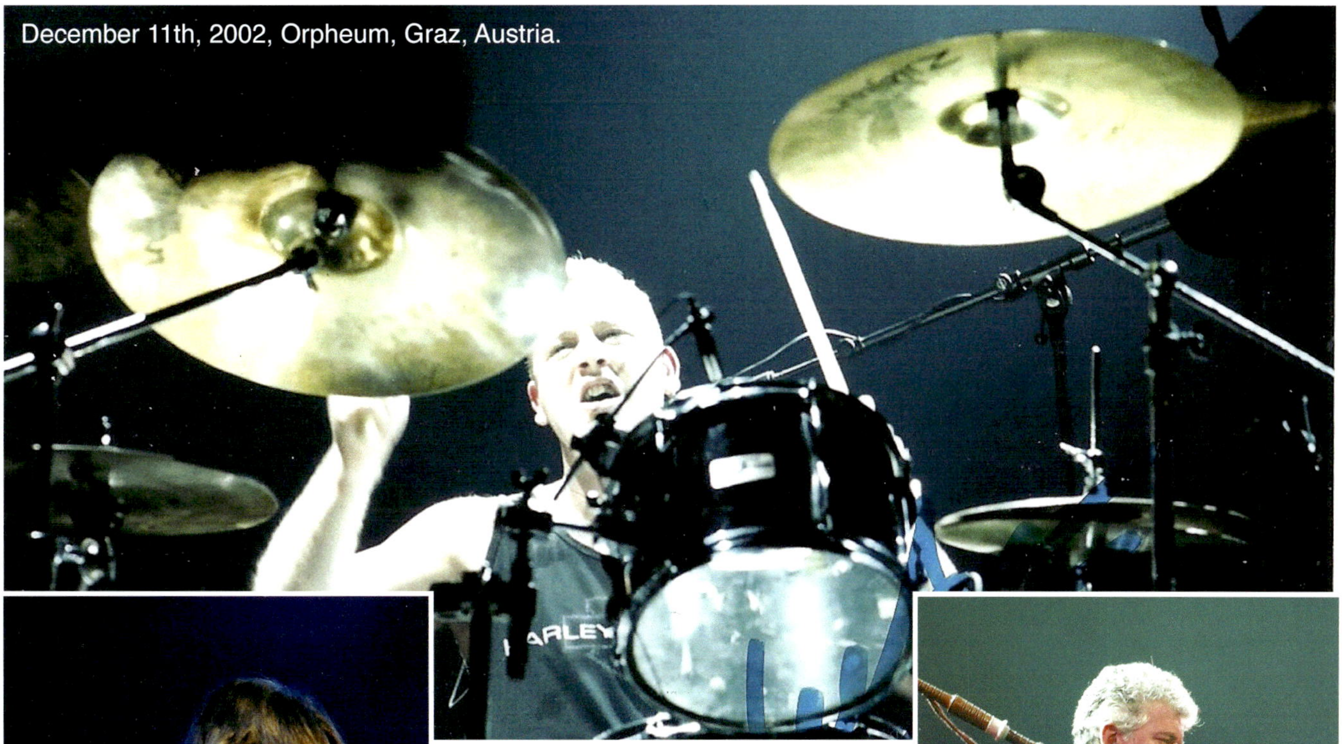

December 11th, 2002, Orpheum, Graz, Austria.

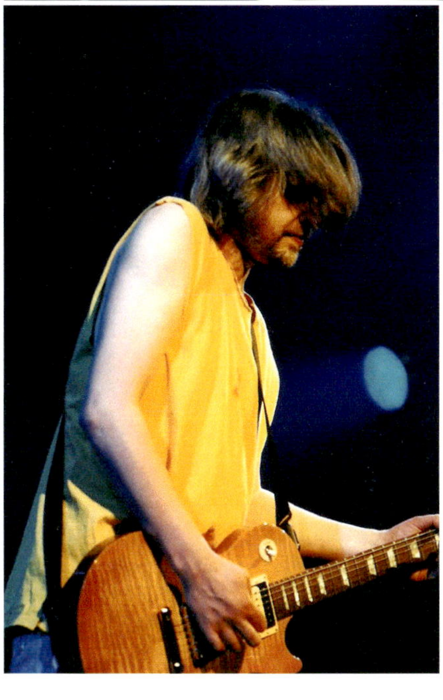

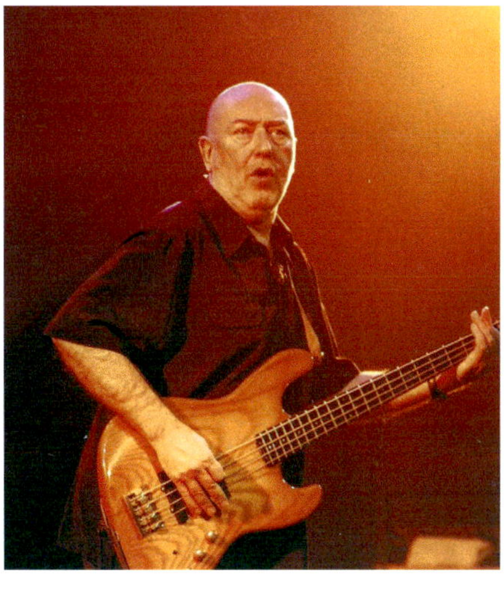

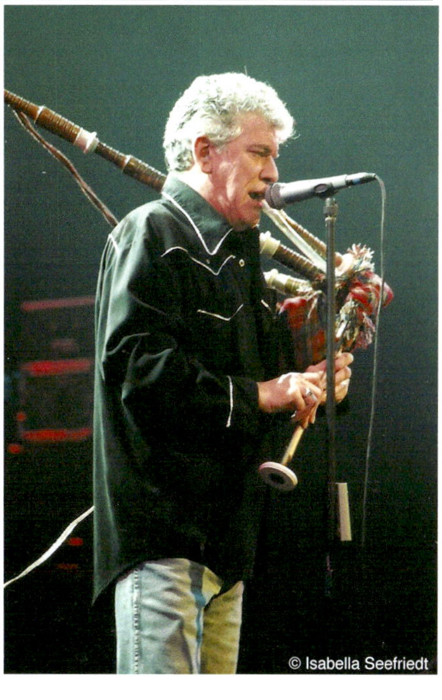

© Isabella Seefriedt

2003

2003. Manny Charlton Band issue *Klone This*.

2003. The band focus their touring efforts on Germany, Russia and the UK.

Dan McCafferty, in July '03:
"Well, Ronnie left, so we're back to a four-piece band. He just got tired of touring. And him and his missus have got a business going over here, and she was a partner at one point and it didn't work out, so he's between the Devil and the deep blue sea. But mainly, he just got tired of touring. We're doing a lot of earlier stuff… stuff from *Hair of the Dog*, about six or seven new songs. Or I should say, six or seven new old songs (laughs). Half the set is kind of spoken for anyway. There are certain songs that if we don't play them, people get very unhappy (laughs). We don't want to get them unhappy, know what I mean? But we're now doing things like 'Changin' Times,' 'Not Faking It,' 'Turn On Your Receiver,' songs we haven't done for a few years."

"The first leg has been really fun. We have a laugh every day (laughs), but most of that we couldn't repeat on the radio. It was interesting to see what the reaction was to the changes and it's all been very, very positive stuff. I think the band sounds tougher now than it did, obviously with the keyboards gone. You can do things as a four-piece that you couldn't do previous. It's pretty much straight-ahead stuff, more rock 'n' roll than it was."

2004

2004. Manny Charlton issues *Say the Word*.

June 12, 2004. Metro Doubles issues a two-CD compilation called *Maximum XS*.

2004, Vienna, Austria.

2005

2005. Manny Charlton issues *Sharp*, which is mostly covers.

February – Mid-March, 2005. The band play Europe, focussing on Germany.

Pete on his son Lee and his effect on the band:
"He had all the same favourites as me from what he was hearing as a kid. He was a Little Feat fan and Abba fan because he was in the house with me and all his brothers. They came up with the same influences as me. But then, of course, they go into different things, when you start to leave and go to college and stuff. Lee was in a band with Jimmy at the college together and they were into all sorts of different music. Lee's a great drummer but he's also a really good songwriter—that's what Lee added to the band. When we're on stage live, I mean, it's always been myself and Lee doing the backup vocals; we're doing all the harmonies on stage. So he's not just a drummer; he's a singer and songwriter. So he adds a lot to it."

March 21 – 27, 2005. Nazareth put into motion yet another Russian tour, followed by additional European dates.

December 1 – 8, 2005. The band mount a tour of the Ukraine.

2005, Spielberg, Austria.

2005, Spielberg, Austria.

© Isabella Seefriedt

2006

August 4, 2006. Former Nazareth keyboard player John Locke—*The Fool Circle*, *'Snaz* and *2XS*—dies, in Ojai, California, from cancer at the age of 62.

October 28th, 2006, Graz, Austria.

© Isabella Seefriedt

2007

2007. Manny Charlton issues *Americana Deluxe*.

April 18 – 21, 2007. Amidst a typical year of European, Russian and North American dates, the band get back to Brazil for a few shows.

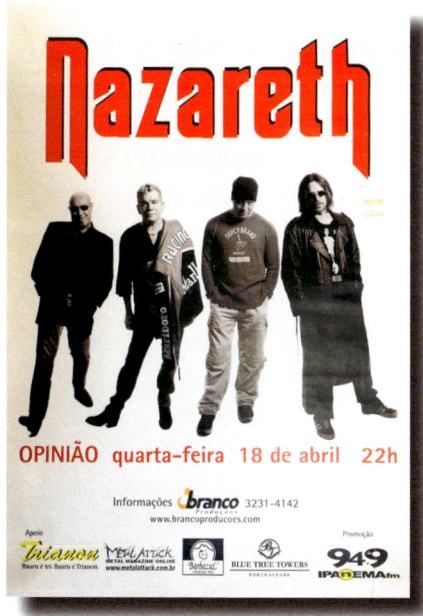

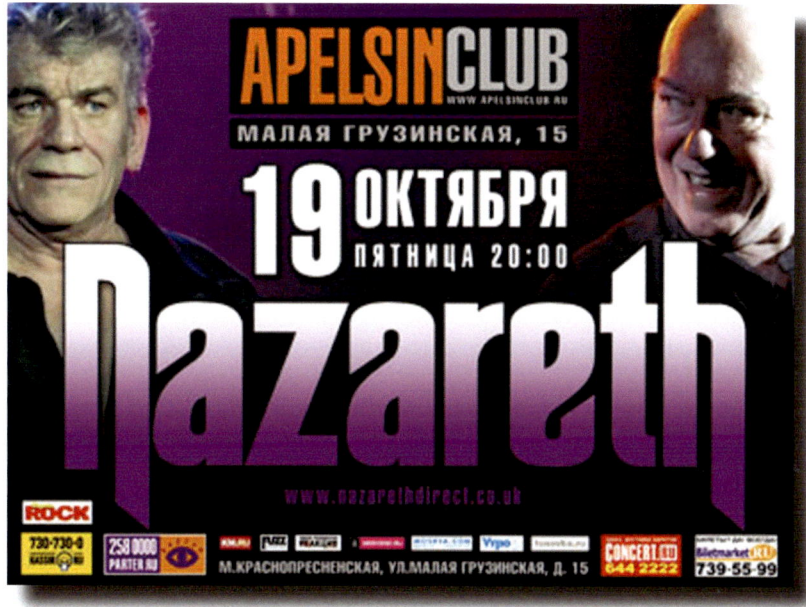

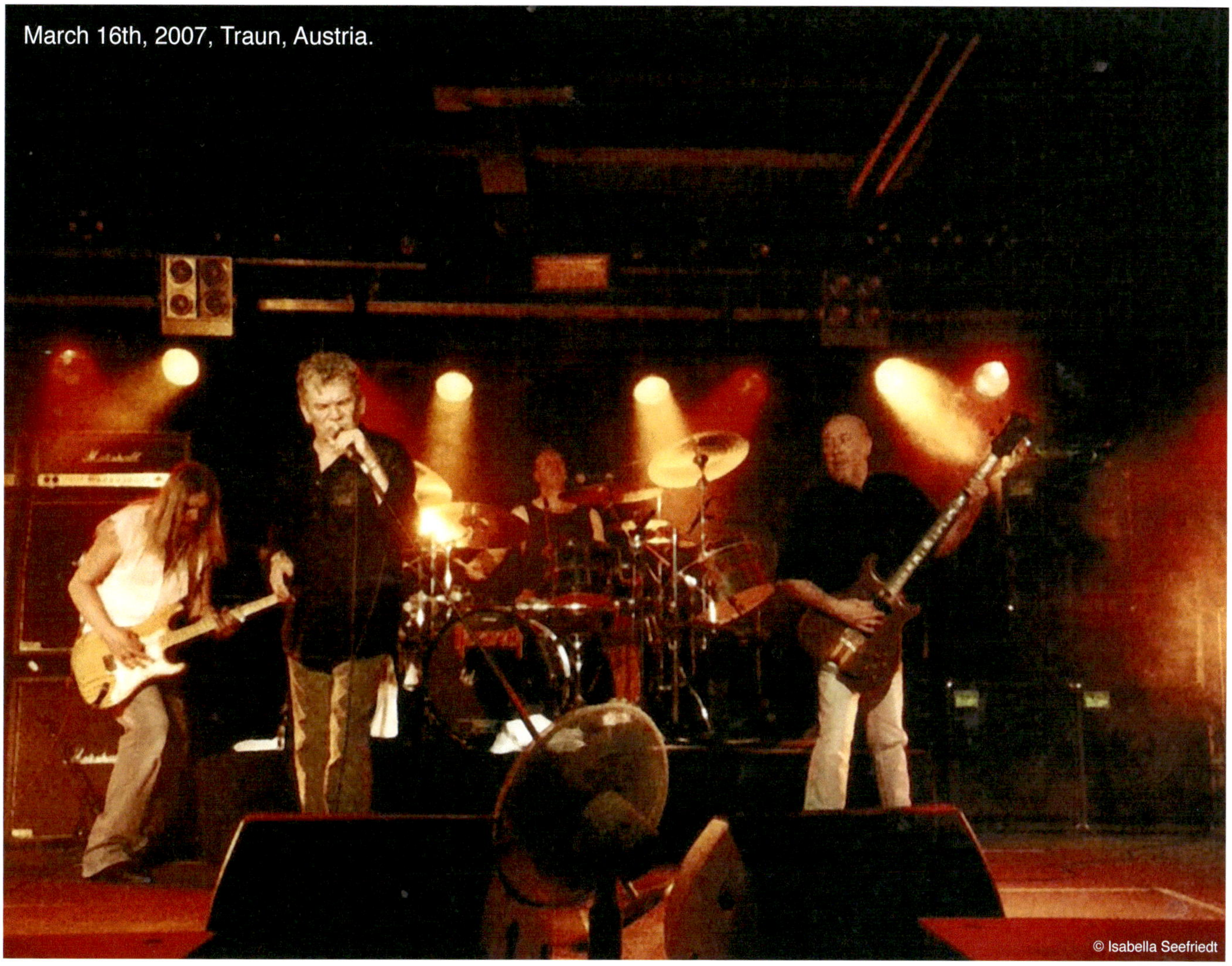
March 16th, 2007, Traun, Austria.

© Isabella Seefriedt

2008

2008. Manny Charlton issues *Then There's This*.

January 25 – May 2, 2008. Nazareth conduct an intensive European tour, including at the beginning many UK shows.

March 31, 2008. Nazareth issue, on Edel, album No.21, *The Newz*, the band's first record to feature Pete's son Lee as drummer.

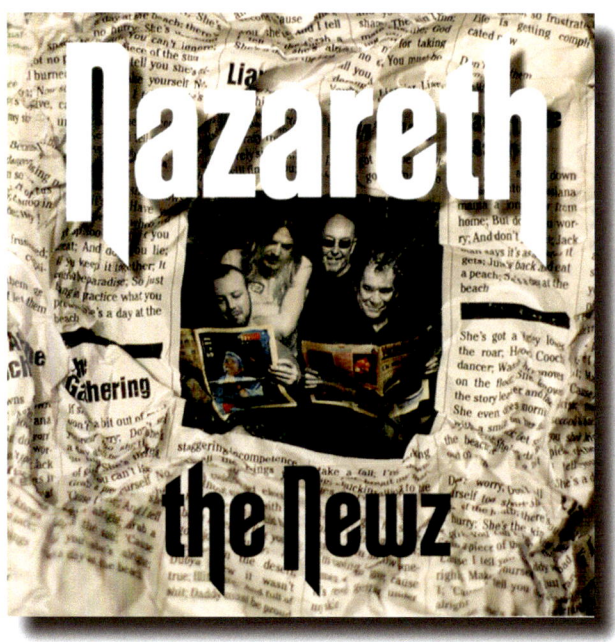

Dan McCafferty:

"With this album, I just think it's the chemistry of the guys in the band—Lee, Jimmy, Pete and myself. It's taken a step forward. We learn from each other, and we're all enjoying it a lot and having a good time. I think that comes across on the record, and it certainly comes across in the live shows. And certainly a lot of writing was done for this album; we came up with the 13 songs that we did, and it was hard to do that. There are a lot of good lyrics on it and everybody wrote. When Jimmy came in with 'Goin' Loco,' we went, oh, this is really different. And we got behind him to make it even better. It was a hearty, very productive album to make."

"I wanted the energy level higher this time, you know what I mean? I think we wanted to do that. And I wanted it to be accessible; I wanted people to be able to understand the songs, think a little bit, but not like *War and Peace*. I wanted these songs to entertain people, but yeah, 'Liar' (laughs), that's probably the heaviest thing we've ever done."

"And Yann, the producer, he really helped a lot too. We wanted it to sound like an album that was made today, but keep the spirit of the band. It was all done by computer, in Switzerland. It took six weeks basically, and maybe Yann did a couple of remixes for us, and that's a couple weeks, I guess. It was done very quickly. He has worked all over the world, but he's based in Switzerland so that's where it was done. I'm quite impressed by the whole thing pretty much. I don't want to sound like I have a big head, but I do like it (laughs)."

Pete Agnew, on Yann Rouiller:

"He's a drummer as well. But he's a studio engineer. This is the thing: a lot of producers are producers. They sit next to the engineer and tell them what they want. Well, Yann is the engineer. He sits there and he's got an assistant if he wants, but again, he does everything. He's recording on his computer, and he sits there and he looks at it and gets all the sounds personally. Yann is excellent. He's a studio man. He's been the fifth member of the band since we met him. Dan and I met Yann in 2006. We went over to see him in a studio there, Zurich, and we spoke to him back and forth for about a year. 2007, we went to record *The Newz*, and he was a very young guy and we thought, I hope he knows what he's doing. But he was great to work with. He's a great drummer, great guitar player, great singer. He's very, very good at everything."

"It's funny, in the studio, when you do a vocal, incredibly high or whatever, a producer will talk to you and maybe play it on the piano and say, 'I want you to sing that.' No. Yann just sings it. You go, hang on a minute; you're singing this impossible thing. So he's a very, very talented man, just brilliant. He's one of these guys that listens to what you've got to say, about how you want the song, and then he's going to get the sounds for you. And he's always got a lot of suggestions."

"He'd never done a rock album with a band like us before, so he was a bit nervous going into the thing. But we told him what we were trying to create. We told him we didn't want to sound flash, with an Aerosmith-type production. It's more nitty-gritty, like they just invented the studio, that kind of thing. And I think we achieved that. It sounds like the record could have been made in the '70s, but it was made now (laughs)."

"There were so many kinds of different things to play on this album. There are a few straightforward things like 'Day at the Beach.' There's the opening track, 'Goin' Loco' and 'Liar.' There weren't actually two tracks the same. It was funny actually, because when we did the album, Roger Glover, who's a good pal of ours, his girlfriend live in Switzerland, so he came up to the studio just to visit for a day. After we had done most of the album, that was one of the things he commented on. He said, 'It must've been a lot of fun playing bass on this album' (laughs). He noticed it right away. And I said yes, it was."

May 14 – 29, 2008. The band mount a pretty extensive Brazilian campaign.

October 8 – November 5, 2008. After the usual European dates and a few shows in North America, the band conduct an extensive tour of The Ukraine, including shows in Russia, Moldova and Kazakhstan. Then it's back to America followed by more Europe to close out the year.

Pete Agnew in November of 2008:
"We've been asked to do another album next year, but I don't know if we're going to manage that. I mean, this year has been unbelievable touring-wise. So far we've done more than 180 shows, and we're finishing in America. We're only doing ten shows or so there but we had to go there, for our 40th anniversary tour. We couldn't miss it out. We're going to do a big North American tour next year, but we figured we'll drop in the ten shows this year."

"We just got back from Russia, and we've come straight out here. We're finishing America, and we got a few dates in Europe in December, then we've got some time off, then we'll go into rehearsals to change the set for next year in January, and then we start all over again touring. So we don't know if we're going to manage to fit anything in. Because we've actually got a lot of material ready that didn't go on the latest album that was very, very good, but we wanted to play around with it a bit more. We've got enough to do an album. We could have it ready, but we just don't think we have the time to prepare it, because of the amount of touring we have coming up again next year. We might get to recording towards the end of the year, but I can't promise that one."

April 18th, 2008, Spielberg, Austria.

2009

February – May 2009. Nazareth play dates across Europe.

May 29 – June 7, 2009. The band return to Brazil for shows.

July 9 – August 8, 2009. The band conduct an extensive tour of Western Canada, with a few shows in the East tucked in at the end.

Dan McCafferty: "We're doing four from the new album and the rest is pretty much greatest hits. We do a song called 'Sunshine' which is really big in Canada, so we do that when we come to Canada. But the rest of the set is songs you really couldn't *not* do, because, I mean, you buy a Nazareth ticket, you want to hear 'Razamanaz,' 'Hair of the Dog,' 'Love Hurts,' that stuff, and we're not in the business to piss people off so much."

August 16 – September 4, 2009. The band play shows in Poland and the Czech Republic.

September 8 – November 17, 2009. The guys play Kazakhstan, Latvia, the Ukraine and Russia in what is the band's most extensive tour of the region ever.

Pete Agnew, on playing Russia:
"It's a completely different country, compared to what it was like when we first went. Completely different. The country and the people, there's potential. There is the mega-rich and you've still got the poor, but you've got a kind of middle class now that they never, ever had before. What you would call the middle class, anyway. People have got a bit more money, and everybody's got a mobile phone, cell phone. I mean, if you go to Moscow and St. Pete, it's just about as good as going to any large city in the world—you've got everything."

"And then you've still got places where we play. Deep Purple were out the same time as us playing Siberia and stuff like that. Some of that is still a bit rough. But things are improving. The hotels are improving, things like that. You see a big difference. But when we first went it was just shocking. And the train rides, they can be monumental. You can be on a train for three days. But when you see the airlines, then you see why people would go on the trains for three days. Everybody says to us—they ask you all these questions at press conferences in the places that we play—and they say, 'Do you gamble? Are you a gambler?' And of course Dan was going no, and I'm going, 'Yeah, we are—we get on Russian planes.'"

April 7th, 2009, Vienna, Austria.

"'The Toast' is a funny song—Lee, our drummer, wrote that. You see, we play a lot in Russia, and when you play in Russia, you play early, you play seven o'clock shows, and then everyone, the promoters, they always want to take you out to dinner. And dinner always takes about four or five hours, because it's very slow service there. Plus they're waiting to make a toast. These guys stand up, speaking in Russian, holding up a vodka glass, 'I'd like to make a toast.' And we have an interpreter and it goes on forever. So that's the other reason the dinners take so long—there are so many toasts. So Lee wrote it. We've always joked about that: 'Oh, here we go; couldn't we just go to McDonald's? It would save a lot of time.' 'No, no, we're going out.' And we have 759 toasts. So that's what the song is all about—it's really about Russia. And doing the talking there, that's Alan, our agent. He's a very funny guy. He's about 65 years old and we gave him a couple of beers and said, 'You've got to put this thing on there.'"

Pete Agnew

The 2010s to 2022

December 2nd, 2018, Graz, Austria.

To reiterate what I said way back in beginning of this book, what made the penning of this tome so delightful is the fact that way up into Nazareth's fifth decade, the band was making some of its loudest and proudest music since the early days, at least as far as this writer is concerned. I'm a big fan of 2008's *The Newz,* but I'm even more invested in 2011's *Big Dogz* and 2014's *Rock 'n' Roll Telephone*, which, sadly, was the last for Dan McCafferty as the lead singer of Nazareth, who was forced to tap out due to crippling chronic obstructive pulmonary disease, or COPD and has since succumbed to the affliction.

In a parallel world, we must give a shout-out to Manny Charlton, on every record from the '70s through to the end of the '80s, who despite being in a self-professed form of retirement for years, found himself making all manner of solo album, all of them very independent and under the radar but joyfully and sincerely delivered nonetheless. Until his death in 2022, he remained the only member of the classic lineup to make solo albums besides Dan, who had only done a covers album in 1975 and a pretty strange low-key record in 1987 called *Into the Ring*. However, in 2019 McCafferty would deliver *Last Testament,* a heart-wrenching, earthy and sometimes Celtic record of reflection, and a more than fitting close to a career.

Meanwhile, Pete, Lee and Jimmy weren't throwing in the towel, hitting the tour trail after Dan's departure, first with Linton Osborne singing and then settling upon Carl Sentance, who was indeed the post-Dan front man on a surprise new studio album from the band in 2018 called *Tattooed on My Brain,* followed by *Surviving the Law* in 2022.

As it stands here in early 2023, it's anyone's guess what happens next in the Nazareth camp, or with respect to the very nature of the music industry itself, for that matter. Suffice to say that Nazareth, after half a century, have nothing left to prove, quite pertinently on the strength of the music they made throughout their fifth decade, much less the 40 years previous. Part of me wants to see five more records with Carl, so that a new legacy is established, one that perhaps sees Pete replaced by another one of his sons!

2010

February 5 – February 20, 2010. The band conduct a UK tour, followed by mainland Europe, west and east.

June 30 – August 1, 2010. The band conduct an extensive cross-Canada tour.

August 2010. *Malice in Wonderland* is reissued by Salvo Records, who add seven BBC live bonus tracks to the original record. Also reissued in expanded versions by Salvo at this time is *Razamanaz, Loud 'n' Proud, Rampant, Hair of the Dog, Greatest Hits, Expect No Mercy, No Mean City* and *The Fool Circle*.

August 14 – 28, 2010. The guys conduct another tour of Eastern Europe.

October 11 – 23, 2010. The band return once again to Brazil, followed by more European shows.

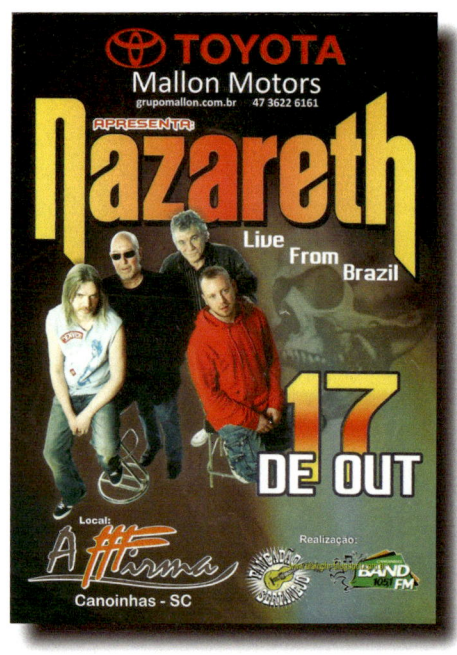

May 6th, 2010, Vienna, Austria.

2011

2011. Salvo Records reissues '*Snaz*, *The Catch*, *Cinema*, *Move Me* and *Boogaloo*.

February 24 – March 31, 2011. The band play Brazil, followed by Russia.

April 15, 2011. Nazareth issue, again on Edel, *Big Dogz*, which is produced by the band's guitarist Jimmy Murrison in conjunction with Yann Rouiller.

Pete Agnew:

"We were trying to not do *The Newz* again, but a bit more rhythm and blues, if you like. And we used very, very little overdubbing; it was kind of live in the studio. Obviously you've got to do overdubs for solos and stuff like that, but we didn't go over the top with it. We were trying to make it studio live, if you like, and I think we've kind of done it, because most people who've phoned me have kind of mentioned that."

"We don't ever record unless we all like a song. Because we've written quite a lot of songs, it takes for us to say 'We all like that one.' But I like 'Big Dog's Gonna Howl,' obviously, as it's a good fun kind of track. I love 'When Jesus Comes to Save the World Again' and I like 'Radio,' because it tells you of a time, well, in our lives definitely. 'Lifeboat,' we don't like to get political, but that one kind of comments on how things are going these days politically, and it hits it on the head. 'Time and Tide' is basically Jimmy, our guitar player, talking about his time in the band. I like 'Claimed' because it's a groovy number. I like the whole thing, actually."

"You now, in the early days, what you used to call hard rock, it all came from the blues, rhythm and blues, Chuck Berry, and that's the way we grew up. Our early albums are like that and things changed a bit in the middle, and poppy in some cases. But this time we just felt we'd like to just go back and groove. They're modern songs, but with that approach. We wanted to sound like a three-piece Delta band, really. So we wrote these modern songs, but we thought, how would we play those things in 1973?"

April 20 – June 25, 2011. Nazareth tour Europe, with most dates as usual taking place in Germany.

June 30 – August 12, 2011. The band conduct another impressive tour blanketing Canada.

September 18 – October 14, 2011. Nazareth conduct another quite thorough tour of Russia.

November 11 – 19, 2011. The band return to Brazil for shows almost every night.

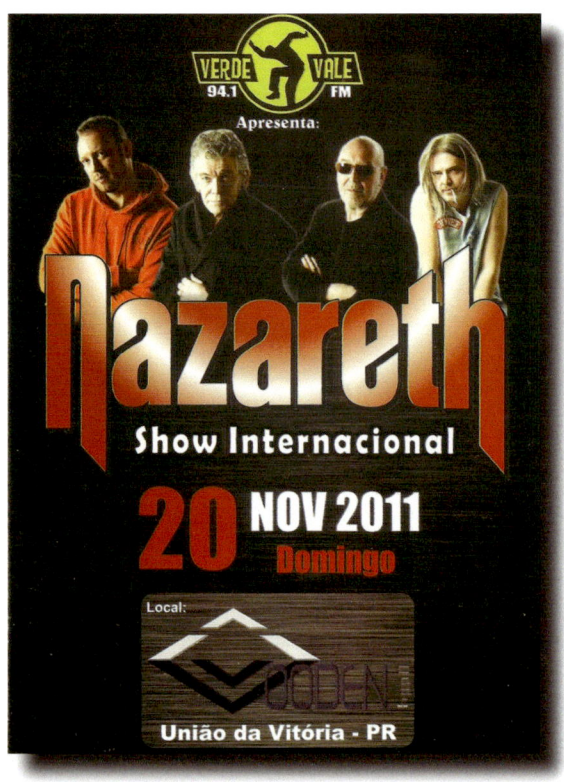
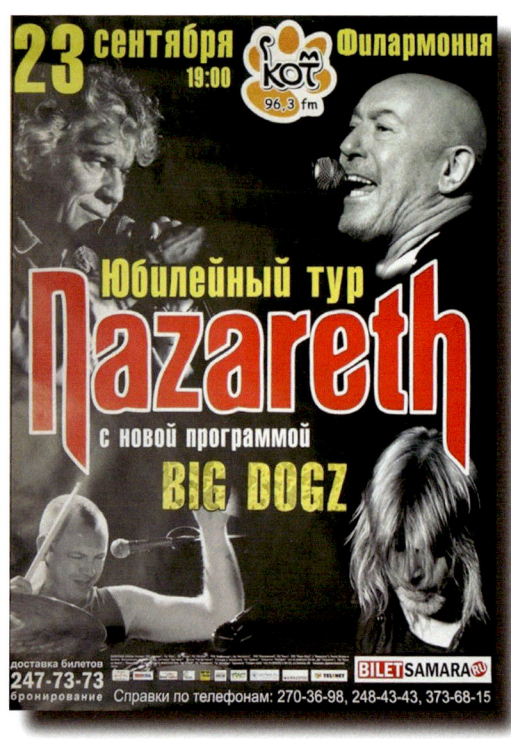

2012

February 2 – February 10, 2012. The band play Brazil yet again.

March 10 – March 23, 2012. Nazareth conduct a brief UK campaign.

April 19 – June 29, 2012. The band begin touring in Germany and cover much of Europe once again.

Pete Agnew on the intricacies of touring with Jimmy Murrison:
"We have a song on *Big Dogz* called 'Sleeptalker' because he's a big-time sleep-talker. I mean, if you get in the room next to him in a hotel, you really don't want to be there, because the guy can talk and talk and talk all night, and he does do this. Jimmy actually wrote the song about himself. And what we did at the end of it, we put a sort of sleep sequence, if you like, a dreamy kind of instrumental part, and we had a whole lot of people who knew us coming in and saying a word here and a word there and a little line there. One of the women who is speaking—that's his wife (laughs). And you've got our agent Alan again, and you've got a drummer mate of ours. There was no other place, Martin, where you could do that on the album—it could only be at the end. You couldn't do it in the middle, because it would be a bit weird. So we thought, well we could either end the album with a great big bang, or we can end the album with, 'Oh, what's this?'"

July 5 – 28, 2012. The band do another one of their intensive tours of Western Canada.

September 20 – October 30. Nazareth conduct another involved Russian tour, with other Eastern European territories covered as well.

November 9 – 24, 2012. The band return for another short tour of Brazil.

2012, Feldkirchen.

2012, Judenberg.

2013

2013. The Manny Charlton Band issue *Hellacious*. Vanilla Fudge and Cactus legend Tim Bogert guests on bass plus there are cameos by Vivian Campbell and Steven Adler.

February 22 – March 9, 2013. Nazareth play ten dates in Brazil.

March 27 – June 2, 2013. The band play Russia and other Eastern European territories.

June 7 – July 15, 2013. The guys play the US, Mexico and Canada, with a number of shows cancelled at the tail end. A handful of European shows round out the year.

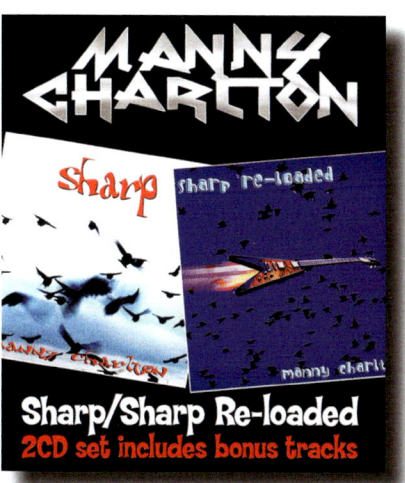

August 2013. Dan has to leave the stage at a show in Switzerland after three songs due to his worsening health. This follows upon an on-stage collapse at a Canadian show in Cranbrook, BC the previous month.

Dan McCafferty on the cause of his ailment:
"Something to do with my misspent youth, I would imagine. And also, well, I didn't help it with the smoking, but I've stopped smoking ages ago. I did my share at the time of many things. But the other thing is, my father died of emphysema. So I've heard the theories from some doctors I've spoke to, that it could be a gene as well. Because I have a friend in the village I live in, she has COPD as well, and she's never put anything in her mouth smoke-able ever. So who knows, you know? You can only play with the cards you're dealt, young man."

August 28, 2013. The band announce the retirement of Dan McCafferty, due to ill health, specifically chronic obstructive pulmonary disease.

Dan McCafferty:
"I've had COPD for a few years. Up until last year I could manage. I was getting through the shows and stuff. Then what happened was, I went in and made the record and I was kind of struggling. I went into it and I was okay, and then

I went to the States, and I had to go to the hospital with an ulcer which is a completely different thing. It sounds like I'm falling apart. And then of course, because you lose so much blood doing that, I wasn't very well. So I only managed to do about four gigs in Canada and then I had to quit. I just wasn't well enough to play. Then we came back home and finished up the album. We had a little bit of a break and then went to do a gig in Switzerland and I couldn't breathe after about three songs. So I decided it was time to hit it on the head. Very sadly, I must say. Because, well, because it's a job I've had for about 45 years (laughs). So it's a bit of a bummer."

"At the moment I'm working on Rock 'n' Roll Telephone. I'm doing a lot of interviews, talking to people like yourself, all over the world. But when the album gets released, then I'll go and… there are a couple of offers in the fire, recording and stuff. But I'm trying not to think about that at all. I'll wrap this up and tie it in a bow and say, 'Goodbye, baby' (crying voice) to another one of your children (laughs). It's true. And then I'll think about what I'm going to do next."

2014

February 22, 2014. Scotsman Linton Osborne joins Nazareth as lead singer, replacing Dan McCafferty. A number of shows are cancelled when Osborne contracts a virus.

Dan McCafferty, in 2014:
"We have Linton Osborne, who is a great singer. And he has already performed in Scotland. I think they wanted to see how it was going to go. And then there are two or three shows in Russia. And then they're going to the Czech Republic and Canada in July I believe. Good luck with that. I know Linton well, because he's a local guy. Well, he's local-ish. For the size of your country, he'd be a next door neighbour, but in Scotland, he's local. And he's a good singer. I've known Linton for years; I've seen him in different bands or whatever, so good luck with that, boys, really."

June 3, 2014. Nazareth issue *Rock 'n' Roll Telephone*, their 23rd record and the last to feature Dan McCafferty as the band's vocalist. Producing once again is Yann Rouiller.

Dan McCafferty:
"We just thought it was a great title (laughs). Especially with the old British telephone boxes; these things are a thing of the past now. But what happened was—and this is true story—we were doing gigs in Russia last year, and Jimmy was going through security at the airport and he left his phone. You always take your phone out of your pocket and that kind of stuff. And in Russia, not having a phone is really being cut off. But everybody's got phones now, so it wasn't a problem, really. But he did get wound up about it a lot, of course. A lot of it is like, I'm stuck in Russia and I can't even speak to my girlfriend, or my wife, or whatever—and never both at the same time, by the way (laughs). Sorry, that was a really bad old joke. But anyway, there's humour in the song and I think it's a really cool track. And it just seemed like a good title. There's no reason why you think it's a good title; you just think 'That's a good title.'"

"All through its history, this band has always done what we feel like doing at the time. Obviously people change. I mean, you get older and wiser—or stupider (laughs). You know, I'm not making any claims in which way I got. But still, you do what you think is good, and then hopefully other people will think it's good. That's always been our criteria. So nothing really changed on this album. It's just that on this one, I mean, Lee and Jimmy have been writing a lot of songs last couple of albums, and they just come up with so much stuff and it's all good. So it's a case of pick the ones you wanna do and let's make a job of them."

"We kinda know what we're doing when we go into the studio. Things can change, obviously, but generally speaking we have a plan. As we do in life, we have a plan. And the thing was, we've played together for so long, Pete and I obviously for a million years, but Jimmy's been with Nazareth for nearly 20 years, and Lee's been there for 11. So you can speak to the people. It's like, 'What about trying this? Could you sing that again, Dan?' And nobody gets upset. It's like everybody's got their eye on the gold ring. They want to make a good record."

"As for the songs, I like 'Boom Bang Bang' for obvious regions, nudge nudge, wink wink. You know, you get it; there's a lot of humour in there. And I also like 'The Right Time,' because it's a very hopeful song. 'Speakeasy,' I think is a hoot, really good. 'Winter Sunlight' is about as romantic as it gets for me. Really, it's a pretty varied, interesting album, he says, blowing his own trumpet. But I really do think that."

Pete Agnew:
"A great album that proved to be the end of an era. Sadly, only a week after recording was completed, Dan was forced to quit Nazareth. Throughout our career, other musicians came and went, but Dan's departure marked the end of an era. He knows we wish him well and we know he wishes us well, as he has mentioned on several occasions how delighted is that we found a singer of Carl's calibre to take his place. It's funny though; sometimes I swear I can still hear his voice in the dressing room after a gig going, 'Will somebody shut that fuckin' door?!' I miss him."

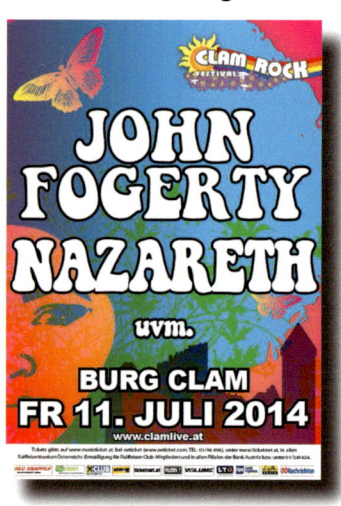

June 25 – July 19, 2014. The band, now with Linton Osborne singing, conduct an extensive Western Canadian campaign.

July 26 – August 16, 2014. As expected, the band participate enthusiastically in the European festival season, following up with a German tour.

2015

2015. Manny Charlton moves to Cordova, Spain.

Manny Charlton, on his reason for leaving Texas and relocating to Spain:
"Blood. DNA. I've got family here. I always wanted to come to Spain to retire, so to speak."

January 16, 2015. Linton Osborne announces on his Facebook page that he is no longer Nazareth's lead singer.

February 13, 2015. The band announce Carl Sentance as their new singer. Sentence had sung previously with Persian Risk (Phil Campbell's pre-Motörhead band), Krokus (briefly) and with Geezer Butler's solo band.

Pete Agnew:

"Carl's got a way different sound compared to Dan and this is what we wanted. The stipulation was—well, two stipulations—he had to be a great singer and he had to not sound like Dan. We didn't want a Dan sound-alike because we would've been crucified if we'd done something like that. And you wouldn't want to do something like that. When we did all the auditions and stuff, the stuff that was being sent to me, a lot of people wanted to try to do the Dan sound-alike but it's not what we were looking for. We tried a couple people, tried a couple different things, and that didn't work. And then a friend of mine said, 'There's a guy you want to have a look at, this guy, Carl Sentance.' He was quite keen to join if we wanted him, and when he came to do an audition with us, within a couple of verses of 'Silver Dollar Forger,' we said this is the man, this is great, wonderful singer. So it worked out. And he's good on stage; he's got a wonderful presence on stage, a great act, if you like. And I thought, it all works really fabulous."

April 17 – December 25, 2015. The band tour extensively, with all the dates taking place in Europe.

October 4th, 2015, Graz, Austria.

© Isabella Seefriedt

2016

2016. Manny Charlton issues *Solo*.

January 30 – July 17, 2016. The band tour Europe, getting in a few dates in Brazil as well, plus one show in Israel.

Pete Agnew, on the legitimacy of the band's lineup at this point:
"I used to get the question about how we still called ourselves Nazareth having only one original member in the lineup, but I don't get asked that hardly anymore these days and I could give you a few examples why. Bands with only one original member include: The Eagles, Guns N' Roses and AC/DC. That pretty much covers the most famous bands in the world. But you could go on and name a few more, like Status Quo, Whitesnake, Uriah Heep, Foreigner, Blue Öyster Cult, REO Speedwagon, Sweet, Little Feat, and if you want to get really picky, Deep Purple, with Ian Paice being the only original. So there you go—we're in good company."

"I'd even go a step further and say I'd like to think that the guys in the band as it is now would carry on the name even without me and I'm sure there would be very few complaints from the many fans that we're currently playing to in concert. You must remember that Jimmy and Lee have been in Nazareth for 26 years and 22 years respectively (both longer than Manny) and have written songs for, and performed on six Nazareth albums—counting the one we are currently recording—accounting for almost a quarter of the total output of the band's recordings. You said yourself, Martin, that you put three of these albums in your top six Nazareth albums, so that alone says it all."

"Anyway, time will tell, but I'm 75 this year (ouch) and the fans who used to come to see the original band aren't getting any younger either, so now we're seeing more and more people coming to our concerts who have never seen the original lineup and completely identify Nazareth as the guys who are up on that stage now. Long may that continue even after I've shuffled off to the big bass amp in the sky."

July 19 – July 27, 2016. The guys conduct yet another Western Canadian campaign; then it's an intense blanketing of Europe to finish out the year.

November 21st, 2016, Graz, Austria.

© Isabella Seefriedt

November 21st, 2016, Graz, Austria.

© Isabella Seefriedt

2017

January 19 – 23, 2017. The band play the Rock Legends Cruise.

March 30 – July 15, 2017. Nazareth conduct a tour of Europe but also, in April, execute a couple of shows in India.

Carl Sentance, in 2017:
"I've become a bit more confident, and of course then I didn't know what to expect. It was like rabbit in the headlamp. Now it's just a bit more confidence and it feels like a family now. It's been great. We have been working solid. I only had a chance maybe three months ago to start listening to different albums that I didn't have a chance to listen before. Now I hear all the stuff and I've picked a few songs out there that I like and I thought would work. It might take me another ten years to learn all the other songs, but I'm getting there (laughs)."
(w/ Marko Syrjala, MetalRules)

May 18, 2017. Although Andrew Carnegie had already built a library in the place of his birth, Dunfermline, Scotland, additions over the years included a museum and art gallery that opened on this date. There is a display dedicated to hometown heroes Nazareth, which Pete and Dan have visited, Pete having donated his first bass guitar to the cause.

July 22 – August 5, 2017. The band conduct a Canadian tour, covering the west as usual, but also Central Canada. Then it's back to Europe to close out the year.

2018

January 19 – August 1, 2018. The band play their regular European stomping grounds, east and west, before returning to similarly familiar territory—Western Canada, in August, with a few Ontario dates as well. Then it's mostly Germany for the balance of 2018.

October 12, 2018. Nazareth issue, on Frontiers, their 24th record, *Tattooed on My Brain*. On vocals is Carl Sentence and producing is a returning Yann Rouiller.

Pete Agnew:
"We did almost like three years with Carl live. We all knew each other very, very well by that time. And when we got to the studio, it was a case of, he's never recorded with us, and everybody's got their own way of recording. But it was great, because he's been in the band for three years. We recorded pretty much the same way as we would record with Dan. It's just a different guy coming through the speakers. But I've got to say, he's pretty much an incredible first-take singer. When the guy goes in to sing, every time he does a take, it sounds perfect. He's like, 'Oh, let's try that again,' and I'm thinking, why? (laughs). So he's really easy to record with. And that was it—we'd been with him for three years so we were used to Carl being the singer with Nazareth."

"We did Carl's songs first, because people were still writing and working at home and in other rooms, rehearsal rooms in the studio. So we recorded his songs first. That was great, because when you're recording with Nazareth, if you can't sing your own songs, you're really up against it. So you're singing the songs you're comfortable with because you wrote them, which was a great way to start recording."

"And then we moved on to the other songs that other people had written. There could easily have been 18 tracks. Due to the amount of great material we had, our biggest problem was having to decide which songs were to be left out. Personal favourites for me are 'Secret Is Out,' 'Pole to Pole' and 'Tattooed on My Brain' but I can play this album right through without wanting to skip a track. However, even though we were all delighted with the finished album, there was a definite nervousness in the camp during the run-up to its release. This was the first album without Dan, so we knew that judgement day critics were going to be harsh. The reviews couldn't be just oaky, or even just 'good'—that was never going to cut it. No wiggle room here: our fans had to love this one, and to our great happiness—not to mention relief—they did. Overwhelmingly. The media reviews and fans' comments were ecstatic."

"In these days when music is 'streamed'—or to use the right word, 'stolen'—instead of being bought from record stores, it's sometimes hard to measure an album's success, so we have to settle for the fact that Tattooed on My Brain was streamed untold thousands of times and hit No1 on the Amazon rock chart on and off for a few of weeks. So we rejoiced knowing that by today's standards we had a long-awaited hit record. Although what we all really know is that by today's standards we just handed out a $50,000 business card. And here's the kicker: we can't wait to get started on another one! Go figure."

2019

2019. The band tour extensively, with almost all of it, all year, in Europe. However, the guys play Brazil in late October, into November, and make a return visit to India, for the Shirock Festival on October 16th.

June 25, 2019. The New York Times article on the 2008 Universal warehouse fire lists Nazareth as one of the band who lost original masters in the blaze.

June 21, 2019. Dan McCafferty issues a video for a song called "Tell Me," from his forthcoming solo album.

October 18, 2019. Dan McCafferty issues a solo album, called *Last Testament*.

Manny Charlton, on Dan:
"Dan, fantastic vocalist, great writer, great lyrics. I really miss him when it comes to doing music and stuff (laughs). Yeah, he's a fantastic vocalist. And never, ever, ever was a prima donna. I've met vocalists since and before who are complete prima donnas. Ask Jeff Beck about vocalists (laughs). Jeff Beck decided he wasn't going to have any, and he's never worked with another vocalist. Dan was great, just one of the guys, and there was a rumour going around that AC/DC wanted him as a replacement for Bon Scott. But Dan would never have left Nazareth. Him and Pete are joined at the hip (laughs). They've been buddies since schoolchildren; like five years old, they've known each other. I was always the new boy (laughs)."

December 2nd, 2018, Graz, Austria.

© Isabella Seefriedt

December 4th, 2018, Vienna, Austria.

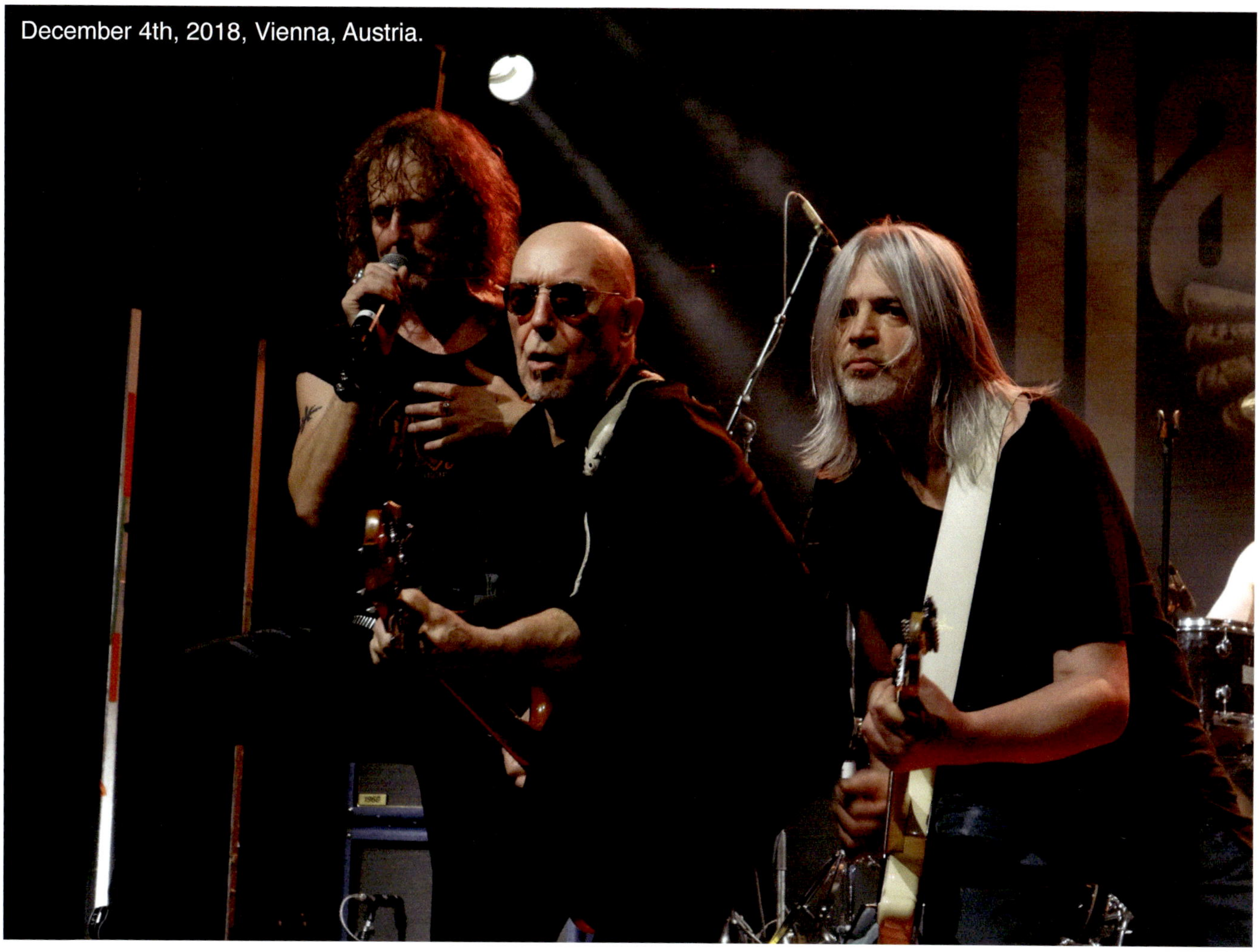

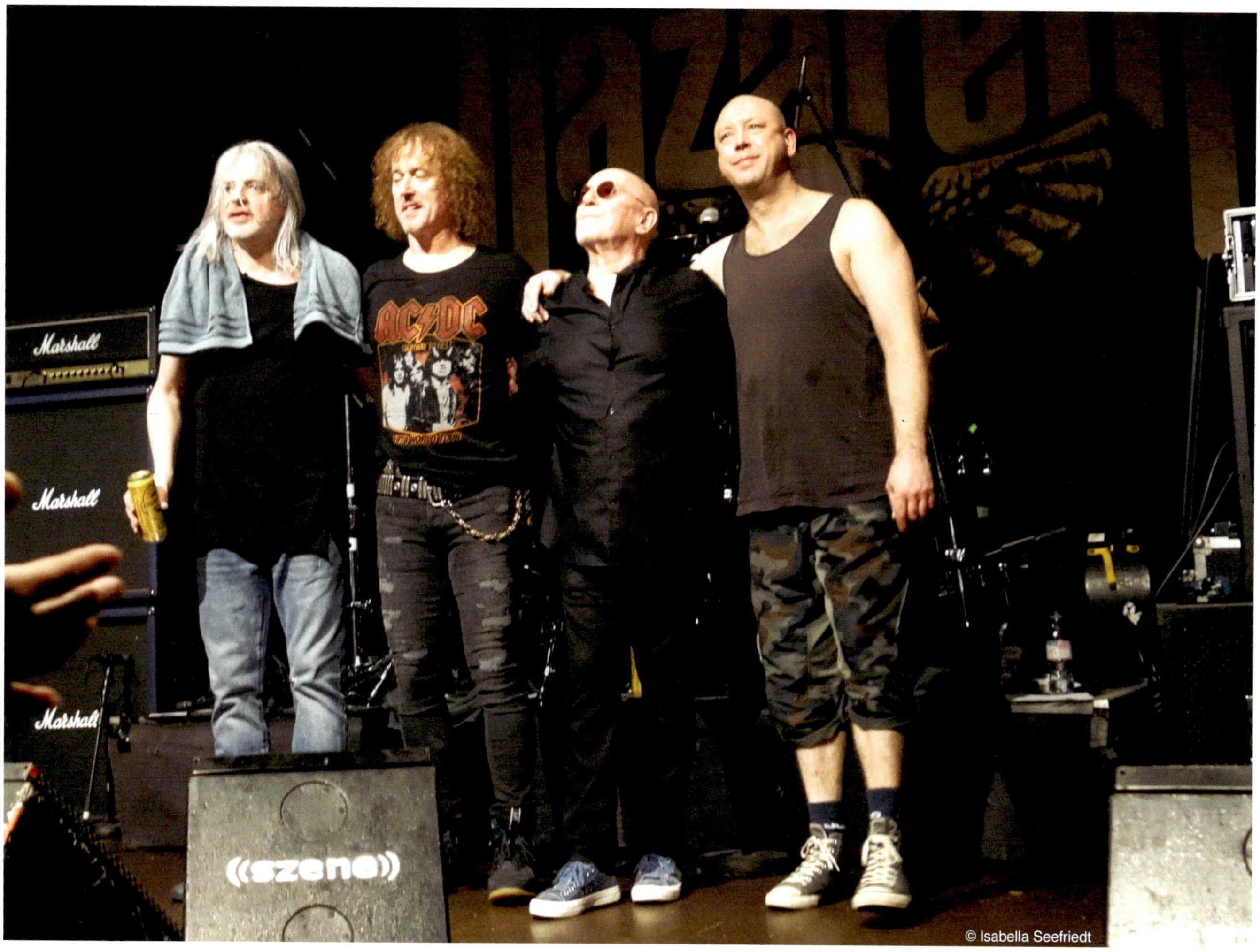

© Isabella Seefriedt

June 29th, 2019, Eisenstadt, Austria.

June 29th, 2019, Eisenstadt, Austria.

2020

January 10 – March 7, 2020. The band tour extensively, mostly in Germany and Russia, making Nazareth one of the most prolific of classic rock bands in the months leading up to shows being cancelled due to the worldwide Coronavirus pandemic.

Pete Agnew:

"I'll be seeing Dan tomorrow, because I've not had a chance to see him these last few weeks. I was in Canada up until the end of September. We did the Canadian tour. He lives only five minutes from me. I live in one village and he lives in the next village down at the seashore. So I go to see him every now and again. He likes to be brought up to date with what we're doing and he loves to hear the stories."

"He has good days and he has bad days with the breathing stuff. If he gets the slightest little bug, it's really bad, for his breath and that. But he can't go along too far walking and stuff without being terribly short of breath. But he's done a new album as well. See, he can't travel with our band. He can't come up and do a show but he can still record. Because as you know, when you go in to record, you can record one line at a time. You can record one word at a time if you like. He can sing a verse, a line of a verse, have a cup of tea and then sing again."

"The studio we used for Tattooed on My Brain, well, it's the studio we used for Rock 'n' Roll Telephone. And the reason we used it, is it's right close to Dan's house. When we did Rock 'n' Roll Telephone, he wasn't getting any better then. It was good to be just recording around the corner so he could just nip down when he was needed to sing. And it was good. So he's recorded a solo album in there with a guy from Prague, the Czech Republic."

"But he'd been having breathing problems for quite a while. When we did Big Dogz, it was probably right around that time, those few years leading up to Rock 'n' Roll Telephone—that's when it got worse. But for Rock 'n' Roll Telephone, he was fine. We did like about a month of the album and we were supposed to come to Canada. Well, we came and we did some dates in the States, and then we came up to do Canada. And when we were in the States, we had to cancel a couple of shows. And then when we went up to do Canada, I think we only managed about four shows. I think Cranbrook was the last place that we actually got up on the stage, and he just couldn't do it anymore. So we had to cancel that Canadian tour."

"And then we came back and we finished recording. We spent another month recording Rock 'n' Roll Telephone and he did the vocals and everything. But then after that, when we finished the record, a few days after we finished it, we went out to do a festival with Joe Cocker and ourselves, and Krokus, which was a band that Carl used to sing with, funny enough. So we went to Switzerland to do that, and we went on the stage that night and he struggled through sort of a few songs and then he just couldn't breathe anymore. He had to come up and say that's it. And that was the day he went. Because he tried to do that a few times and he said, 'No, no, I can't do this to the band anymore. That was my last attempt.' That was five years ago now. Time flies, doesn't it?"

Dan McCafferty on what he's going to miss the most in retirement, playing live or making records:

"Oh, I'm really going to miss the road. Oh God, the two things I love. Obviously I've been doing this for 50-odd years, so I'm kind of fond of playing music. The studio was great, because you are having a bit of fun, taking a punt; if something doesn't work, let's do this, let's try that. Because we were never a formula band, really. But the road I love, because, well, you meet new people on their own turf. And they don't care if you traveled 300 or 400 miles that night to play to them. They'll say, 'Hey man, I paid 20 bucks' (laughs), and you have to do perform and I kind of liked that. It was very enjoyable and it was personal. I mean, you see people's faces and they're smiling at you. Or they're going, 'You suck, man' (laughs). Generally speaking they are smiling at you. So yeah, I'm going to miss them both—very much."

"What am I most proud of? Making 24 recorded albums, I guess. And playing just about every place in the world that had a plug. I mean really, I've enjoyed much it. I thought it was great. And it's funny, since I got sick, the amount of people who run into me from other bands and say, 'Oh, come on, Dan, get better' blah blah blah. So at least you know you had made an impact, that you made a few ripples in pool."

2021

February 21, 2021. With live gigging a distant memory worldwide and not exactly slated to resume any time soon, the Nazareth clan work toward a follow-up to *Tattooed on My Brain*.

Pete Agnew:
"Because we've been locked in for all this amount of time, there are so many songs. It's going to be hard to decide what to use. I mean, Jimmy, he's sent me 14 songs he's done. And Lee only really started writing last month and Lee's got five. Carl, I'm sure he'll have a few. But Carl, what he did was he recorded a solo album. He's living out in Austria now and he wrote and recorded a solo album, during the summer of last year, and Yann, our producer, mixed it; I think he's still mixing it. But he'll have a lot of material because he writes songs all the time. Put it this way: it's not going to be like it was at Morin Heights when we did *Play 'n' the Game,* when we had nothing, absolutely nothing, and you go into the studio and you're just jamming. It won't be like that with this new album because with no touring the guys have done nothing *but* writing."

"You know, what I always like is that first week in the studio, when you get all the drum sounds but more importantly, you've got everybody in there and you're wondering what are we going to be doing? What sorts of songs are we going to be doing? That's when you listen to all the material that everybody's got and you start to choose. 'We can do that one, change that, change that…' I always look forward to that first week. There's a great buzz. Everybody is going in and you're not really sure what you're going to be doing and it's great. Despite right now going fuckin' stir-crazy (laughs), me and the guys absolutely have that to look forward to."

June 29th, 2019, Eisenstadt, Austria.

2022

April 15, 2022. Nazareth issue their milestone 25th album. *Surviving the Law* finds the guys working once again with producer Yann Rouiller. The band's sound is rougher and heavier this time, as Carl Sentance settles into his role with a second album fronting the band.

July 5, 2022. Guitarist and sometime producer through the glory years, Manny Charlton, dies at the age of 80, on a visit to Texas to wrap up some of his financial affairs. Tragically, he had lost his son six months previous.

November 8, 2022. Vocal legend, all 'round nice guy and rock 'n' roll ambassador Dan McCafferty succumbs to his chronic obstructive pulmonary disease, passing at the age of 76. Now the band playing poker on the front cover of *Play 'n' the Game* has left the table, save for one. But Pete Agnew carries on, at the spry age of 77, delivering a revitalized version of Nazareth to the world.

ACKNOWLEDGEMENTS

Thanks once again to my faithful copy editor Agustin Garcia de Paredes, who applied his eagle eye to this book and hopefully helped me keep the typos down to an acceptable number. Agustin is also the administrator of the Facebook page for my History in Five Songs with Martin Popoff podcast and has the most complete collection of my books of anyone I know. Plus he's got a whip-smart band and he saw Nazareth in concert in Barrie in 2018.

Digging deeper, Nazareth expert and buddy Robert Lawson (who has his own Nazareth book, Razama-Snaz!), conducted a peer review of the book. His wise and conscientious scholarship on all things Naz applied to these pages made me look less stupid.

I'd also like to thank my good buddy Kevin Julie, who helped assemble a bit of a press archive, handy for the odd key quote.

And yes, cheers to those lovely photographers! Thank you to Roni Ramos Amorim, Rudy Childs, Richard Galbraith, Wolfgang Gürster and Isabella Seefriedt for helping make this book, in a visual sense, sing like Dan. Of course among these fine collaborators, Roni needs to be singled out for his collecting, scanning and photographing of his top-shelf Nazareth collection. His kind contribution in the field of images helped so much to make this a treasure trove in book form.

Special thanks to Pete Agnew for permission to use the official Nazareth logos.

ABOUT THE AUTHOR

At approximately 7900 (with over 7000 appearing in his books), Martin has unofficially written more record reviews than anybody in the history of music writing across all genres. Additionally, Martin has penned approximately 110 books on hard rock, heavy metal, classic rock and record collecting. He was Editor-In-Chief of the now retired Brave Words & Bloody Knuckles, Canada's foremost metal publication for 14 years, and has also contributed to Revolver, Guitar World, Goldmine, Record Collector, bravewords.com, lollipop.com and hardradio.com, with many record label band bios and liner notes to his credit as well. Additionally, Martin has been a regular contractor to Banger Films, having worked for two years as researcher on the award-winning documentary Rush: Beyond the Lighted Stage, on the writing and research team for the 11-episode Metal Evolution and on the ten-episode Rock Icons, both for VH1 Classic. Additionally, Martin is the writer of the original metal genre chart used in Metal: A Headbanger's Journey and throughout the Metal Evolution episodes. Martin currently resides in Toronto and can be reached through martinp@inforamp.net or www.martinpopoff.com.

Sources

Sources cited throughout this book are credited "in situ," i.e. right at the end of the quote. Quotes with no accreditation at the end are from the author's own chats with the Naz guys or other speakers deemed relevant to the tale. The exception are some of the stories from Pete Agnew, who graciously contributed some of his own written musings to the cause. Pete also diligently went through the document correcting for accuracy and conducted a late-in-the-process interview with me to cover some of the gaps. His time and care spent on hammering this into improved shape is much appreciated.

Martin Popoff – A Complete Bibliography

2023: Nazareth: A Visual Biography, Dominance and Submission: The Blue Öyster Cult Canon, Wild Mood Swings: Disintegrating The Cure Album by Album, AC/DC at 50

2022: Pink Floyd and The Dark Side of the Moon: 50 Years, Killing the Dragon: Dio in the '90s and 2000s, Feed My Frankenstein: Alice Cooper, the Solo Years, Easy Action: The Original Alice Cooper Band, Lively Arts: The Damned Deconstructed, Yes: A Visual Biography II: 1982 – 2022, Bowie @ 75, Dream Evil: Dio in the '80s, Judas Priest: A Visual Biography, UFO: A Visual Biography

2021: Hawkwind: A Visual Biography, Loud 'n' Proud: Fifty Years of Nazareth, Yes: A Visual Biography, Uriah Heep: A Visual Biography, Driven: Rush in the '90s and "In the End," Flaming Telepaths: Imaginos Expanded and Specified, Rebel Rouser: A Sweet User Manual

2020: The Fortune: On the Rocks with Angel, Van Halen: A Visual Biography, Limelight: Rush in the '80s, Thin Lizzy: A Visual Biography, Empire of the Clouds: Iron Maiden in the 2000s, Blue Öyster Cult: A Visual Biography, Anthem: Rush in the '70s, Denim and Leather: Saxon's First Ten Years, Black Funeral: Into the Coven with Mercyful Fate

2019: Satisfaction: 10 Albums That Changed My Life, Holy Smoke: Iron Maiden in the '90s, Sensitive to Light: The Rainbow Story, Where Eagles Dare: Iron Maiden in the '80s, Aces High: The Top 250 Heavy Metal Songs of the '80s, Judas Priest: Turbo 'til Now, Born Again! Black Sabbath in the Eighties and Nineties

2018: Riff Raff: The Top 250 Heavy Metal Songs of the '70s, Lettin' Go: UFO in the '80s and '90s, Queen: Album by Album, Unchained: A Van Halen User Manual, Iron Maiden: Album by Album, Sabotage! Black Sabbath in the Seventies, Welcome to My Nightmare: 50 Years of Alice Cooper, Judas Priest: Decade of Domination, Popoff Archive – 6: American Power Metal, Popoff Archive – 5: European Power Metal, The Clash: All the Albums, All the Songs

2017: Led Zeppelin: All the Albums, All the Songs, AC/DC: Album by Album, Lights Out: Surviving the '70s with UFO, Tornado of Souls: Thrash's Titanic Clash, Caught in a Mosh: The Golden Era of Thrash, Rush: Album by Album, Beer Drinkers and Hell Raisers: The Rise of Motörhead, Metal Collector: Gathered Tales from Headbangers, Hit the Lights: The Birth of Thrash, Popoff Archive – 4: Classic Rock, Popoff Archive – 3: Hair Metal

2016: Popoff Archive – 2: Progressive Rock, Popoff Archive – 1: Doom Metal, Rock the Nation: Montrose, Gamma and Ronnie Redefined, Punk Tees: The Punk Revolution in 125 T-Shirts, Metal Heart: Aiming High with Accept, Ramones at 40, Time and a Word: The Yes Story

2015: Kickstart My Heart: A Mötley Crüe Day-by-Day, This Means War: The Sunset Years of the NWOBHM, Wheels of Steel: The Explosive Early Years of the NWOBHM, Swords and Tequila: Riot's Classic First Decade, Who Invented Heavy Metal?, Sail Away: Whitesnake's Fantastic Voyage

2014: Live Magnetic Air: The Unlikely Saga of the Superlative Max Webster, Steal Away the Night: An Ozzy Osbourne Day-by-Day, The Big Book of Hair Metal, Sweating Bullets: The Deth and Rebirth of Megadeth, Smokin' Valves: A Headbanger's Guide to 900 NWOBHM Records

2013: The Art of Metal (co-edit with Malcolm Dome), 2 Minutes to Midnight: An Iron Maiden Day-by-Day, Metallica: The Complete Illustrated History, Rush: The Illustrated History, Ye Olde Metal: 1979, Scorpions: Top of the Bill - updated and reissued as Wind of Change: The Scorpions Story in 2016

2012: Epic Ted Nugent, Fade To Black: Hard Rock Cover Art of the Vinyl Age, It's Getting Dangerous: Thin Lizzy 81-12, We Will Be Strong: Thin Lizzy 76-81, Fighting My Way Back: Thin Lizzy 69-76, The Deep Purple Royal Family: Chain of Events '80 – '11, The Deep Purple Royal Family: Chain of Events Through '79 - reissued as The Deep Purple Family Year by Year books

2011: Black Sabbath FAQ, The Collector's Guide to Heavy Metal: Volume 4: The '00s (co-authored with David Perri)

2010: Goldmine Standard Catalog of American Records 1948 – 1991, 7th Edition

2009: Goldmine Record Album Price Guide, 6th Edition, Goldmine 45 RPM Price Guide, 7th Edition, A Castle Full of Rascals: Deep Purple '83 – '09, Worlds Away: Voivod and the Art of Michel Langevin, Ye Olde Metal: 1978

2008: Gettin' Tighter: Deep Purple '68 – '76, All Access: The Art of the Backstage Pass, Ye Olde Metal: 1977, Ye Olde Metal: 1976

2007: Judas Priest: Heavy Metal Painkillers, Ye Olde Metal: 1973 to 1975, The Collector's Guide to Heavy Metal: Volume 3: The Nineties, Ye Olde Metal: 1968 to 1972
2006: Run for Cover: The Art of Derek Riggs, Black Sabbath: Doom Let Loose, Dio: Light Beyond the Black

2005: The Collector's Guide to Heavy Metal: Volume 2: The Eighties, Rainbow: English Castle Magic, UFO: Shoot Out the Lights, The New Wave of British Heavy Metal Singles

2004: Blue Öyster Cult: Secrets Revealed! – update and reissue 2009); updated and reissued as Agents of Fortune: The Blue Öyster Cult Story 2016, Contents Under Pressure: 30 Years of Rush at Home & Away, The Top 500 Heavy Metal Albums of All Time

2003: The Collector's Guide to Heavy Metal: Volume 1: The Seventies, The Top 500 Heavy Metal Songs of All Time

2001: Southern Rock Review

2000: Heavy Metal: 20th Century Rock and Roll, The Goldmine Price Guide to Heavy Metal Records

1997: The Collector's Guide to Heavy Metal

1993: Riff Kills Man! 25 Years of Recorded Hard Rock & Heavy Metal

See martinpopoff.com for complete details and ordering information.